MW00699265

EASY TARGET

I stood in my living-room window, looking down at the river, listening to the rain nick at the window and watching the water cascade down the glass in a slow, dark sheet to the sash.

Janice. I should call Janice. But it was too late, both on the clock and inside my head. Sooner or later, I would call her. What I would say, though, was something else. If I told her about Marian Tawney, would that be the end of things? Or would a silent lie be worse? Even with three marital DOAs under my belt, I didn't have a good answer to that one.

I was still standing in the window, big as life, when the first bullet crashed through the glass and smacked into the ceiling behind me.

Bantam Crime Line Books offer the finest in classic and modern American mysteries.
Ask your bookseller for the books you have missed.

Cupid

Robert Sims Reid

BANTAM BOOKS
NEW YORK · TORONTO · LONDON · SYDNEY · AUCKLAND

This novel is a work of fiction. Names, characters, places and incidents are either the product of the author's imagination or are used fictitiously. Any resemblance to actual persons, living or dead, events or locales is entirely coincidental.

CUPID

A Bantam Book / January 1991

All rights reserved.
Copyright © 1990 by Robert Sims Reid.
Cover art copyright © 1990 by Joe Devito.
No part of this book may be reproduced or transmitted
in any form or by any means, electronic or mechanical,
including photocopying, recording, or by any information
storage and retrieval system, without permission in writing from
the publisher.
For information address: Bantam Books.

ISBN 0-553-28824-5

Published simultaneously in the United States and Canada

Bantam Books are published by Bantam Books, a division of Bantam Doubleday Dell Publishing Group, Inc. Its trademark, consisting of the words "Bantam Books" and the portrayal of a rooster, is Registered in U.S. Patent and Trademark Office and in other countries. Marca Registrada. Bantam Books, 666 Fifth Avenue, New York, New York 10103.

PRINTED IN THE UNITED STATES OF AMERICA

RAD   0 9 8 7 6 5 4 3 2 1

This, at long last,
is for Gayle.

Cupid

Chapter 1

The first I knew of the Hudson shooting was when the 9-1-1 dispatcher phoned me at home. Of course, I didn't know right off that it was Hudson who'd been shot. But I found out plenty soon enough.

The call came on a Saturday night in mid-October. I was reading through a stack of U.S. Geological Survey reports, daydreaming about a fossil-hunting trip I wanted to make to eastern Montana next summer. There was a shooting, the dispatcher said, officers were still at the scene and the whole piece of business remained more or less in progress. Sam Blieker, my sergeant, wanted me to go to work. The dispatcher gave me an address in Ragtown, a down-at-the-heels neighborhood south across the river from the abandoned Corso lumber mill. Then she hung up. She was out of breath.

Saturday night. I was home. I was dressed. I was alone. I was sober. I also had an unmarked car, which I'd driven home for the weekend after working late Friday afternoon.

Saturday night and gunshots. If I told you that after nearly twenty years those words no longer gave me at least a moderate rush, I would be lying.

Saturday night and murder. If I went on to tell you that after nearly twenty years those words no longer led the way finally to a deep and expanding sadness, a sadness spiked with wonder, like some many-limbed animal digging its way through the warm, moist dirt of my heart, well, that would be lying, too.

It took me less than ten minutes to drive to the Esther Street address. I parked near the alley just as Blieker pulled up in a blue sedan identical to the one I drove. Ordinarily, Frank Woodruff, the lieutenant in the Detective Division, would have been there, too. Oddly enough, though, Woodruff was in Los Angeles, doing a training stint with one of the LAPD homicide units.

There were four black and whites in the street. Ray Bartell stood at the gate of the crude fence, ready to keep out the crowd should one happen our way. The red and blue overheads were shut down on all the cars except Bartell's, which lighted the scene like a grotesque dance floor.

There was an ambulance at the curb.

I nodded hello to Bartell as Blieker and I stepped through the gate and walked along a dirt path to the door of the tiny old stone house. Arnold Slayton, the Uniform shift boss, was at the door. Light from inside spilled around him.

Blieker nodded toward the door. "Dead?"

"Damn near." Slayton zipped up his black leather jacket. He has black hair, which he wears with military style whitewalls around his ears and neck. The haircut makes his ears look larger than they are. His tangled black eyebrows sneak up on each other across the bridge of his nose. "You got here fast," Slayton said. "They haven't even had time to move him yet."

"You called fast," Blieker said. Then he looked at me. "Leo, when he goes to the hospital, you go along. Ardell Wings is on the way down. He and I will do the crime scene."

I said that sounded fine to me.

Blieker straightened his tie. Rain or shine, day or night. Spring, summer, winter, fall. Sam Blieker wears a necktie. And a brown suit. Or a blue suit. And a white shirt. Always a white shirt.

"Soon as I heard the dispatch," Slayton said, "I asked for detectives. I figure, you get a report of shots fired and a guy down, you need detectives. Why wait an hour to make the call? Then it took probably ten or fifteen minutes before my guys finally worked their way into the house."

"Any problems?" Blieker asked.

"Zip."

"Any suspects?" I said.

"Correct me on the problem aspect," Slayton said, laughing. "We don't have a suspect. I guess you could say that's a problem."

"You might say that." Blieker fondled a cigarette, then

thought better of it and stuck it behind his ear. "What about the guy inside?"

Slayton shook his head. "Whoever he is, he's got three new belly buttons."

That was when I stepped closer to the door and looked over Arnold Slayton's shoulder. At first, all I could see were med techs and cops. Med techs kneeling over a body on the floor, cops standing around to watch. Then one of the med techs leaned away and I saw the face of the man on the floor.

"I'll be goddamned," I whispered. I kept staring at the man, wanting to be sure I wasn't wrong about the face. "I'll be go to hell."

Blieker stepped around Slayton and through the door. "Sonofabitch." He whistled and looked back at me. "Well, well, it really is, isn't it?"

I felt myself start to get light-headed, almost giddy, and fought it off.

"Is *who*?" Arnold Slayton looked at me and his eyebrows collided head-on. "What are you talking about, Banks?"

"I'll be goddamned," I said again, ignoring Slayton. Then I stepped away from the door and wandered back out to the street, with my stomach suddenly feeling like a sieve.

The man on the floor was Sky King Hudson.

There were people in the street now. Freaks. Figures draped in GI clothes and serapes and jeans. Like some goddamned time warp, it was, ghosts flitting out from under a rock nobody had kicked over for fifteen years.

I pulled off my glasses and folded them into the pocket of my plaid wool shirt. I took a deep breath and felt the cold air sting the inside of my nose, then watched the steam dissolve as I slowly exhaled. The air smelled good, the way October always smells in that part of town, dead leaves mixed with diesel fumes from the Burlington Northern train yard down the block. October smelled even better when I was a kid back in the Midwest and people burned their leaves in the gutter. But that was another life. The town where I live now is in a cramped alpine valley, which is subjected to too many temperature inversions and too many people. Put those two factors together and sometimes you get air so rotten you could get cancer just discussing it. The Big Sky Country. That's what they call Montana, after a great book about mountain men by A. B. Guthrie. The trouble is that everybody wants a piece of that sky.

It snowed by fits and starts. Two more women walked out of the shadows in the alley behind the narrow house. One of them, the dark one in a red mackinaw, looked familiar. She carried a baby slung on her hip and her long skirt licked at the top of a pair of knee-high moccasins as she came out of the dusty alley into the street. The two women stopped with the small crowd milling behind the ambulance and my unmarked car.

"They'll be hauling him in a minute," I said absently to Ray Bartell, "the guy in the house." Bartell has been on the Rozette Police Department for seven or eight years. Still a young cop, really. Or at least it seems so to a guy like me, a guy who's been around about as long as a glacier. The department is small enough—about seventy officers—that we're acquainted, but big enough that some cops go for years and never get to know each other much beyond, *Hello, what happened?* Bartell seems like a good cop, though. He has to be. Bad cops don't survive the loss of a partner the way Bartell had survived the death of Paul Culp a few years back.

I reached through Bartell's open window and switched off his overheads before they gave me a headache. "I think everybody knows we're here."

"You going along to the hospital, Leo?" Bartell pulled out a handkerchief and blew his nose. Snow was landing on his hair and shoulders.

I gave him a distracted nod, looking at the crowd that was collecting near the ambulance. "I'm the official witness, case he says anything before he turns into evidence." Evidence. That's what becomes of the victim of a homicide, which was what this case would be as soon as Sky King Hudson stopped wasting oxygen.

I picked out faces that I recognized, trying to attach each face to the low rumble of names idling away at the back of my mind. Jerome Running Rabbit. That was the small Indian standing off by himself under the streetlight. Wanda Bjork-lund. And Cajun, the tall sonofabitch in the floppy leather hat, the one who would talk to cops if you thumped him a little when you picked him up, made it look like an earnest roust.

And Maid Marian. Marian Tawney. She was the woman in the red mackinaw with the kid. At first, I was surprised not to have recognized her. Not that she was less beautiful. Just changed. Her face seemed sharper now, more sculpted around the eyes and cheeks. And the kid. Somehow, motherhood did not fit into any of my impressions of Marian Tawney. She still had the hair, thick auburn hair that fell below the middle of her back. I remembered her from those nights in Angel's Bar, dancing against the bank of colored lights, her breasts shadowed globes through a gauze blouse and that wild auburn hair whipping along the lean slope of her back and ass as she whirled and spun. I wondered how many fathers it had taken to make that baby. None of them had done the kid any favors.

"There's beer at my place," Bartell said. "After shift. Whenever you wrap this up." The uniform guys often ended the night with a few belts at somebody's house.

"I'll see." Even as I said it, I knew I wouldn't stop by. I'd been exceptionally rational since my third marriage cracked up. Come to think of it, whenever I'm single, I never pull the kind of stunts that always get me divorced.

"You know any of these maggots?" Bartell asked.

"My squandered youth," I said, wincing slightly. My back was hurting. It always hurts in certain weather. Perfect it should flare up tonight, with the perpetrator himself headed for a slab. I would have told Bartell all about it, except that before I had the chance, they carried Sky King out to the ambulance. The crowd parted, silent at the sight of a man being worked on as though he were a broken car. Sam Blieker trotted after the gurney, trailing cigarette smoke and bad humor.

"Can you still handle this, Leo?" Blieker said. "I don't want to put you in worse a bind than you're in just being here."

I ignored Blieker and climbed through the double back doors of the orange, white, and blue ambulance.

Blieker stared at me a minute, then shrugged. "Make a note, he happens to say anything. I'll be in touch."

I nodded and pulled the doors closed. The ambulance started and I turned to look at the man on the gurney, who now wore only a pair of inflated Mast pants. The male nurse on the crew was busy with an IV, while one technician frowned at the heart monitor and the other drove.

"He going to make it?" I asked nobody in particular.

"Don't know," the nurse answered. "He was straight-line when we got there. But we got this pulse now, without CPR."

I grunted and stretched my back. I looked down at Sky King's pale, grimy feet. The nails grew over the ends of his toes like blunt claws. Then I looked at Sky King's face: gray and puffy, the mouth a useless gash, blank eyes behind flaccid lids, dusty brown hair still tied in a ponytail, which drew back from a surprisingly thin widow's peak and showed a disturbing amount of gray. Then I looked at the pressure bandage that kept Sky King's guts from leaking out. Then, quietly under my breath, I started to laugh.

Leo Banks was just what the Rozette, Montana, Police Department needed in the late sixties and early seventies. Not much over twenty and fresh out of the Navy, I'd spent my last year and a half doing petty investigations at Bremmerton, a job that was mostly paper. I'd never been a civilian cop, so I didn't bring bad habits to a profession fearful of habits that cannot be described as wholesome. Yes, sir, I was welcomed with semiopen arms.

Those blue, uniformed arms were only semiopen because my first experience in Rozette, Montana, was getting semiar-rested.

I came to Rozette on a freight train, after separation from the Navy and a substantial binge in Seattle, which left me a lot more than semibroke. In those days, there was a big mean cop named Dave Johanson on the Rozette department. Johanson used to be a professional wrestler. My first day in town, he popped me for panhandling. He cuffed me, threw me in the back of his patrol car, then drove around town while he read through the separation papers he'd dug out of my hip pocket. After he finished reading, he started to talk, and soon after that he took the cuffs off and put me in the front seat and then he kept on driving and kept on talking. Then he bought me a hamburger. Before I knew what happened, I had a job in a bookstore and Dave Johanson kept coming around. He was just too goddamned mean to let me climb back in a boxcar. I told Johanson lots of times that I was only in Rozette long enough to get myself together and head back home to Illinois. He seemed to know, though, that if I ever left town there was nothing ahead of me but road.

After I'd been in Rozette for about a year, Johanson handed me a Police Department application. Seven of us applied for two jobs. We get hundreds of applications now, but in those days, when hair was something God gave people so they'd have a place to put flowers, becoming a cop wasn't much of an attraction. I wasn't long on the job when the transfer came from patrol into drugs. I was pulled off the street and spent a couple of months buried deep at the station, letting my hair and beard grow. By the time I was turned loose, I didn't look like me anymore.

"You got any problems setting these people up? People your own age, even sympathies, maybe?" Captain Zimmer had asked me that just before I went undercover. Vietnam was still gasping then. Guys my age weren't supposed to trust anybody over thirty, which meant that guys like Zimmer weren't supposed to trust guys like me, either.

What problems? You make the buy, then stick a gun in the chump's ear and take him down. I was young and stupid. Zimmer was right not to trust me, but not for the reasons he suspected. If I'd told him how much I looked forward to getting under peoples' skin, regardless of their age, politics, or recreational habits, he'd never have given me the job. And who knows, if I'd realized that about myself, I might never have taken it. Zimmer retired not long after that and went to work as a night watchman at one of Corso's logging outfits. I can retire soon myself. I'm still plenty young enough to have a good time, if I can still recognize a good time when it's happening to me. At least there's a pension waiting at the bottom of this rock pile. Poor Sky King, though, there was no pension in his future at all.

The ambulance pulled up to the Emergency dock at St. Francis. I threw open the double doors, then jumped out

ahead of the gurney. In the rush that followed, I was only a
bystander, the guy who stood in the corner near the victim and
flashed my badge every time somebody told me to leave. The
job suited me just fine. I knew that Sky King wasn't going to
say anything, because the first thing the medical people did
was stick an airway down his throat. Then they opened up his
groin and started three or four units of blood under pressure
into his femoral artery. Then one of the doctors cracked his
chest, so they could depress the aorta and slow the internal
bleeding, and so when the heart eventually stopped, they
could have a go at massaging it back to life before pronouncing
Hudson officially dead. Every time the nurse squeezed the air
bag, inflating Sky King's chest, his left lung popped out
between the aluminum jaws of the chest spreader, like an
animal peeking outside its cage, then settled back again as the
lung deflated. Yes, boys and girls, Sky King's voice was only a
memory.

*You dig all this shit? I mean . . . can . . . you . . . dig
it?* Sky King was dragging out Baggies from every nook and
cranny of the old primered VW beetle.

Can . . . you . . . dig it? The words, the rhythms. All
stale, so totally . . . hip . . . they are embarrassing now,
bromides to brave days of new freedom through enlightened
politics and chemistry.

Got the bread, man?

You bet I had the bread. Old Leo always had the bread. I
remember how Sky King had shaken a bag of pills like a kid's
rattle toy. It was about dark, in the summertime, and my skin
was crawling from the heat, from being on the outside and
dirty for over a week, setting up this deal.

Hey, lady! Crack us a beer!

There was a woman standing in the door of the small frame
house and for a moment, I didn't recognize her, with the dusk
and all, but then I saw it was Marian Tawney, the woman from
Angel's Bar they called Maid Marian. She was barefoot,
wearing hip-hugger jeans cut off at the crotch and a white
T-shirt and when I walked into the house ahead of Sky King,
she stepped aside and I noticed that she smelled like strawberries. Strawberries. Strawberry Fields, and there was a
Cream album spinning on the turntable, "Sunshine of Your

Love," filling the dim pungent room with beautiful raunch. I
turned and reached under my T-shirt for the stack of bills, the
money that would complete the deal. Then I would reach for
the Model 36 Smith I carried in an ankle holster, and make the
arrest. I should have been paying more attention to Sky King
Hudson and less to the topography of Maid Marian's tank top.
The blade flashed once in the last of the sunlight as Sky King—

Pig motherfucker!

Sky!

It was Marian shouting and when I instinctively grabbed at
my throat (it never hurt, I still can't believe it) and turned away
and doubled over, going for the gun, Marian Tawney shouted
again just before Hudson buried the knife near my right
kidney and I toppled onto the floor, knowing I'd done it
wrong, should have kept the deal outside, where my
backups—Paul Culp and Frank Woodruff that day—could see
from inside the van down the street. But I'd fucked up and
now I was bleeding to death out on the floor of some dump I'd
never leave alive.

—I don't give a fuck, he's a narc!

You fuckin' killed him!

Yeah . . .

Oh, Jesus Christ.

*. . . yeah . . . probably did (laughter) . . . killed the
motherfucker!*

You better split . . . Oh, God . . .

Asshole!

Get out of here!

"We're going into surgery now." The doctor sounded a
million miles away and for a moment, I thought he was another
doctor, a doctor from years ago talking to somebody about me.
He was young, this doctor at work on Hudson. Younger than
me, younger than the doctor who'd stitched me together years
ago, but he ran the show like he knew what he was doing. He
wore surgical greens and white Nike shoes.

"Any chances?" I chewed on a toothpick as I spoke. There
were nearly a dozen people around the figure in the gurney, all
of them talking, but it seemed quiet.

The doctor shrugged. "You hear that heart monitor?" He
spoke with his hands, using his words as sutures.

I heard it.

The doctor shook his head. "Sounds more like a bad band before midnight than a heartbeat. Inside an hour it'll sound like your TV set when the station signs off."

"I'll need any clothes that may be on him or under him," I said.

"I'll try, but we've got a little more than that on our minds."

"I understand . . . it's real important." Doctors. They always have something bigger and better on their minds. I spit out a sliver of toothpick and watched as everyone began organizing the tangle of equipment for the trip upstairs.

Strawberries.

I opened my eyes and saw the woman's face. I couldn't hear Sky King now and I could smell the strawberries even stronger, feel the hot, damp gentle pressure against my throat, the sweaty heat of her thigh against my cheek. I started to say something.

Don't talk.

My head was in her lap and her hair tickled my face as she bent over me, pressing the towel against my neck. Her breasts, the nipples hard, mashed into my forehead as she rocked back and forth.

I called an ambulance.

Marian Tawney rubbed her eye. Her hand was covered with blood, my blood, and now it was smeared under her eye, like war paint.

Partners.

Right here.

It was Frank Woodruff, standing out of sight behind Marian Tawney.

Culp? Culp?

He's got Hudson out in the van. We took him down when he drove off . . . just before we got word she'd called for an ambulance.

I felt the pressure grow against my throat and I fought to stay awake. The muscles around my eyes tingled, straining to hold focus, while I tried to comprehend the crimson stain on Marian Tawney's tank top. I thought about Hudson between those same thighs and I tried to roll away, but Marian Tawney hushed me as she would a child. Woodruff wasn't so gentle.

Lay fucking still . . . you die on me and I'll break your goddamn neck.

I lay back and tried to take a deep breath, and when I did, the pain in my back was so goddamned bad it was paralyzing, like my skin had been nailed to the back side of my belly. My back hurt so bad I didn't even worry that I was bleeding to death out my neck. I heard a siren wail and gritted my teeth against being moved. There was a trickle of sweat on Marian Tawney's face, a trickle that left a thin, pink trail through my blood smeared on her cheek.

Die on me and I'll break your goddamn neck.

Once a man crouches next to you and makes a threat like that, he becomes a friend who never goes away. Paul Culp, though, was gone forever.

So I didn't have an ounce of grief for the man who continued dying as we took the elevator upstairs to OR. My only regret was that Culp and Woodruff weren't there to savor the moment with me.

Outside the elevator door, I stopped at a small matchwood desk and chair. I was restricted from going farther, badge or no badge. Hudson would have to die without me.

I stood in the green anteroom and listened to the soft hydraulic squeeze as the double mechanical doors into surgery pressed closed. Time to wait, time to be glad that for Leo Banks, tonight the buck stopped here, not inside on a table. I took out my notebook and made a note that at approximately four minutes after midnight, Sky King Hudson had gone into surgery. Inside an hour, the doctor had said. I sat back in the chair and watched the numerals above the elevator doors wink one way, then the other along the scale as the car moved up and down.

An hour.

I got up and wandered into the nurses' lounge and filled a Styrofoam cup with cold coffee and slowly drank. Anything could happen in an hour. Maybe Hudson would live. Christ, who knew these days. Miracles do happen, and they don't need an hour. Not for a miracle. Miracles can happen in a heartbeat.

* * *

Sky King Hudson had plea-bargained for thirty years, which included the drug charge and the attempted homicide on me. Thank Christ Hudson took the cash when he Bogarted after carving me up that afternoon. Otherwise, the possession and sale might have been down the toilet and the knifing reduced to disorderly conduct, since there was always the risk that twelve respectable citizens could decide that I had obviously enticed the innocent Hudson into a criminal act, and then had the bad manners to frighten him with the prospect of prison. I knew he'd been paroled almost a year ago. I knew, too, that one of the conditions of the parole was that he not get within smelling distance of Rozette. Hell, I could pop Sky King on a PV, if he weren't about to be dead.

Because she had the courtesy to save my life, Marian Tawney walked. I didn't mind that so much—saving my life had to be worth something, even if she did have felonious bad taste in men. I'd seen her once or twice at Hudson's court appearances, where I went to kill time between getting out of the hospital and going back to work. After that, I bumped into her two or three times when I happened to be walking through Angel's. I was in uniform then, since the whole Hudson disaster had turned me into Celebrity Narc. Marian Tawney never had much to say. Usually just a nod. She had her reputation to protect. Until tonight, I hadn't seen her for nearly ten years, not since the mid-seventies, when hippies became topics of nostalgic chitchat.

I had been sitting for about half an hour when the doctor came out and told me Hudson was dead.

"I need the body, along with the dressings, clothing, tubes, and evacuated fluids. Leave all the tubes connected. Just snip them off at your equipment." I wasn't wasting words on the doctor's ego now, not when we were dealing with courts of law instead of temples of mercy. I didn't know if Blieker and Wings had recovered any bullets at the house, and I wasn't taking any chances that one might have been sucked from Hudson's belly by a vacuum tube. "Just cut all the tubes and wrap the whole works in the sheet he's laying on. And bags. Can you tape some paper bags over his hands?" If Hudson had fired a gun that night, there might be gunshot residue on his hands and the bags would preserve it, evidence that might influence how the case was finally resolved.

"Right," the doctor said, looking at the green-clad nurse on his left to see if she understood. He'd been practicing Emergency Room long enough to know when the serve changed. The nurse went back into the OR to get Hudson.

"I need to know your name." I took out my notebook and looked at the doctor.

"Meyer," the doctor said. "Donald Meyer."

I phoned for a coroner while Donald Meyer waited for the elevator.

"You know his name?" Meyer glanced toward the door to surgery.

"Hudson. Sky King Hudson."

"What—"

"Gene. But they always called him Sky King. I don't know why . . . he tried to kill me once." I laughed nervously, like a boy telling a new friend an old and beloved secret.

"Interesting," Dr. Meyer said, getting on the elevator.

A moment later, the nurse wheeled out the gurney with Hudson's corpse wrapped in a sheet. His hair spread from under the top of the sheet like a banner.

"We'll be going down to three," she said, punching for the elevator. "You can wait there. I don't know what happens then."

"The coroner. He gets the body. Then I can leave." I guided the gurney onto the elevator and a few seconds later, I was alone with Hudson in a large darkened hallway lined with unmade beds.

I put on my glasses. Then I lifted the sheet to look at Hudson's face. The eyes were partially open, a dull gaze that drilled through me more certainly than Hudson's knife had nearly fifteen years ago. My glasses began to feel heavy on my face and the years seemed like shovelsful of dirt thrown at my feet. I took off my glasses slowly with both hands and put them back in my shirt pocket.

"Asshole," I whispered. "Goddamn puke-bag mother-fucker." Hudson kept staring at me. I said the words again, this time aloud.

"What is it?"

I dropped the sheet and jumped back.

"What's going on out there?" A nurse stood in a lighted doorway about twenty feet down the hall.

"Therapy," I said.

"You scared me," the nurse said.

"Me, too," I said, slumping against the nearest bed. "Scared me half to death."

Who knows what goes on in a man's mind? Blieker and Wings were almost done when I got back to the house. They had measured and sketched all the pertinent details inside the three-room house, and Ardell Wings had shot a complete set of photos. Now they were bagging and tagging evidence: scraps of bloody clothing cut from Hudson by the ambulance crew; a nearly empty quart of vodka; a bag of weed, mostly seeds and stems; two plastic vials, with a spent bullet in each.

"Whoever shot him missed twice." Blieker pointed out two damaged areas in the wall to the left of the door. He and Ardell Wings had already recovered the slugs, which had copper jackets and appeared to be .38 caliber. "We figure whoever shot him was sitting across there, on the bed, when Hudson came through the door. At least a couple of shots missed. Three didn't."

"So how come he didn't just jump back out the door?"

Blieker smiled. "Check behind the chair." He pointed to the ragged armchair on my left, where a sawed-off pump shotgun rested on two nails hammered into the cracked lathe and plaster wall. There was blood on the wall between the door and the chair, and three splintered holes, from which they had removed portions of the cores of three more bullets. The copper jackets, along with lead fragments, apparently remained inside Hudson.

"He wasn't much on backing down, was he?" I said.

Blieker laughed. He snugged up his rubber gloves, then removed the shotgun, noting the time to Wings, who was keeping the evidence log. "Twelve-gauge Mossberg. Safety off." He jerked back the slide and caught the ejected live round on the fly. "Loaded." Blieker lay the shotgun on the floor with the other evidence then put the shell in a small brown paper bag.

The room smelled like incense and body odor and dope, the essential perfume of America's underground. The corners of the ceiling were choked with cobwebs, and the floor held heaps of dirty clothes and dog-eared magazines and beer cans. The walls were covered with posters—save the whales posters, posters of defunct rock 'n' roll bands, get-out-of-Vietnam/Chile/Nicaragua/El Salvador/Lebanon posters—and a pair of horned cattle skulls. There was a cheap guitar with three broken strings, an unassailable mountain of 8-track tapes beside an amp, a tape deck, and speakers. In a room no bigger than a small closet were a dingy sink and hot plate. The bathroom was smaller still, and looked like it harbored enough diseases to alter the course of civilization. And it all stank of incense and body odor and dope, without even a hint of strawberries.

Blieker put all the separate items of evidence into one large plastic garbage bag and set it near the door, along with the aluminum case containing Ardell's camera gear.

"The guy next door told us Hudson moved in here about seven months ago," Ardell Wings said, buttoning his brown corduroy jacket. Wings is a small man, a dark bookish guy with thick glasses, who always looks out of place at a crime scene. "He's been out of the joint about—"

"About a year ago," I said. "Anybody know why it happened?" I stood in the door, leaving it open for fresh air.

Blieker shook his head. "Slayton's people did a preliminary canvass of the neighborhood and the bystanders. They asked for names and got them. Asked for information and didn't. Everybody's either too dumb or too scared to talk."

"And Hudson too dead," I said.

"No shit." Blieker took a last look around, then switched off the bare overhead bulb, which provided the only light inside the house. He paused, then said, "I'm assigning this case to myself. I want you involved, but I don't want your name down as lead investigator."

"That'd be best." I appreciated Blieker's gentleness with my ego. Normally, I would likely have worked the case through with Red Hanrahan, my regular partner, who was out of town for the weekend.

"It's not you. It's just that in court . . . Christ, if I'd known it was Hudson got croaked, I wouldn't have called you down here at all."

"Forget it." I tried not to sound elaborately casual. "What do you want me to do from here?"

"I'm still thinking about that." Blieker finished filling out a receipt for the items seized, then left a carbon of the receipt on the cot.

The three of us gathered up our goods and carried them out to Blieker's blue Dodge. Wings got in on the passenger side, while Blieker want back and locked Hudson's house.

"You all right?" Blieker asked, walking me to my car. He flipped up the collar of his dark blue overcoat and pulled on a pair of heavy gloves. Seeing Blieker bundle up, I felt cold.

"Sonofabitches," I said. "Most people, you know, when they live in a shithole like this, it's because something went wrong, they lost their job or never had anything to start with. But guys like this . . . these people . . . they had a plan. They all *believe* this is the way people *should* live."

"Everybody's got to be someplace," Blieker said. "You keep tabs on him after he got out?"

"Why?" I guess I flared at the question more than I should have. Probably a hangover from the week after Hudson was released, when Frank Woodruff pulled me in for a chat on the impropriety of certain types of revenge.

"Just asking," Blieker said. "That's all."

"I know. It's a logical question. I don't have an alibi, if that's what you're getting at."

"No . . . " Blieker was exasperated. I liked that. It's good for him. He said, "Give it a rest, huh?"

I'm unaccustomed to having other people make decisions on cases that I work. This is a consequence of ten years of fending for myself with various degrees of success. I wondered aloud where the investigation was headed.

Blieker rested his hip on the fender of my car and thought. "What time is it?"

It was coming up on three A.M.

Blieker straightened abruptly and bunched his coat around

his shoulders. He and Wings would haul their evidence back to the station and get it locked up. Then they would pack it in for the night. "You head on home from here," he said. "Try to get some sleep."

"And tomorrow?"

"Say, ten o'clock at the station. We'll go over it all from the start, arrange for the autopsy, make assignments, solve this sonofabitch."

"Always the optimist."

"Might as well," Blieker said, "it doesn't cost anything."

"That the same as saying talk's cheap?"

"You got to look forward to something, Leo. It's only . . . normal, for Chrissake."

"I look forward to payday."

Blieker laughed and started for his car. "I guess that's a start."

"Peace and love, baby." I flashed Blieker the peace sign as he walked away.

Peace and love, I snarled, getting in my car. I drove away from the curb and turned into the alley, where I saw a woman walking toward me. Marian Tawney. The red mackinaw was thrown loosely over her shoulders, and she carried a bundle against her chest. I cranked down my window as I pulled up beside her. The air was stinging cold.

"The baby?"

"He's nursing. Gets real uptight if I stop. But I saw the lights. I wanted to talk to somebody before you all left."

"Get in."

Marian Tawney walked around the car and slid in beside me. She adjusted the mackinaw, pulling it closer around her chest. I heard a smacking noise from inside the bundle of blankets.

"I live just a couple of blocks over," she said. "When I heard all the sirens, saw the lights, I was afraid it might be here. So I walked over."

"You getting along okay?" I asked. Her face was startlingly drawn, which I hadn't noticed earlier from a distance. I looked for some clue to tell me what kind of life she'd been living. I didn't find one. I knew, though, that the next time I looked in a mirror, I'd look older than the last time I'd looked before running into Marian Tawney.

"I'm getting along." She took out a cigarette and cracked her window to vent the smoke. I watched the tip of the cigarette and her fingers as she lit it. Her hands were steady. I was glad to see she didn't have the shakes.

"You should quit that," I said. "If you're going to nurse the baby, anyway. One of my ex-wives is a dietitian. She used to give me a lot of shit about health . . . before she threw me out."

"How many ex-wives you got?"

"Enough."

"I been working at this co-op day-care center, about the last year and a half."

"You see him much? After he got out?"

"I thought what I wanted most of all was to have him out," she said. "It wasn't."

"How old is the baby?"

"You know when he got paroled." She drew calmly on the cigarette. "Figure it out."

I stared ahead through the windshield. Down the alley, a cat wandered in and out of the bright sphere of a streetlight in the next block. Crazy. It was like I was trying to put my hand on the pulse of the moment, the way she'd put her hand on my pulse one hot summer evening a long time ago. Was that too much to ask? To ask of yourself the ability to make something last, even if it's something awful?

"What I wanted to know," she said, "I wanted to know if he's really dead . . . or if he'll be back. That's what I wanted to know for sure. If he's really gone this time."

"Why?"

"I just want to know, that's all. Just tell me if he's dead." Her voice was deep and strong and the wind sucked the smoke from her mouth through the window.

"He's dead. I didn't drive a stake through his heart, but he's dead."

"Thanks."

"You know why it happened?" Maybe it was a bad time to talk business, but it was bad business I had on my mind.

She was quiet for a long time. Then she said, "You

know . . . knew him. Deciding who killed him would be like drawing straws." She took a short drag on the cigarette and then a longer one.

"That's okay," I said. "I figure you'll talk to me when you're ready."

"What's that supposed to mean? You think I'm lying?"

"People lie all the time," I said. "Even when they don't know they're doing it. I think you came back down here looking for me for a reason. And I think once you got here, something held you back."

Marian hauled the baby closer to her breast and opened the door. She started to get out, then stopped. "It was me, you know. That burned you. I forget why it was, but I made you when he brought you to the house that day. I was just real scared. That's what I wanted to tell you. It's been on my mind a lot. Since he got out."

"Yeah. I always figured." I used to wonder how I'd feel if I ever knew for sure. I wanted anger, knew that anger was healthy, but the best I could do was disappointment, and disappointment is not exactly a rare commodity with Leo Banks. "I'll give you a lift. It's pretty cold. For the kid."

Marian Tawney shook her head and smiled. "You take care of yourself," she said.

"You too. You're sure about the ride?"

She smiled again and said, "It's not far," and closed the door. For a time, I sat in the alley and watched her walk away. Snow began to flash like fireflys in the headlights. If I sat very still and concentrated, I could see her dancing, whirling through the colored lights and smoke, before everything tumbled to earth.

Chapter 2

I gouged my shin on the corner of a coffee table as I walked back into the living room with another can of beer. I jumped away from the pain and when I did that, the beer slopped over my knuckles and I started to swear, but caught myself. I'd been trying to cut down on my obscenities. People—not cops, but regular people—tend to stare at you when you use *fuck* like punctuation. People had been staring at me plenty lately.

"Fuck!" I rubbed my shin, then caught my balance and stumbled around the table to the couch. There wasn't anybody to stare at me in my own home. I could say *fuck* all I wanted. This Sunday, now grinding to an end, had not been one of my better days.

The Rozette City Police Department's Detective Division is in the basement of City Hall. That means that there are no windows. And because of a stroke of architectural genius, the basement was dug below the level of water and sewer lines. That means that you have to go upstairs to find a water fountain or use the can.

"Keeps the suicide rate down," Captain Fanning likes to say. "No windows to jump out of, no toilets to drown yourselves in." Fanning always neglects to point out that there are plenty of pipes to dangle yourself from, and nobody has to go farther than his own person to find one or more guns.

Sam Blieker was uncharacteristically animated when I wandered into his office at the Division that Sunday morning. He was nursing coffee and talking with Jack Tracer. Tracer, a prosecutor in the County Attorney's office, was tugging at his salt and pepper mustache while he read over a group of police reports. His glasses were balanced on the end of his bulbous nose, which is always the color of a plum, about the same shade as a '65 Mustang I had when I was a kid.

"Better than your average reports." Tracer slid the sheaf of papers onto Blieker's desk. "Howdy, Leo."

Tracer is somewhere over fifty. When his first grandchild was born a few years ago, his hair immediately began a disappearing act that finally left him with just a fringe above his ears and collar. In court, Tracer can make justice seem as terrible or as gentle as the situation requires. He speaks with the aid of large, expressive hands that dish off words and phrases with the dexterity of a point guard feeding a power forward on the break.

"Relax, Jack," I said. "I didn't do Hudson."

"No, but I can hear the envy in your voice."

I hoped he was joking.

Blieker told me that he'd deviated from his plan of the night before. He'd come to work a couple of hours ago and called Dr. Odell Molyneaux, the medical examiner. Molyneaux was scheduled to meet with the attorney general the next day in Helena, so he wanted to post Hudson as soon as possible. Thomas Cassidy, another of the detectives, was at the morgue now.

I pulled up a chair beside Tracer. "I take it no new and dramatic leads have presented themselves overnight."

Blieker's smile was grim. "Ansel Williams. He's the guy who lives next door to Hudson and was his landlord. It was Williams called 9-1-1, when he heard a noise out back. He didn't recognize the noise as a dispute or shots, exactly. Just some kind of vague noise that woke him up, got him pissed off enough he decided to call the cops, teach a lesson to whoever it was interrupted his sleep."

Blieker reached under the desk and tugged at his socks. Then he went on. "Before you start asking me a lot of questions, I'm going to give you a blanket answer: I don't know." He slid the reports that Tracer had just read across the desk toward me. "These are from Slayton's guys last night. No leads, like I said, but it looks like they've got a pretty healthy list of alleged witnesses in the neighborhood." Blieker's smile brightened. "Have a nice day. "

"Beats selling vacuum cleaners or encyclopedias," I said.

Tracer cleared his throat. "Too bad we couldn't have got Hudson some more time." He was the attorney who'd handled my near-death. "That's always bothered me. But I figured—must've told you at the time—figured that even if we took him to trial, the sentence would have been about the same. So there was no percentage in going to trial. Hell, I don't have to tell you about the way some juries manage to dig up a soft spot."

No, Tracer didn't have to explain plea-bargaining. Not after all these years. The sentence hadn't bothered me then, and it didn't bother me now. "Think of it in a cosmic sense, Jack. If Hudson had served one day more, or one day less, then his whole life after that might have been completely different. He might not have been standing in front of bullets last night. You get my drift?"

Tracer got it.

I wasn't in the mood to participate in a psychological autopsy on myself, so I started for the door.

"Jack and I are drafting a search warrant," Blieker said. "For another search of Hudson's house." His investigation the night before had brought forth no reason to believe that anybody but Hudson lived in the house, and the dead have no expectation of privacy. Even so, a search warrant was reasonable precaution to take before reentering the house after it had been sealed. Since we still didn't have a suspect in the shooting, there was always the outside chance that Hudson was killed by somebody who could claim residence at Hudson's place. We'd run into claims like that on other cases over the years, and I can tell you it's a lot easier to spend a couple of hours on a search warrant rather than a couple of months having some defense attorney try to get all your evidence tossed out.

Blieker went on: "We get done, hunt up a judge and everything, then I'll pick up Ardell Wings and head on back over to the house. Last night . . . you looked like seeing that place was taking you pretty far away. You don't—" He stopped and looked at Tracer, then back at me. "I mean, there's no investigative reason why you have to go back there . . . and at the same time there's none for you to stay away. That's one of the reasons for not putting your name on top of the case. I guess what I'm saying is you should stop in or stay away, whatever you think you need to do."

I sensed another incision in my psyche, so I didn't waste a lot of words telling Blieker I understood.

"Whatever you decide," Blieker told me, "can you get together with us by, say, three this afternoon?"

I could, and I would. In the meantime, I enjoyed a crisp morning stroll through Ragtown.

Fifty years ago, Ragtown amounted to eight blocks of cramped, identical bungalows across the Holt River from the old Corso lumber mill. The houses were all owned by the Company back then, but over the years they'd been sold off, once in a while abandoned, now and then burned down. Somewhere along the line, the name Ragtown was applied. The name stuck like a bad reputation, and the neighborhood grew as the Company houses began to decay and the decay spread to surrounding blocks. Today, vacant lots give the neighborhood the look of a place seen in black and white newsreel footage. Feral dogs roam the streets, sleeping at night under rusted out cars, swayback porches, the green skirts of tall spruce trees that drag the ground, or dense willow thickets near the river. Wild dogs everywhere. They should have called the place Dogtown. Over the years, I'd arrested countless people in Ragtown, tossed dozens of houses. The house where I'd been cut was in Ragtown, and I've never gone back into that neighborhood without remembering that day, and wondering what it would have been like to cap that nightmare by putting a handful of bullets into Sky King Hudson. Now, somebody else had capped the nightmare for me.

Ansel Williams was trying to beat the odds in Ragtown. He was a foreman at Corso, who had retired before the mill shut down for good. His white frame house was newly painted and the lawn was in good shape. And now, despite all that, some numskull had gone and committed a murder right there in plain sight from his bathroom window. Now he couldn't even do his business and read the newspaper, without being reminded of the trash outside. Ansel Williams wanted justice. He wanted me to arrest somebody. Unfortunately, he didn't have a clue as to just who I should arrest. He was in bed, sound asleep, as though he still had to make the early shift at Corso the next day.

And that was pretty much the story of my Sunday tour through Ragtown. I managed to locate all the people named in the reports from Patrol, as well as add three of my own. I avoided Hudson's house like a disease. By three o'clock, I left with no more direction than I'd had when I arrived.

Back at the station, I found Thomas Cassidy, Ardell Wings, and Blieker sitting around Blieker's office. Wings and Blieker were talking, while Cassidy scribbled in a spiral notebook.

I sat down next to Cassidy and said, "Your next epic?" Cassidy wrote a book once, and now he considers himself the resident representative of the literate world. Every day, he reads *Doonesbury* and explains it to the rest of us. I'm not sure what his book was about. It went out of print before I bought a copy, and somebody stole the one copy at the city library. Cassidy claims to be working on another tome. He says Judge Walter N. Clay is helping him out with the moral and commercial elements.

Cassidy didn't bother to look up. "I just took a guided tour through the insides of your unfinished business, Mr. Gene Sky King Hudson, Esquire. Some people might call that having an experience." He looked up then and smiled as he crossed his legs and lazily kicked a tassled cordovan loafer.

"You're too pretty for this line of work," I said. With that, Blieker coughed pointedly and we got down to business.

Business didn't amount to much. The second search of Hudson's house had turned up nothing to indicate who Hudson had been hanging with or what he had been up to. Cassidy's aforementioned guided tour at the morgue revealed that Hudson had died of gunshot wounds, which we all knew before Cassidy spent the day having an experience, while he padded his pockets with overtime. Then I weighed in with equally astounding noninformation. After half an hour of pointless brainstorming, Blieker broke us up for the day.

Driving home, I thought about the one name that hadn't been in the reports, the one piece of work I hadn't done that day. Marian Tawney. I couldn't shake the sense that there was something she'd wanted to tell me early that morning in the alley, some reason beyond nostalgia that she'd carried her nursing baby through the snow to catch me. She'd told me she lived nearby. I could easily have looked her up. Should have looked her up, maybe. But there would be time to see her later, after I was sure if I was looking to catch a killer or an apparition.

I live in two alcove rooms in a big old house on Eau Claire, a street at the fringe of the Defoe district. The house is on the Holt River, just across from downtown Rozette. At night after I fold out the Hide-A-Bed, I like to lie and look out at the city lights. The house is really a mansion, built in the last century by a timber baron named Ronald Hollingshead. My niche on the third floor used to be the servants' quarters. The baron's only child, Miss Leona Hollingshead, still owns the house. Inside that wax museum she calls a home on the first floor, she clings to life with the aid of about four thousand cats and an oxygen tank. She collects the rent in person, and dispenses lectures on morality to anyone unfortunate enough to cross her path. I moved in almost two years ago, after my third wife gave me the air. Except for several boxes of books and papers in the kitchen, I'm almost unpacked. Even after two years, though, I still notice the odor of cooking grease and space heater exhaust that go with seedy apartments.

"Deirdre, you were the best." I toasted the air my third wife had given me and drained off half the beer. Deirdre is a loan officer at a Rozette bank. Sometimes I resent like hell that she has a job good enough she could unload me just like that. When I'm rational about it, though, I know that the split was much tougher on her than I like to remember. I'm glad her job is good enough she didn't have to stick around and be miserable. I stared at the can of Budweiser in my hand and tried to remember how many had preceded it. I always feel charitable after about three beers, and downright sentimental after five. By seven I'm depressed and after nine I just plain don't give a shit. It only takes one, though, to have me choking down guilt.

I swear to God Deirdre is my last wife.

I'm glad Deirdre's job was good enough she couldn't stick me for alimony.

I'm glad, too, that none of my wives and I shared any children. I may be many things in this life, but being a good role model—or even a vaguely adequate one—for children is not one of the things that I am.

"Sharon, you were second best." I took another large swallow. Sharon was my middle try at wedded bliss. She left me to marry a carpenter and they moved to Billings.

Alice, the first, was a bitch. The dietitian. The last I heard, she was working in a hospital in Denver. Probably doing medical experiments on people.

The only thing I could say for sure about my wives was that each time out of the chute, I got a little closer to picking the right one. Of course, by starting out with Big Al, a real testicle pulverizer, I had nowhere to go but up. I started to get another beer, but there wasn't enough beer in the world to get me back to feeling sentimental about Big Al.

It was probably wrong that I felt as happy as I did about Sky King Hudson getting stiffened up. Until my fourth beer, though, I'd enjoyed being happy too much to get concerned over the moral and mental health implications of dancing on graves.

"To you, Sky King Hudson. To your rigor mortis, life's last hard-on."

Almost twenty years . . . one fifth of a century. What happened to all that time? The years in uniform. The first big cases as a detective. I thought about all the people, living and dead, I'd dealt with and they all ran together, a wall of faces . . . *Banks . . . Banks . . . Banks! We want Banks!*

What did they want? My help? My forgiveness? More likely, my blood.

Sometimes, I believe that my partner, Red Hanrahan, understands what they want. Hanrahan is a good Catholic and an even better Irishman, so he understands guilt and defeat like a shark understands water. He's such a good Catholic, he gave me a St. Christopher medal once. I told him I was a confirmed Secular Humanist and it was more likely I'd become a Druid before I followed him through those big oak doors at St. Paul's. But Hanrahan insisted. The funny thing is, I wear the damned thing. Of course, I didn't start wearing it until after the Church decided St. Christopher wasn't a saint anymore.

"Now, lad, you can't be doin' this." It was Hanrahan talking like Pat O'Brien to me, while I was talking about another divorce. "You've got to be settlin' down now."

Or, "Easy, Leo, me boy. Let's save one for the next communion," when I got up for yet another six-pack after Jimmy Shell got the death sentence. I thought about calling Hanrahan that Sunday to tell him about Sky King Hudson, but Red and his brood were still at his mother's in Butte.

I mashed the aluminum can and dropped it on the floor beside the couch. I got up and started to pace around the apartment. It was quiet. My back ached a little. My footsteps sounded expectant on the bare hardwood floor. I looked at my watch and saw that it was ten minutes before midnight. Sunday the thirteenth was almost over. Hudson had been dead for nearly twenty-four hours. I felt expectant, too, but there really wasn't anything I was waiting for, except perhaps morning, when I could go to work. I got another beer and went back to the couch.

Any way you looked at it, it was a hell of a deal. Sky King Hudson was dead. Even sober, I had been delighted. Hudson is dead. Pushing up daisies. It was as though I had stored all the euphemisms for death in a small jeweled trunk inside my mind, and now I opened that trunk and began trying out its contents on Hudson, just to see how they fit.

Sky King Hudson is feeding worms. That one wasn't bad. Had a kind of frontier ring to it.

Sky King Hudson is underground. Poetic justice there, since the sonofabitch had come from hell in the first place.

Sky King Hudson caught a bullet. Damn right, pardner, caught three of them right in the belly.

Sky King Hudson has gone the way of the buffalo. Amen, brother, and may the ghosts of all those beasts trample his ghost into nothing.

Sky King Hudson is terminated. Ah, high tech death, the absolute fucking end.

I wished to God I could have spent Sunday afternoon the way I'd spent Saturday, when I went up to an abandoned coal mine south of town and dug for several hours in a bed of pumicite that outcrops there, looking for fossil leaf prints and wondering if I should have worked harder to stay in school.

Paleontology. That's what I'd studied a long time ago, before

flunking out of the University of Illinois and doing my hitch in
the Navy. Brachiopods and trilobites. I stumbled back into
that world when I was laid up after getting cut by Sky King
Hudson. The books kept my mind off my rage, and when I was
able to get up and around, hiking in the mountains with a
shovel and rock hammer was as good a way as any to get my
legs back. Wading through the books seemed much easier than
when I was in school. But then lots of things probably are
easier when you aren't drunk *all* the time and trying to fight a
revolution on the side. I'd come back with two nice prints,
genus *Sequoia*, I think. In a day or so, I'd catalog them and put
them with the rest of my collection, which Miss Hollingshead
lets me store in the basement—an appropriate place for fossils
if ever there was one.

I was starting to feel like a fossil myself. This was especially
true whenever I thought about Blieker and Frank Woodruff.
It's hard to imagine that Woodruff is a lieutenant and Blieker a
sergeant. I've got more time on the Department than either of
them and they're both a couple of wheels now, have been for
a long time, while I'm still just a basic patrolman. It's my own
fault, though. I've never applied for sergeant, never put in my
letter and taken the test.

"I coulda been somebody, I coulda been a contender." I
laughed and kicked my feet up on the coffee table. "A
mother-goddamn-fuckin' contender." I yawned and clawed my
fingers through my hair. Now I'd gone and said *fuck* again.
What's a guy supposed to do?

For a nonrated detective, making sergeant almost always
means an automatic transfer back into uniform and I'm happier
where I am than I figure I'd be as any kind of a sergeant, or
even a lieutenant in Uniform Patrol. Woodruff was smooth
enough—political enough—to maneuver his promotions and
stay a detective, and Blieker had lucked into a transfer back
after only a year in uniform. But office politics unsettle me, and
I have absolutely no faith in luck. I'd decided a long time ago
to stay put. Red Hanrahan wants to be a sergeant. Being a
good Irishman, he understands perseverance in the face of
impossible odds. And being the father of four, he also understands money. I hope he makes it, even if it means I'll need a
new partner.

I sat up and looked around the apartment, at the plain white walls, which still bear the shadows of pictures that had been hung by previous tenants and taken down when they packed up and moved on. I ought to paint, get rid of the ghosts of what some other poor sonofabitch thought was worth looking at while he sat around this dump listening to his hair grow and trimming his toenails. And get a rug, maybe, one of those bargain Persian kind of rugs they sell at Sears. Put a little color in the place, make it look a little less like a room in some hospital on the skids. At least the second floor separates me from Miss Hollingshead's feline circus. I've never known for sure if she needs oxygen because of disease or cats.

And at least it was quiet that Sunday night. Sometimes, the young couple downstairs get to rooting around at each other and I have to turn on the TV to drown out all that groaning and yipping. What must Miss Hollingshead think, living below that nymph and satyr? And how can they get up for that much romance? Considering the menagerie on the ground floor, the whole middle apartment must reek of cat piss. Jesus Christ, you can smell it in the stairway if you have the stomach to use the inside entrance. Those two must really be in love.

I got up again and resumed pacing.

I went to the window and looked down into the deep yard, which is bounded on the west by a tall arborvitae hedge and on the east by a stand of willows. The arborvitae extends like a row of tall thick green tails from the corner of the house to a levee and the headgate of an irrigation network, which Ronald Hollingshead built to water this whole part of town. Of course, this wasn't town at all back then, but Hollingshead's ranch. People still pump water from the ditches, which run for three or four miles downstream. Every summer several dogs and a child or two fall in and drown. Water is a valuable commodity here in the West.

Just east—upstream—from the Hollingshead property, Leeds Park begins as a narrow, grassy strip, then opens into a broader pocket of cottonwoods and brush at the mouth of Bride's Canyon. Leeds Park is bordered on the north by the Holt River, which drains the canyon. This late in the year, the water is down, leaving exposed bed between the water and

the levee. A big rain, though, and the river threatens the park
and Miss Hollingshead's backyard.

"We used to picnic in the gazebo out back near the river,"
Miss Hollingshead told me once. The gazebo is still there.
"And Father used to trout fish from the headgate. And shoot
antelope from the front porch."

Yes, Miss Hollingshead.

"With his associates from Chicago and New York City, and
once from London, England."

Of course, Miss Hollingshead.

Besides outliving all of Father's money, the old gargoyle was
crazy as hell.

The dancing.

It was the dancing—what the dancing means late at night
just before I sleep—that I'd never gotten over. Sometimes,
and always by surprise, it is as though I can reach out and
touch her, Marian Tawney, still dancing through the smoke
there in Angel's. What is it about some women that makes
them lodge so in a man's memory, like emotional cancer? She
was beautiful, but there were women more beautiful. Her
body had probably harbored enough chemicals to stock the lab
of a medium-sized high school. She'd fathered a child by one
of the great scum-balls of all time. She'd almost cost me my
life.

Was it just the dancing? I watched the river glint under the
lights from downtown. In the curve of the river, I imagined the
curve of her breasts and hips.

*Steady there, Leo, me lad. Let's not be gettin' psychoana-
lytical now, eh? Let's leave that for the nonbelievers.*

It was the dancing. I remembered the way she'd shoot her
arms into the air, as though trying to seize time itself. It wasn't
that the dancing was everything, but that in those precise
moments, everything was the dance.

And now she was just another exhibit in the zoo.

Dancing.

My mind went whirling away, spinning around and around
and around and the axis of it all was a knife, the knife Sky King
Hudson had planted in my back.

How can these four walls contain me?

I started to pace again, back and forth across the small living

room. I headed into the kitchen for another beer, then stopped
and sagged against the doorjamb. I would go to bed. Get a
good night's sleep for a change. Sky King Hudson was dead.
What better way to celebrate than a good night's sleep?

But would the world stop spinning long enough for sleep?
Who would pull the knife from my back this time? Three wives
and twenty years on the force had only quickened the pace.

I stepped around a pile of magazines just inside the kitchen.
I opened the refrigerator, then looked down and watched as
my hands opened another can of beer. I'd started drinking
beer about as much as I was saying *fuck*. If I kept up at this
rate, people would be staring at me before I even opened my
mouth.

Chapter 3

"You're a wreck, Banks," Vic Fanning said when I walked in Monday morning. He was standing in his office door, waiting for me. "How many times have I told you the goddamn personal appearance policy. Now, I know what you're about to say." Fanning held up his hand and shook his head. "But I got to tell you, Leo, I don't think anybody ever choked to death pulling his tie all the way up. And I don't think anybody ever went Chapter Eleven over a haircut and a shave."

Captains, they always feel obliged to start clubbing you over the head with policy.

I didn't really mind Fanning climbing me about hygiene, because I was late that Monday morning. Monday the fourteenth, the day after Sunday the thirteenth. I could at least argue the cleanliness and godliness issue. There wasn't much I could do about being forty minutes late except eat it. What the hell.

With the two-inch heels on his glossy black cowboy boots, Fanning stands only as tall as my nose, and I'm hardly six feet. Fanning's gray hair is always cropped and mashed flat against his head, like a cast iron skullcap. He always wears monogrammed dress shirts, always heavily starched. Sometimes, when he sweats a lot, which is often, he changes to a fresh shirt in the middle of the day. I usually don't change to a fresh shirt until about Wednesday.

I looked back at Fanning and grinned. "There was this guru in Nepal—"

"Don't start off the day giving me shit. You're late." Fanning turned back into his office and then stopped. "And where'd you get that tie?"

I was wearing a black tie with a bouquet of hand-painted red roses. The tie must have been six inches wide and forty years old.

"You got some special policy on neckties, other than I got to wear one?"

"That's the ugliest necktie I ever saw."

"What the fu—"

"What?"

"Nothing."

"Sounded like you were about to say a word commonly used by vulgar people when they talk about the human reproductive process."

"Not me. You must have me confused with somebody else, Vic."

"Yeah, sure. Well, I'll tell you, that tie gives ugly a bad name."

Beth McCoy, our secretary, scratched her scalp with a pencil point as I walked past her desk. She had on a green and red flowered blouse that looked like it needed water.

"So does your mother." I straightened my tie for Beth McCoy, then turned left into the open area I shared with Red Hanrahan, Thomas Cassidy, Harold Hoopes, and Linda Westhammer. There are two other similar areas—pits, we call them—in the City Hall basement, where a total of fifteen detectives work. Then there are Fanning, Woodruff, and Blieker, who have private offices.

"At least I've got a mother," Fanning shouting after me.

I was relieved to hear the little guy laugh. Needling Fanning is too much fun to pass up, yet always a calculated risk, since at least half the time, Fanning wouldn't know a joke if he was dying of it.

"A saint, she is," Fanning called.

"You mean a nun," I said, pressing my luck. I loosened my tie further and flopped into the chair behind my desk. Red Hanrahan was reading the sports section of the *Rozette Free Independent*. Harold Hoopes was gone. Linda Westhammer was working on her mouth with a lipstick. Cassidy was on the phone.

"Yes, ma'am . . . sure . . . no, I'd be upset, too, if he told me to do that . . . and then what'd he say? . . . yeah . . . yeah . . . yeah, it would hurt . . . no, I've

never seen one that big . . . he's just putting you
on . . . sure . . . I'm positive of it . . . absolutely . . .
no, they don't get that big, nobody's does . . . no, I'm not an
expert, but we've got one. Just a minute, I'll ask." Cassidy put
his hand over the phone. "Linda, what's the biggest dick you
ever saw?"

"You're scum, Cassidy." Linda Westhammer put the cap on
the lipstick and dropped it into her purse.

"I was right, ma'am, they don't get that big . . .
yeah . . . yeah . . . we will. Just let me know if he calls
back again . . . right, goodbye." Cassidy looked down at the
report as he made some notes, then glanced up through his
bushy red brows at Linda Westhammer. "We should get
married, Linda."

"Your old lady'd love it." Linda is a small, tightly wound
woman with blond hair that she wears in a frizz. She's one of
half a dozen women on the Department, all of whom regularly
get more or less clubbed by innuendo.

"She's history." Thomas Cassidy unzipped his leather jacket
and stretched. Cassidy's tie was patterned like a *snakeskin*, for
Christ's sake. Why wasn't Fanning giving *him* shit?

"Over my dead body," Linda Westhammer said.

"Suit yourself." Cassidy leered across the office at her. "I'm
patient. It'll give you something to look forward to on your
deathbed."

"I'd rather look forward to the autopsy," Linda Westhammer
said.

"Patient like a crow waiting for road kill." Cassidy reached
across to Hanrahan's desk and snatched part of the paper. "You
guys seen *Doonesbury* today? Where you hiding *Doonesbury*,
Hanrahan?"

"Speaking of hiding," I said, "where's Harold today?" I
hadn't seen Harold Hoopes for over a week, yet Hoopes had
the cleanest desk in the office. He could clear a case in less
time than most detectives could read it. Creative investigation, he calls it.

"He's off sick," Hanrahan said.

"Getting a root canal," Westhammer said.

"Probably he'll be gone for the week," Cassidy said.

."Probably hide out for a week, stuffing potato chips down his neck."

"Fuck," I said.

"That's it!" Westhammer shouted. She jumped up and ran to my desk, her palm outstretched. "Pay up, sucker."

"What the fuck's she talking about?" I said to Hanrahan.

"You forgot?" Hanrahan kicked his feet up on his desk and laughed. He's a big man with a full red mustache and curly red hair that he tries to keep plastered close to his head. When he laughs, he rocks the room and his hair springs free.

"Forgot what?"

"It's Monday."

"So?"

"Monday—"

"*Fuckless* Monday," Westhammer said, slapping her palm on my desk. "Fork over the cash."

Then I remembered. I'd bet Westhammer that I could go a whole day without saying *fuck*. I'd made a big production of it. Even Vic Fanning remembered, and now he was in our office waiting for me to pay over. Christ, Harold Hoopes probably even remembered, and he wasn't even at work Friday when we made the bet. My hubris was going to cost me five bucks.

"Unless you want to go double or nothing," Westhammer said, offering to let me run before she set the hook.

I thought for a moment, and then said, "I can't fuckin' do it," and handed over the cash. Linda slapped me on the shoulder and swaggered back to her desk.

"So what's new for business today?" I tried to sound unconcerned and in control, as though I wasn't up to my eyeballs in a homicide that had cost me the longest Sunday in recent memory.

Hanrahan reached across his desk and handed me half a dozen case files. "Mostly junk. Monday morning stuff. I already cleared a couple with phone calls. Nothing solves a Saturday night assault like Monday morning sobriety."

"You hear about Hudson?"

Hanrahan nodded. "Sorry I was out of town. Fact is, Blieker's been waiting for you. Wants to see you and me and Cassidy when he gets back. He went over to Jack Tracer's office for a minute."

The surge of anxiety I felt caught me off guard. I looked sharply over at Cassidy. "He make an arrest?"

Cassidy sounded bored. "Relax, Leo. He's just returning the search warrant from yesterday."

I was even more surprised by the relief I felt, knowing that Hudson's killer was still out there somewhere. Maybe there was still a chance he'd come my way. I got up and started for the door, looking back at Hanrahan. "You ready?"

"What makes you think I waited for you?"

"You're my partner. It's your job to wait for me when I'm late."

"Brute. You take me for granted."

"I love it when you're angry." I figured we had some time before Blieker got back. I told Cassidy we'd be back in thirty minutes. Then Hanrahan and I headed up the stairs. We were off on one of the most sacred missions performed by cops everywhere. We were going to coffee.

Sometimes, even a week later, I thought so hard about Hudson being dead that it exhausted me. And as the time passed, I also came to feel curiously empty, as though Hudson's death had eliminated one of my reasons for survival.

By the time Hanrahan and I got back from coffee that Monday morning, Blieker had drawn up a new list of assignments. Ardell Wings was busy cataloging the evidence. Later in the day, he and Blieker would select those items that needed to go quickly to the State Crime Lab in Missoula. Wings would make all those arrangements, which included driving the evidence to Missoula the next morning.

Physical evidence usually falls into three general categories—body fluids, fingerprints, and ballistics. The only body fluid we had from the house was blood. That appeared to be Hudson's, so there's no point right then in hammering the lab for a quick analysis. Beyond that, there were no identifiable prints that we could associate with the shooting. That left bullets.

From the autopsy and the house, we had recovered both substantial parts of lead cores, copper jackets and assorted fragments of both. The cores and jackets were of a size consistent with .38 caliber, which would include both .38 special and .357 magnum ammunition. We agreed that ballistics was our most pressing concern among all the physical evidence. If we didn't know what sort of shooter we were looking for, it made identifying the weapon that much more important. Finding a needle in a haystack is a little easier if you at least have an idea of which haystack to start with.

As soon as the meeting was over, Blieker wanted to take Cassidy with him to the Parole Office, where they would start in with the background, past and present, on Hudson. That left Hanrahan and me with . . . what?

Blieker was apologetic. "I guess there's not a whole lot left, Leo." He sucked on a tooth and drummed his thick fingers on the desk.

I started to make a crack about Blieker's talent for understatement, but held back. He was only trying to balance what he saw as the needs of the case with my need not to be frozen out. Why make an old friend's load any heavier?

Cassidy wasn't shy at all. "Think of yourself as a valuable resource, Leo. Somebody us lesser lights can come to when the going gets tough."

Cassidy wasn't an old friend. "You want the rights to my story?" I said. "Put some reality in your next book?"

Cassidy's smile was cold and slick. "Who'd believe a guy like you, Leo?"

"Some of us do this job," I said to Cassidy, "for more reasons than to pick up girls." I was already feeling patronized, confused and generally pissed off. Mashing Cassidy's round, boyish face wouldn't have cured me. Wouldn't have cured me at all. But it would have helped.

Cassidy didn't let up. "Lonely at the top, huh?"

Red Hanrahan jumped in before I got the chance to go on. "Don't you have an appointment or something, Cassidy. With your hairdresser, maybe?"

"That's enough!" Blieker might know better than to interfere with my bile, but he wasn't about to let Hanrahan into the act, too. "Leo, I said I'd involve you and I did. I also said I don't want this to be your case. But you know how these things go. You get past the first rush, and then it's just a matter of grinding it out. Right now, I can't see enough work for more than two people. I don't want you that close to this thing. Neither does Jack Tracer."

Knowing Blieker was right didn't help a damned bit. I told him I'd stay in touch with the case, both inside and outside the station. The outside part of that promise made him uneasy. Luckily, he had the good sense to let it go. Thomas Cassidy had the good sense not to say anything more at all. I thought about suggesting that one of them talk to Marian Tawney.

And then I decided, Screw these guys. Marian Tawney was my ace. I'd play her when I was damned good and ready.

For several days, I kept myself pumped up by getting details of the investigation from Blieker or, when I could tolerate him, Cassidy. Finally, though, all of the leads turned out not to be leads at all and the case settled into limbo. I caught myself in the midst of a kind of sick joy over the fact that, just as Blieker had wanted, the case wasn't tagged with my name.

On Wednesday of that week, I found Marian Tawney's name in the phone book and gave her a call. I didn't waste any breath on the old days. I told her that I was willing to risk a paycheck that she'd sought me out in the alley behind Hudson's because she had some information that needed to be told.

"I don't know what held you back," I said, "but I could see it in the way you held your baby, the way you sucked down that cigarette."

"I was nervous, that's all."

"That's my point."

"I almost got you killed once. You don't think telling somebody that is enough to make you nervous?"

"Sure it would. But I also know you didn't need to tell me at all. Not after all these years."

"What about my conscience?"

"I heard about a guy once that had one of those. But that was before the Beatles broke up."

"I guess it was a mistake. Trying to make things right."

"You wait over fifteen years, then just casually flag me down outside a murder scene? Nobody's tried a story that wild since Nixon caught the last chopper out of D.C."

"That's your problem," she said. And then she hung up. As

I sat at my desk, staring down at the phone, I realized how much I'd lived the last years on sheer bile. With Hudson finally dead, I could forgive Marian Tawney for setting me up, but I could also break her skull for holding out on me now. I needed to know the truth about how and why Hudson died. Not just know it, but *find it out*. In a way that I still don't understand, it was as though until I knew Hudson's full story, I would never know my own. I was using murder as metaphor, the same way sex freaks use pornography like a map.

Work, usually a balm, was suddenly no help. Hanrahan and I were passing through one of those deadly times when none of our cases led anywhere. We work crimes against persons. Sex and violence, Hanrahan calls it. That means rapes and homicides. But it also means nickel-and-dime fistfights. Lots of nickel-and-dime fistfights. Deals where everybody was drunk and the loser wants to press charges. Offsetting penalties, replay the down. No victim, no crime. Lots of time and frustration for the fortunate detective assigned the "case."

Hanrahan and I spent a lot of time those next few days tracking down reports that some creepo sleezoid banana had been taking pictures of little kids around all the local elementary schools. Vic Fanning, in his public relations zeal, had seen to it that word of this phantom photographer and his wheels had been published several times in the *Free Independent*, as well as broadcast on the TV and radio stations. For the past two weeks, Red and I had been chasing frantic reports about the Monster Molester, and I for one was getting damned tired of it.

"You know what I want?" I said one afternoon to Hanrahan while we were watching Mansfield Elementary on the north side.

"Yeah. You wanna sleep with a movie star."

"Be serious. I'm talking about something realistic."

"A million bucks." Hanrahan took another cookie from the bag he'd picked up earlier at a bakery, then watched through the telephoto lens on his camera as the kids fanned out across the playground. If we were lucky, we'd get a picture of the guy who was taking pictures of the kids.

"After I get a million bucks." I took a cookie for myself. Red has this theory that if everybody ate one cookie a day, the world would be a better place. So far, I'd had half a dozen and I didn't feel any better. Just fatter. And when I tried to tell Hanrahan what I really wanted, I found I didn't really know.

I had dropped the cookie back in the bag when I heard a black and white dispatched to a report of two guys in a blue car taking pictures of kids at Mansfield School. Red Hanrahan straightened in his seat and poised his camera.

"We're here," Hanrahan hissed. "I don't see the sonofa-bitches." Then he looked down at his camera. Then he looked over at me.

"And we're in a blue car," I said. I rolled my eyes and reached for the radio mike, but the frequency was jammed with traffic, other officers asking for more detailed descriptions of the fiends, which the unwitting bimbo in the dispatch center breathlessly provided.

. . . gray jacket . . .

I looked at my gray sleeve.

. . . wearing a necktie described as "weird" . . . second male subject described as "fat" . . .

"I've lost forty pounds!" Hanrahan shrieked.

like Bluto . . .

"That does it!" Hanrahan grabbed the mike out of my hand. By now I was beginning to hear sirens, lots of them, and they were getting closer. "That's us!" Hanrahan screamed into the mike. By now, the children were like startled deer, unsure whether to stand and gawk or run for cover.

Unit identify.

"Who do you think it is, it's us!"

Repeat, unit identify.

"Us! Hanrahan and Banks!"

The uniforms all acknowledged that they understood, then one by one, they drove by and waved, four of them—Collie Proell, Ike Skinner, Marie O'Conner, and the one and only Chester Boyles, who still worked for the Sheriff's Office, despite nearly being canned after firing a warning shot with a shotgun at a bank vice president during a false holdup alarm. Considering that Chester was on the street, both Hanrahan and I felt lucky not to be riddled with bullets.

"Where's the complainant?" I asked the dispatcher. Once I pried that information out of her, I drove around the block and

Hanrahan and I walked up to the front door of a small white shingled house across from the school. I pressed the bell. Inside, a voice shrilled: "They're here! Oh, dear God, somebody help me, they're at my door right now!"

I cupped my hand to the window in the door. Through the lace curtain, I saw a young woman waving one hand wildly toward the door and gripping the telephone with the other. I took out my badge and held it to the window. The shrieking stopped. A few moments later, the door inched opened, then stopped at the end of a brass chain.

"We're the police." I showed the woman all my teeth. "Is there a problem?"

Years ago, I'd been cut by a drug-crazed Neanderthal and stood at the brink of the pearly gates, only to be jerked back into life in the form of Celebrity Narc. Now Hanrahan and I were Celebrity Child Molesters. For a couple of days, it was fun, a good joke, a crack in humpty-dumpty's shell. A couple of nights in a row, I even went out to the movies and it felt good, being around people who weren't in any obvious trouble.

But it didn't last. The monotony returned, humpty-dumpty remained on the wall and once again I was spending my nights pacing inside my apartment, drinking beer and watching the lights of town on the river. Before Hudson's death, I'd never understood how easy it had been to focus my life when there was someone out there in that world for me to hate. Now, I wasn't sure I liked it all, this final retribution.

This being free.

Chapter 4

It's expectations that always get us in trouble. In our town of about seventy thousand souls, we understand when burglars, robbers, and even rapists fall through the cracks. These crimes go on all the time and people generally understand that the cops can't put the arm on everybody.

But murder is something different. Rozette has about half a dozen homicides a year, and as a rule the people around town expect the local constabulary to throw out a net and drag in the guilty fish. There just aren't enough people murdered here to turn homicide into an abstraction. Most of the cops I know could take or leave public pressure. What gets to us most is the unrelieved grind of pushing a case to the brink, only to find out that there is no brink; there is only more push. By the time Sky King Hudson had been dead for two weeks, Sam Blieker was starting to walk around with the look of a guy who was about to invent his own brink.

"At first we thought it had to be drugs," Blieker told me one afternoon at coffee. "Hudson took his fall for drugs. He had some THC in him when he got croaked. But there's nothing that takes us that way except general suspicion."

"People get murdered because of sex, money, or booze," I said, launching into my *film noir* theory of detecting. "Everything else is just an elaboration of that."

"Including drugs?"

"Including drugs," I said. "Maybe especially including drugs. Sex, money, or booze. You find where those things went wrong, you find your killer."

Blieker was not impressed. "You're a genius, Leo," he said. "A genius. You should be an attorney."

Ardell Wings had come back from Missoula to tell us that the gun which had killed Sky King Hudson was a .38 Smith & Wesson revolver, only perhaps the most common handgun in the world. After much deliberation, Blieker decided to withhold that information, despite at least three phone calls a day from Robert Tolliver, the police reporter for the *Free Independent*. Tolliver was suffering through a news drought, and he kept looking to Blieker and the Hudson case for rain. This information about the gun would be no great secret to the killer, so I suspect that Blieker held back just for the sake of holding, the way you hate to break a five dollar bill because then it spends faster. Sooner or later, Tolliver would catch onto this and make Blieker pay—probably by saddling him in print with some outrageous quote that Blieker had thought was off the record. I considered trying to warn Blieker off, but we've had that discussion before. Blieker was an adult. If he wanted to goad Tolliver into making him look stupid, that was his business.

The worst part of all about those two weeks was that I still couldn't shake the memory of Marian Tawney dancing. One night, I got out the phone book again, checked her address, then drove by the tiny brick house on Benton, not two blocks from Hudson's place in Ragtown. Thank God I still had enough brains not to stop. The problem was that her ghost was about the only thing still moving on that whole past life to which I still clung with a grip tight as death. It takes so little to change a life. An arch of fate's eyebrow here, a nudge of her hip there. Who knows.

Maybe if I'd seen Marian Tawney dancing before I started copping, maybe I'd have gone back to school and learned paleontology for real. Maybe we'd have hit it off and settled down and had kids who became professors and artists. Maybe I'd have saved myself and three women three marriages.

Or maybe I'd still have gotten myself stabbed, only gone to prison for it instead of into a blue uniform.

Who knows? Who the fuck knows? Maybe Thomas Cassidy knows, from all those books he says he reads and tries to write. I don't.

Late one afternoon, I was sitting at my desk, mulling over these cosmic subtleties, when the phone rang. It was Herm Fenstermacher, the Uniform Patrol boss on afternoon shift, who was calling to inquire if there were any detectives around who might be interested in investigating a dead body. The body was in Leeds Park and it was underground. Or mostly underground, Fenstermacher said. Red and I were the only dicks in the shop at the time, so off we went.

A dead body, I mused. How appropriate that it should happen on this particular day. Everybody should get a dead body the day before Halloween.

It was getting along toward dark when Red Hanrahan and I pulled up in the parking lot along the Holt River at the east edge of town. There were three black and whites in the lot, and a brown Datsun pickup. The pickup and one of the black and whites were empty. Ike Skinner sat with a civilian in the second black and white, and Herm Fenstermacher waited in the third. The canyon was already steeped in shadow, the chilly purple hue of evening, illuminated by the bright orange and gold torches of autumnal trees, cottonwoods near the river, and tamaracks along the mountainsides. If I held my face just right to the chilly breeze, it seemed as though I could smell elk. As I walked up to Fenstermacher, the scene made me think of football games and hayrides and pretty girls. Fenstermacher was just finishing up a coughing fit. Once he stopped, I could hear wind sifting through the dry leaves all around us.

"We got the guy found it." Herm blew his nose into a dingy handkerchief. "Guy name of Victor Reinholtz. That's him there with Skinner." He looked into the handkerchief before folding it and cramming it into his hip pocket.

There's something ironic about talking about corpses with Herm Fenstermacher, who could pass for dead himself. Herm has mousy brown hair and a chest caved in enough to catch rainwater. He holds the undisputed world record—eight minutes, forty-three seconds—for coughing without pausing to catch his breath. Even more amazing, he'd managed to smoke two cigarettes and drink a can of beer at the same time.

Reinholtz had been out for a walk, Fenstermacher told us, testing out the new Nikon his old lady had given him for his birthday. He saw this coyote out near the eastern boundary of the park, near where the park turns into National Forest, and he figured he'd get a good picture of it, so he put on a 400mm lens and focused in.

"The coyote, he was lickin' at something on the ground and once old Victor saw what it was he was really lookin' at, he saw it was a human hand. So old Victor, he says, 'Oh, my oh my,' and he takes time to run the coyote off before he calls the cops. A real deal, eh?" Herm balanced a Camel straight on his lip and set it on fire.

Red and I decided to leave the crime-fighting gear in the trunk of the car, since we were quickly losing daylight. The only thing we took along into the woods was a spool of yellow plastic barrier tape to cordon off the area around the grave. There was no need to rig up lights and rush the job tonight; the thing in the ground wasn't going anyplace. Not before morning, anyway.

But . . . some poor bastard was going to have to spend the night before Halloween guarding a cadaver.

We followed Fenstermacher into the trees, where an unsuspecting Collie Proell stood watch over the scene.

"You said nothing but bones," Red Hanrahan said. He stopped to pull loose a strand of wild rose that had snagged on his pants.

"Yeah, bones. Nothing but bones. You know, though, we never did no digging. And there's a lot of fallen leaves. Nobody moved nothing, not so much as a leaf. I just put Proell on it and pulled back and called Leo."

"I hope Proell didn't mess with the grave," I said. There's nothing a detective likes less than having to reconstruct a crime scene that somebody has *helped* him on.

"He did that, you guys just let me know when that grave's empty. I'll fill the sonofabitch up with three hundred pounds of policeman."

Fortunately for Collie Proell, we found him hunched down against the trunk of a cottonwood, nursing a chew of Beech Nut and generally minding his own business. Proell was at the far edge of a clearing about fifteen feet wide by twenty feet long. The clearing was blanketed with fired cottonwood leaves, which rustled as the three of us skirted the area and made our way to Proell, who stood to greet us.

"It ain't moved," Proell said. He was nearly as big around as the tree trunk he leaned against. Before he'd started enforcing the laws of man, Collie Proell had enforced Nature's Law for two seasons as a backup nose guard for the Denver Broncos. When he moved between me and the setting sun, Proell cast a shadow over an already gloomy scene. Proell pointed to an area of disturbed leaves near the center of the clearing.

At first, I thought I was looking at a gnarled root that had been dug up and torn loose by an animal. Suddenly, though, the image clicked, just as it probably had for Victor Reinholtz, and I recognized it as a hand. After that, it was impossible to interpret it as anything else.

"Nothin' but bones," Collie Proell said.

"How long you been on shift?" I asked Proell.

"About an hour." Proell glanced around nervously. "Why you asking that?"

I looked at my watch. It was after six-thirty and the dusk was thickening as we spoke. "How do you feel about ghost stories?"

"Whadya mean?"

"We're talking night of the living dead here," Red Hanrahan said.

"I look like Boris Karloff to you?" Proell straightened to his full height, which in fact made him look a lot like Karloff looked when Karloff played the original Frankenstein's monster.

"I'll see you get relieved about ten o'clock," Herm Fenstermacher said. "I'll *send* somebody."

"I ain't spendin' the night in the woods with no *dead body*!" They probably heard Proell all the way down in Denver.

"It'll be easy," I said.

"Oh, God," Proell moaned. "Oh, shit."

The four of us strung yellow barrier tape from tree to tree around the clearing. We talked about procuring chains to fasten Collie Proell to a tree, a large tree, but that proved not to be necessary. We offered to get Proell some garlic and silver bullets and a very large crucifix, but all Proell asked Herm Fenstermacher to bring him were a bag of groceries and a flashlight, a very bright flashlight and a very big bag of groceries.

"And lots of toothpicks," Proell said. "I can tell this is going to be a multi-toothpick kind of job."

Herm promised Proell the world, then hurried off so that he could complete the errand before dark.

"It'd be best if you kept on the outside of the barrier," I told Collie Proell.

"You don't have to worry about that."

"And keep everybody else away."

"Yeah, well you just remember, if anybody comes soft-footin' up on me, I ain't responsible for the consequences."

"Don't worry," Red Hanrahan said. "You're the most irresponsible guy I know."

"Hey, fuck you, Hanrahan," Proell said. "Fuck the both of you."

I stopped once and looked back through the underbrush at the clearing. The hand seemed to reach toward me from under the mulch.

"Ugly," Hanrahan said.

"Ugly as hell," I said. Uglier than Hanrahan knew. Uglier than I'd ever tell him.

Hanrahan kept shaking his head as we walked back through the trees. "Nothing but bones."

"Jesus Christ," I said, "I hope so."

Halloween day itself was a wonderful experience. I was tired and ill-tempered when I arrived at the station. Before going home the night before, Red and I had spent nearly two hours interviewing Victor Reinholtz. I had also taken time to contact Dr. Odell Molyneaux, the medical examiner, for technical advice on opening the grave. Dr. Molyneaux, in turn, told me to contact Dr. Janice Bowie, who taught archaeology at Rozette Junior College. Dr. Bowie was supposed to meet Hanrahan and me at the station at seven A.M. I was late.

In the days ahead, I would try to convince Hanrahan that I had no idea of what to expect in the way of a female archaeologist. He remained convinced that the whole thing was a conspiracy between me and Dr. Molyneaux. That's because Dr. Bowie turned out to be a tall, slender woman in her early thirties, with big dark eyes and feathered black hair that didn't look the least bit scientific.

"Call me Janice," she said, offering a hand.

I managed a smile, despite the hangover detonating deep inside my brain.

Within an hour, we had rounded up the tools necessary to complement our regular photography and evidence-gathering gear. Basically, that equipment amounted to two shovels, three hand trowels, a Pulaski tool, two five-gallon buckets, a wire mesh screen for sifting dirt, a metal detector, and a large plastic case full of assorted sized bags and containers. Once our excavation and evidence search was done, the coroner would supply a heavy black plastic body bag. We spent another thirty minutes briefing Fanning and Blieker. Then we were off on our woodland adventure.

"The main thing," Janice Bowie told us from the backseat as Hanrahan drove through the deserted streets to the park, "is you don't just dig the thing up."

"The Transylvanian approach," Hanrahan said.

"I beg your pardon?" Dr. Bowie was obviously not prepared for Detective Hanrahan.

"You know," Hanrahan said, "a wagon, a tired old horse, a dim lantern and a hunchback named Igor. The Transylvanian approach."

Janice Bowie tapped me on the shoulder. "Does he have a license for this sort of thing?"

In an effort to recover her professional sensibility, Janice Bowie went on to explain that it was best to dig a trench along the grave and several feet below the object to be recovered, then work into the grave laterally. "That way," she said, "you recover and protect as much as possible."

"Dig a trench," Hanrahan said. "I told you we needed a hunchback, Leo."

I decided not to tell Dr. Bowie about my fossil-hunting days and the fact that I had more than a passing knowledge of the kind of work that lay ahead. "We're pretty good with bodies above ground," I said. "But for the grave, we needed a specialist. Not," I glared over at Hanrahan, "a hunchback." I wasn't really upset with him. We both knew the awful chore that awaited us; if Red could keep us loose, he was doing everybody a favor.

"Your job," I told Janice, "is to convince a jury later on that we're not just a couple of grave robbers."

Janice said, "I still don't understand why Dr. Molyneaux didn't come himself."

Hanrahan glanced back and grinned. "He said you're an expert at digging up bones. You had any experience digging up bones that still have the meat on them?"

"No."

"Ask me that question about Molyneaux again in a couple of hours."

"Sometimes," I said, "nature is not a pretty thing."

And nature did not disappoint us that day. After photographing the general scene, I scanned the area with the metal detector and succeeded in finding only a rusty bolt. I got several positive readings, but those objects were underground and would have to wait. I was optimistic, though, since one of those readings was in what seemed to be near the body's center mass.

Hanrahan and I slowly brushed away the leaves and it was then that we learned that animals might have worked on more than the hand. Judging by the position of the hand, the face, whatever remained of it, seemed to be about eight or ten inches underground, in an area where several small burrows opened. Mice. Then the coyote picked up the scent and got to the arm. Another few days and there would have been bones all over the park.

Hanrahan began digging first, working on the access trench, putting the dirt into buckets, which Janice Bowie and I sifted through the wire screen, looking for whatever evidence we might find. We found only rocks and roots. Still, either Hanrahan or I periodically scanned the mound of sifted dirt with the metal detector. We didn't know the cause and manner of death, but the one metal reading we'd had earlier could mean that a bullet was involved; neither of us was willing to risk losing even the tiniest fragment.

After an hour, I spared Hanrahan in the trench, and an hour after that, Janice and I began carefully using the trowels to clear out the grave. Taking Janice's advice, I collected the ends of several roots, which appeared to have been severed when the grave was dug. By determining the species of root, along with the amount of regeneration, perhaps a botanist could come up with some additional information about when someone first put spade to earth at this particular little excavation site.

I knew by the smell and by the proximity of the exposed arm that we were getting close to the body itself. I stood up and took several deep breaths, while Janice continued to work.

"Let's take a break." I offered her my hand.

"Better not." Her use of the small trowel was unceasing and deft. "You might not get me back down in here again."

Then her trowel suddenly bit into flesh. She dropped the trowel, turned aside and wretched.

Wordlessly, Hanrahan reached down and took her under one arm, while I took the other. Once Janice was out of the trench, I scrambled out after her and followed her and Hanrahan to the edge of the clearing.

"Sorry," Janice said, catching her breath.

"For what?" I said.

"For that display. Not very professional."

"Red and I should thank you," I said, "for distracting us from our own stomachs."

"Giving you the chance to feel manly," she said, sounding disgusted.

"Just luck," Hanrahan said evenly. "Today, ours was good, yours bad. Got nothing to do with being tough. I'll get the stuff." He walked to one of the cases we'd carried in.

"What stuff is that?" Janice wrinkled her nose and breathed through her mouth.

"Surgical masks," I said. "And Vicks VapoRub. You put a gob of Vicks under your nose, then wear a mask. That stinks, too, but at least it doesn't make you puke."

Red Hanrahan handed Janice a molded blue mask. "Welcome to the world of forensic archaeology."

Dr. Molyneaux figured that the girl had been dead for between six and ten days. She was about twenty-two years old. He fixed her age by judging the development of her pelvis and the joints in her hands, both of which display quite predictable changes into the early twenties. She was blond, a natural blond, whose hair had grown below her shoulders before it stopped growing.

The girl had a red, blue, and yellow dragon tattooed on her left buttock, which I dutifully photographed. Dr. Molyneaux felt that the tattoo was very recent, not healed, and not even scabbed over. This led to speculation that it was applied postmortem. Her killer's signature, perhaps.

There were no fillings in her teeth, which led me to comment that there was no way to investigate her identity through the dental records of similar missing persons. Here, Dr. Molyneaux corrected me by pointing out that such perfection was, in itself, an identifying characteristic.

A black graphite crossbow bolt with red fletching was imbedded in her spine. The metal tip, which consisted of three razor-sharp flanges, was the object we'd picked up on the metal-detector. The bolt had entered just below the rib cage to the left of the keel sternum and penetrated her heart, which was now in a miserable state of disrepair.

The girl from the grave was nude and she didn't have a name. It was Red Hanrahan who first called her Linda Leeds.

"Are you missing any twenty-two-year-old girls with perfect teeth?" Dr. Molyneaux asked. He closed the cooler door and looked at me as I studied the crossbow bolt. The bolt was inside a plastic bag and the bag was sealed with red evidence tape. The bolt was about ten inches long. The point was slightly bent, probably from its impact with bone.

"If somebody in Rozette has a girl of this description missing," I said, "they haven't told the cops."

"Unless the killer is the only one who knows she was available to be missing," said Hanrahan. He finished packing our camera gear and snapped the metal case shut.

Dr. Molyneaux polished the thick lenses of his glasses on the tail of his lab coat and smiled at Janice Bowie, who had insisted on staying through the three-hour autopsy. "Which one of these clowns did the most digging?"

"Detective Banks," Janice Bowie said.

"That was so he could fondle Linda's breasts," Red Hanrahan said.

"I told you I'd still respect her in the morning," I said. Red and I both knew from experience that we'd feel worse if we couldn't dredge up a few laughs.

Janice Bowie laughed. And now that I thought of it, she'd been first-class company all day, not at all squeamish about climbing down in the trench, and not in the least bit outraged by Red's and my grim humor.

"Do you have anywhere to go with this?" Molyneaux asked.

"We're kind of like Lindbergh," I said. "We know we're going to Paris. We just have to hope we get there before we crash."

The four of us stood in front of a large grated duct, which vented fresh air into the morgue. Molyneaux wrapped his instruments in a white towel, leaving them for his diener to clean tomorrow. He'd already hosed down the stainless steel table. Now, he shut off the lights and opened the door.

"I have to leave the fan on. Otherwise, by tomorrow I won't be able to get anybody in the rest of the building to stay at work." He ushered us out the back door into the unlighted parking lot along the river.

The evening felt like cold weather. Canadian cold. It was the right time of year, a time of swirling leaves and ghosts and unexpected snow. The time of year when, once upon a time, the girl from the grave probably had fleeting thoughts of Santa Claus. But if you thought about things like that, it only made you crazy.

"Thanks for working late." I offered Molyneaux my hand.

"An appropriate night for it," he said. "Now Red has a real ghost story to tell his kids."

"I don't think I'll tell them this one." Hanrahan opened the car door. "This one is true. Better I should give them a set of beads and tell them to stay out of dark places."

Janice and Hanrahan got in the car. Janice had asked us all over to her house for a drink, but Hanrahan and Molyneaux succumbed instead to the allure of home and hearth. I, on the other hand, suffered no such temptations, so I was going to Janice Bowie's alone.

"Good luck with your case." Molyneaux waved and drove off.

The wind was blowing out of Bride's Canyon and the river smelled unspeakably good. It was the first time all day I'd gotten the smell of death out of my nose. I hated to get in the car. I stood for a moment, watching the low clouds scuttle above the traffic crawling overhead on the Defoe Street Bridge. I wanted to breathe in as much decent air as I could. I was thinking about the delicate bite of a paddle in the easy current, when Red Hanrahan leaned across and tapped on the window and it was time to go.

The truth was, we didn't have much of a case at all. A dead girl with no name. No clothes. No belongings of any sort. Not even any dental work. I had rolled a classifiable set of fingerprints from her left hand, the one that hadn't found its way above ground. In the morning I would send those off to the FBI. Most people's fingerprints, though, aren't on file with the Bureau. Linda Leeds she was tonight, and Linda Leeds she might well remain.

I stood in the French doors and watched the leaves drop from a huge cottonwood that slanted above the woodpile in Janice Bowie's backyard. Janice's house sits on two acres, out of the wind at the head of a small ravine south of town. The leaves bumped one by one through the baring branches and finally tumbled through the short gap of empty air. The yard was lighted by a mercury lamp. A large white dog trotted across the yard. It was the kind of big mongrel some kid should name Buster.

"I got the house," Janice said, walking up behind me and handing me another beer. "He got the car and boat and enough money for a new start in Alaska." She was talking about her ex-husband, an engineer named Tom Wysoki. They had been divorced for nearly two years.

"I gave up marrying people," I said.

"There are days when I'd say you made a wise decision."

"Maybe." I didn't say more. I've always found that the best way not to say bad things about your ex-wives is not to say anything at all. Janice deserved better than a dose of Banks gloom.

Janice stooped and put another slab of wood into the wood stove to our right. Her tight jeans stretched even tighter as she leaned forward, exposing a crescent of skin between her jeans and black sweatshirt. The sweatshirt had yellow Oriental characters written on the back. She had taken a shower, trying to get the stench of the morgue off her, and her black hair fell in tight, wet curls to her shoulders. The room smelled of cinnamon, from the three or four sticks Janice had put into a bowl of hot water on top of the stove. Janice smelled good, too, smelled of frangipani. I was the only thing left that still smelled rancid. I lifted my arm and smelled my sleeve. It smelled like a grave.

I turned away from the door and walked back to the gray sofa. The room was done all in wood, with a vaulted ceiling that gave way to a short balcony. The stairway reached up the north wall, which was to my right. I sipped my beer and stretched my legs ahead to the edge of a coffee table. Behind me, a rough cedar bookcase reached nearly to the ceiling and on top of the bookcase sat a deer skull and antlers.

"So how did you become an archaeologist?"

Janice left the stove door open, then crossed the room and sat next to me.

"I like old stuff. And when I was twenty, it was fun to go off during the summer and do fieldwork. I didn't have much money, but with the fieldwork, I could do lots of traveling on scholarships and grants."

"Digs."

Janice nodded. "For me, that part always seemed to be the perfect mix of past, present, and future. And of labor and thought."

"That's pretty scary."

"It's at least more interesting than reruns of *Ozzie and Harriet*."

Janice had met Tom Wysoki when they were both students at the University of Washington in Seattle. Wysoki finished ahead of her, then persuaded her to drop out of the Masters program when he took a job with a consulting firm in Rozette. She was twenty-three. The marriage lasted seven years. At least it lasted seven years on paper. Three years before the end, she'd heard the divorce train on the tracks and gotten into the graduate program at Stanford. Trying to live a commuter marriage did nothing but speed up the train, and by the time she had her Ph.D., she'd had her divorce for over a year. The job at Rozette Junior College had been a pure windfall, not nearly good enough for her credentials, but still a job that let her stay put and on her own in a place that she liked.

"What will you do next?" Janice asked. "As far as finding out what happened to that girl?"

What would we do next? Well, first we would try to find out who she was. After I put her fingerprints in the mail to the Bureau, I would get on the phone and try to build a fire under someone at the ID lab in Washington, D.C., where the prints would arrive. I also planned to send a set of her prints to the Montana Identification Bureau in Helena. Then I'd double check through Police Department, Sheriff's Office, and Welfare records to make sure there weren't any active missing person cases involving a blond woman in her early twenties. I'd also send out a teletype to all law enforcement agencies in the Pacific Northwest and down the West Coast. Once all those gears were turning, Hanrahan and I would take the crossbow bolt and start making the rounds, first to identify the bolt, and then to see if we could identify anyone who might have bought it.

"We'll also check the tattoo," I said. "See if we can find who did it, and if so, see if he knew the girl's name."

"And then?" She looked at me an instant too long and then looked away.

"We spend a few weeks chasing down all the leads that result from the newspaper and TV coverage. By then, the file will be about six inches thick. Our main job by that point will be to organize it, so when we finally put it away in about a year, it'll be in good enough shape that the guys who get it out in ten years won't go around saying we were such slobs, it's no wonder we couldn't solve the case."

"Isn't that a defeatist attitude?"

"It's a realistic attitude. Cops don't solve very many mysteries. Most of the time, people are killed by somebody they know, and the suspect is apparent. You take legally acceptable steps to document the obvious, then get the case in shape for court. Real-life cops hate real-life mysteries. They make us look bad." I thought about the Sky King Hudson mystery, both Sam Blieker's official version, and my own, which was considerably less material. Eating two homicides within the space of

two weeks would not go down well in the community. At least
Blieker could comfort himself with the knowledge that his
victim deserved to be dead.

Neither of us said anything for a while and I let my head rest
against the back of the sofa. A gust of wind reverberated
against the house. Janice hugged herself and leaned back.
Sometimes the wind, especially this time of year, gets inside
your skin and rattles around over your bones and makes you
shiver. That's the kind of wind that makes you hear things in
the house late at night.

"I enjoyed working with you today," Janice said. "I think I
was sandbagged, though. You know more about digging than
you let on."

"I confess," I said, "I do. I like rocks. Geology. Paleontology.
Strictly amateur."

"I thought you seemed at home in the dirt."

I started to laugh. "Unfortunately, I'm completely at home
in the dirt. All kinds of dirt. But if you meant that well-drained
sandy soil above gravel beds, that stuff today most people
would call dirt—is that what you meant?"

"Something like that."

"Dirt."

"Precisely," Janice said. "Dirt."

"I like to think I know my way around a shovel and
hammer," I said.

"Then why call me?"

"Like I said, I'm an amateur. I may have a good idea of how
to exhume a body, but when it comes to testifying in court, I'm
just another chump off the street. But you, you're an expert."
I tried to say this in a way that wouldn't sound like I'd set her
up, which I guess I had.

"Yes," she said, "I am. And I don't mind telling you I was
prepared to spend the day with a couple of thugs, fighting you
every step of the way to keep some measure of integrity about
the whole recovery."

"Sort of an invasion of the body snatchers."

"Something like that."

I was about to make a crack about depriving her of a juicy
story on the academic cocktail circuit, but thought better of it.

"Anyway," she said, "I'm glad I got the chance to help. To

meet you. Is that terrible? I mean, if that poor girl hadn't died, we might never have met. My God, just saying that makes it sound trite."

"Give you the willies?"

"Doesn't it you?"

"You're asking the wrong guy." I leaned over and kissed her. "I make my living off the disaster of others. Worse than that, I enjoy it, look forward to it. Make disturbed jokes about it. Without tragedy, I'd be bored out of my mind." I kissed her again. I slipped my arm around her shoulder and pulled her close. "I'm glad I needed an expert today."

Janice straightened and pulled away. I removed my arm and crossed my legs, feeling silly and old-fashioned in a way that hadn't come over me for years.

"I think I know a place you'd like," Janice said. "It's over east, on the Smith River. North of White Sulphur Springs." She told me about ancient drawings inside limestone caverns along the river. "The caverns are cramped and dark and the walls smudged with soot. These are places where hunters told their stories and shamen made magic."

"Inside caves," I said.

"That's right. Dark and deep and secret."

"And scientific," I reminded her. "We only pursue these mysteries for the advancement of science."

"That's right. Scientific," she said. "Until you crawl into a tight chamber and put your hand inside the imprint of a hand made thousands of years ago by a man who worshiped buffalo and wind and then you turn out the flashlight. Then you don't think much at all about science."

"I don't like caves," I said. "They're damp and dangerous."

"I think that's the whole point," Janice said.

I told Janice I had to go. Every time I moved, my clothes reeked worse than before. If I stayed much longer, her whole house would smell like the inside of a tomb.

"I have a better idea." Janice went upstairs and came back down with a huge blue robe, which she tossed in my lap. "The shower is that way." She jerked her thumb toward another part of the house.

"But even if I'm clean, the clothes will still have a life of their own."

"Put them outside the door. I'll wash them. They'll be done in an hour." Janice pulled me to my feet and led me to the bathroom, which was at the end of a short hall that passed a dining room on the left and a study on the right.

I shucked off my clothes and deposited them as she'd asked. Then I stood under a hot shower.

It must surely be a sin, the sturdy gothic kind, to find enjoyment in the work I do. It's as though the damage done to my spirit by one death can only be repaired by the next . . . and the next . . . and so on down an endless corridor, which will end someday with . . . what? What will I know at the end that I hadn't known secretly all along. Do answers always have to stop breathing before you can believe them?

By the time the water began to run cold, I smelled of frangipani, too. I toweled off, then bundled up in the robe, gathered up my gun, handcuffs, wallet, and other trinkets, and went out to find Janice.

Only my boots remained outside the bathroom door. The house was nearly dark. I found my way back out to the room where we'd been sitting. I stubbed my toe on a chair and swore.

"I'm up here." Her voice came from upstairs.

The bedroom was long and narrow and the ornate brass bed sat at the far end. I could hardly make out Janice's face and bare shoulders above the dark covers.

"Do you think I'm terrible?" she asked.

"We're grown-up people. If we're going to do this, the only thing it means if we wait till tomorrow is that we'll have one less time together." I draped my shoulder holster over the back of a rocking chair, then put the rest of my knickknacks on a dresser, let the robe fall to the floor, and slipped into bed beside her. She tucked her head under my chin. Her hair was cool and damp. Her breasts were hot against my ribs.

"I'm sorry." She fingered the scar along the right side of my throat. "I've been wondering all day how you got this."

"It's an award," I said. "For chump of the year. I've got one on my back to match." I lifted her chin and kissed her. "What if you'd called me up here and I'd said no."

"That's easy," she said. "You'd have become the victim of one of your disasters."

We both laughed and then I kissed her again and ran my hand down her back and along the slope of her hip and she lifted her knee and rolled onto her back.

"I'm glad," I said, "one of us had the good sense to think of this and do something about it."

"Me, too." She pulled me close and for a long time, neither of us said anything. All in all, it was an extremely good night not to be in a grave.

Chapter 5

When an unidentified someone dies of unexplained violence, there are certain fundamental things that the police must do. Many, if not most, of these tasks are repetitive and dull. We do them anyway, the way football players lift weights, doctors draw blood, and priests mouth a Eucharist.

I started off the day after the autopsy by spending forty-five minutes at the typewriter, hammering out our investigation to that point. Then I packaged the girl's fingerprints for mailing, and made a call to the FBI Identification section in Washington, D.C. While I did this, Hanrahan got Ardell Wings going on the photographs I'd taken at the autopsy. I could get along nicely for the rest of my natural life without seeing most of those photos, but it figured that we would need a photo of the dragon tattoo within the next twenty-four hours.

At about nine o'clock, Thomas Cassidy stopped off at my desk and volunteered his services. Working with Blieker on the Hudson shooting must have given him an appetite for unsolvable homicides.

"Raw material for your next book?" I asked. I usually manage to avoid unprovoked sarcasm.

"What makes you think there'll be a next book? What makes you think that's all I care about?" Cassidy stuck his fists in the pockets of his mauve slacks.

"You're right. Sorry."

"Forget it. People who don't want to get snakebit should watch where they walk."

"I said I was sorry."

"So do you want a hand or not?" Cassidy fell into a chair and put his feet on my desk. He was right. He really should watch where he walked.

"I want a hand. But I'll warn you, it's a boring job."

"There are no boring jobs," Cassidy said. "Only boring investigators."

"Can Blieker spare you?"

"We're down to the typing. The whole thing looks pretty grim, prospect-wise. No suspects, and a victim nobody's losing sleep over. Nobody but you, that is."

I told Cassidy to go forth and do his best not to be boring while he made the official rounds to see if he could get a line on any missing women who matched the description of Linda Leeds. He told me he just remembered a pressing appointment with his urologist. I told him to hit the road.

On the way out, I lavished a few minutes on Vic Fanning, figuring that if I talked to him now, he wouldn't interrupt the rhythm of my day later on. I told Fanning that we didn't have a clue as to the identity of either Linda Leeds or her killer. I explained the manner of death and spent the next twenty minutes listening to Fanning tell me three times all the things I'd already told Janice Bowie that Hanrahan and I would do.

"According to Molyneaux," I said, "she's been dead about a week. You know as well as I do that's a damned cold trail."

"I don't care. We've got to move on this." Fanning straightened his blue and yellow club tie.

"I know."

"We can't afford to let this thing gather any more dust." He smoothed his steel-gray hair.

"I know."

"I've already had two calls from the chief." He drummed his fingers on his desk. His desk bore all the clutter and charm of a stretch of tundra.

"I know."

"And a dozen from the media." He rapped a yellow pencil on the beige telephone.

My God, The Media. That meant we'd escalated without warning from the truly serious to the seriously serious. "I know."

"You and Hanrahan got nothing to do but this case." He straightened his tie again.

"I know."

"I want you back here by four o'clock to talk to the newspeople," Fanning said.

"I don't have time."

"You'll make time. This won't go away, you know. And I want—"

"Goodbye."

It was a relief to check the stubby black arrow out of evidence and get Hanrahan in the car and drive off into the morning overcast.

"So what's first?" Hanrahan squirmed in the seat and took out his Copenhagen. Red always likes a chew when he's on the trail of something. "Her bottom or the bow?"

"The bow," I said. It made more sense to start with the crossbow, because places that sold weaponry are open in the morning. Tattoos are more of a nocturnal pursuit. And before we went searching for the guy who had tattooed the dragon on Linda Leeds's backside, I wanted to get some subcultural directions from my pal Pastor Roscoe Beckett, the owner of Angel's Bar and local Bard of the Blues.

Hanrahan slouched down in the seat and closed his eyes. "You figure it's a sex thing?"

"Could be. No clothes. That's the most obvious. Unless he just stripped her down to make it look like a sex thing."

Hanrahan reminded me that at autopsy Dr. Molyneaux had found fluid in the vaginal vault. Lab tests would determine if the fluid was seminal.

"Sex isn't *always* a crime," I said.

"Convince my wife and her gynecologist. Take my word, Leo, unless you want a huge family, never let your old lady get hooked up with a gynecologist who started life as a Jesuit."

Other than the wound to Linda's chest, there weren't any signs on the body of injury or assault—at least as far as could be determined after taking into account the altered state of tissue brought on by the local fauna and the start of decomposition.

"An identity thing?" I glanced over at Hanrahan. "A way to keep us from finding out who she is. Which could mean that just identifying her will point a finger at the killer."

Red Hanrahan unbuttoned his collar and loosened his tie. "I

don't want to be asking these questions a year from now." He tried to mash his hair down on his head, then stroked his mustache. Then he rubbed his cheek and groaned. "I forgot to shave. You'll have to keep me away from Fanning today. Last time, he said it'd cost me a couple of days off. He said that because he was pissed at you for not shaving in three or four days. Thanks." Hanrahan closed his eyes and pretended to snore.

"You went home early last night. What happened?"

"Halloween. Remember? I sent a herd of goblins out into the world. Had to wait up till I got them all back. Back in the house and back down to earth."

"It's a tough job, but somebody's got to do it."

"I guess." Hanrahan looked over at me and grinned. "And where were you at six o'clock this morning when I called about an early breakfast?"

"I was—" I caught myself and looked at him and he started to laugh. "You bastard, you've never been up at six o'clock in your life."

"Hook, line, and sinker." Hanrahan slapped his thigh and kept on laughing. "It's a tough job—"

"—but somebody's got to do it." I made a right turn and started across the Defoe Street Bridge. "It's not as tacky as you make it sound."

"Christ," Hanrahan said. "I don't think it's tacky at all. I think it's a perfectly fine idea. And she's a perfectly fine lady."

"Right on both counts."

"Just don't wreck her life by deciding you can get away with perpetrating marriage."

"Fat chance."

I'd gotten home at about three-thirty, grabbed too little sleep, showered, and come to work. Even with a dead-end homicide newly draped over my shoulders and Vic Fanning's exhortations still grating in my ears, I felt better than I'd felt in months. Janice Bowie had no idea of the debt I owed her. I whistled a few bars from "String of Pearls," then smiled across at Hanrahan. "If my cheerfulness makes you uncomfortable, let me know . . . I'll stop and let you out."

"No, no, I can handle all the cheerfulness you've got."

I tried to make better time through the sparse traffic, but the streets were still slick. We'd had a heavy fog last night, and the temperature had dropped to freezing. I broke traction once, while turning off of Defoe onto Powers. There were a couple of hunting shops on the south end of town I wanted to check first. The arrow, though, was much shorter than any standard hunting arrow I had ever seen. I had a hunch we were about to ask questions in Hemingway country, when we needed to be charting a course toward a more post-nuclear quadrant on the psychological landscape.

"You ever think how sick it is," Hanrahan said, "enjoying the kind of work we do? Getting your kicks from lifting the rotten body of a dead girl out of the earth?"

"Sure." I signaled a left turn into the Antler. I wondered if Hanrahan had been reading my mind again. "You ever think about quitting? Not quitting the cops, say, but going back into uniform?"

"Sometimes. It makes me feel left out."

And lost, I thought. Especially with homicides.

I said, "You think that makes us a couple of arrogant pricks?"

"That depends."

"You're supposed to say it makes us dedicated men of high principles."

"That all depends, too."

"You're right. A couple of arrogant pricks."

I was right about the stores where we started. More solidly right than I liked to admit. We talked to Homer Nimphius and Eddie Pfouts at the Antler, who told us that anybody could make an arrow like our little red and black gem just by cutting down a standard shaft and remounting either the tip or the fletching, depending on the end at which you started. Neither, however, could describe exactly the type of weapon that might be used to fire such a projectile. A crossbow was the most obvious guess, but the arrow seemed too short even for a crossbow.

"It's none of my business," said Nimphius, who wore a camouflage chamois-cloth shirt. "I mean, it could be a secret and all." He looked at his sidekick and frowned, then looked at me and frowned. "If it—"

I said, "I can't tell you if it's a secret till you ask me."

"Christ yeah, Homer," said Eddie Pfouts. He had a black beard and wore a brown baseball cap with the picture of a bull elk on the front. "Ask the man for God's sake."

"Well, see, I was just wondering if you found this here arrow *inside* somebody."

Red Hanrahan said, "Why?"

"Well, see," said Homer, "a crossbrow, or a compound bow, either one of them'll shoot an arrow just like a goddamn bullet."

"He's right," said Pfouts. "Wham!" He slammed his fist into the palm of his hand. "Homer's right about that, boys."

"So if you found this arrow *inside* somebody," Homer said, "it was either a real long shot, or something less than a compound bow or a standard crossbow. Especially, like I said, with a stubby little arrow like that. Otherwise it might have gone clean through."

"It was found inside the body of a dead woman," I said.

"Inside." Homer whistled softly and shook his head. "Well, there you go."

"You know who did it?" Eddie Pfouts asked.

"We were hoping you could put us on the track," I said.

Pfouts nodded and raked his fingers through his beard. "Yeah, I guess you were. Well, I'm sorry we can't help you with that. But I can tell you something *about* whoever did it."

Hanrahan and I waited for Pfouts to go on. When he didn't, Hanrahan finally prompted him.

"You boys bowhunt?" Pfouts asked.

I hunt with a rifle, Hanrahan not at all.

Pfouts shook his head, as though we had just admitted to character flaws. "Killing something isn't too hard. Not today. You can use a rifle halfway across town." He looked at me accusingly. "Get so far away, it's like the thing you're killing isn't even real. Distance. You understand what I mean?"

I understood.

"Arrow's not like that. Especially not a short little arrow like the one you got."

"That's right," Homer Nimphius said.

"What's your point?" Hanrahan said.

Pfouts looked grim. "What I'm saying, whoever killed your

woman really wanted it done. No accidents, no second thoughts. Doing it like this, he had to stand right there and look at her and decide he wanted her dead and then kill her."

"Wait it out, too," Homer Nimphius said.

"That's right," Pfouts said. "I've killed a lot of animals with a bow, and I can tell you—Homer, too—they don't just fall down and die, not like they do sometimes when you make a good shot with a rifle."

"She was hit in the heart," I said, a comment loaded with ironic hope.

"Well, that'd help, I guess," Pfouts said. "Still . . ." His voice tailed off.

We thanked Homer Nimphius and Eddie Pfouts and left the Antler. I could have lived the rest of my life without hearing Pfout's appraisal of the girl's last moments.

By the middle of the afternoon, we'd tried over fifteen stores, including general purpose sporting goods and hunting shops, specialized archery outlets, and a handful of second-hand dealers and pawns. Nobody had taken us any farther than Pfouts and Nimphius.

"You think we're wasting our time?" By now, our list of arrow questions was like a stuck record playing inside my head.

Hanrahan shrugged. "It's the only game in town."

I told him I was fast getting out of the mood for games.

My mood wasn't improved by the four o'clock session with reporters that Fanning had arranged. There were about half a dozen reporters there, both men and women, along with their technical entourages. Of the group, I knew only the ubiquitous Quentin Davies, who is the senior TV guy in town, and Robert Tolliver of the *Free Independent*. Davies opened with a couple of well-articulated, on-camera questions, while standing with hands on his hips so that his red paisley galluses could be seen. For the most part, everyone was docile. I explained how the body in the park had been discovered. I described the dead girl. No, she had not been identified. And no, according to Detective Cassidy's research, no young women of her description had been reported missing within the last two weeks. Our unidentified young female Caucasian had died as the result of homicide when some person, as yet unknown, shot an arrow through her heart.

"Sort of like Cupid," Robert Tolliver said. It was the first time he'd opened his mouth during the session.

"Sure," I said, "I guess you could say that."

"Are you telling us," Quentin Davies said, "that you think the girl died as the result of a lover's quarrel?"

Everyone in the room looked at Quentin Davies, except his cameraman, who looked away.

Robert Tolliver wanted to know if we thought there was any connection between the dead girl in the park and Sky King Hudson. Tolliver is about ten years younger than me. He has a hawk nose and the look of emaciated health you associate with long-distance runners.

I smiled. "Suppose I said, 'No comment'?"

Tolliver didn't smile back. "Then I'd take that to mean you thought there was."

"There's no evidence of a connection," I said.

"Maybe not, but have you speculated?"

"Have you asked Sam Blieker what *he* thinks? Hudson is his case."

Now, Tolliver did break a smile. "You know Blieker. I might as well write a letter to the Pope."

I agreed. "That would do you about as much good as talking to cops about speculation."

The exchange with Tolliver convinced me that Hanrahan and I had done enough that day to earn our pay. I broke up the press conference, and about twenty minutes later, Hanrahan and I were in a car, on our way home. As I drove, a 737 overflew us on final approach to the airport west of town. Hanrahan craned his neck until the plane was out of sight.

"My father flew jets, you know."

I knew that.

"He was killed in a crash."

I knew that, too.

"Before I was born. He shot down three planes in Korea. Flying off a carrier. Then he died in Florida, teaching rookies how to do what he'd done. I guess he taught them, all right."

"Most things don't make any sense."

"I always wanted to fly," Hanrahan said.

I'd lost track of the jet, but Hanrahan tilted his head, as though he were still following it.

"But I was always afraid. Mom moved back to Butte, where she had me. Moved in with her folks. My grandpa still worked in the mines most of the time I was growing up. He was a good man who thought flying was crazy."

"Miners don't get to see much of the sky."

"It's not what you see, it's what you dream. My grandpa worked in a hole in the ground. He was a good man, but he dreamed of a hole in the ground, too."

"What do you dream about?"

Hanrahan squared himself in the seat and looked straight ahead. "I dream about house payments. You can't fly house payments. You can't crash them, either. But they don't fly worth a shit."

I pulled up in front of Hanrahan's house. It was a pale blue bungalow fronted by a buckthorn hedge. "Lots of people are afraid of flying," I said.

"That's not what I meant and you know it." Hanrahan stared at his house. "That's what I'm afraid of. I'm afraid of what's in there, what it means. You know that."

"You can't control it all, Red. You can't stop all the cave-ins and crashes."

"I know that," Hanrahan said. "A disaster like that, that'd be bad enough. But if somebody just, you know, just fucking *took* one of them, did it just because she decided to walk down this side of the street instead of the other, something stupid like that. Christ, I don't know what I'd do. I don't know what I'd do if I couldn't catch the sonofabitch . . . don't know what I'd do if I did."

"You mean some kind of Butte justice?" I was thinking about a long drop down an abandoned mine shaft, or a grave far out in the woods. Something like that. Something like justice.

Hanrahan laughed softly. "You all the time give me shit about Butte. That's just because you're jealous you don't come from there. Hell's fire, you're even from out of state, Leo. You ain't even *Irish*. What is it you are again?"

"Scottish."

"Yeah, Scotch."

"Scott*ish*. If you're going to harrass me, at least do it right."

"Counterfeit Irish, that's what it is. You're just sore because you're an out-of-stater who ain't even Irish. What can I tell you, Leo.?"

"Tell me good night," I said.

"So good night then, you fuckin' carpetbagger." He got out and was met halfway up the walk by four kids and a dog. Watching them, I wondered how much Red Hanrahan worried about losing himself, too, about leaving behind for his kids the sort of life without a father he'd had. I waved, but none of them noticed and I drove off, feeling a dull envy for my friend and his personal history that went all the way back before the cradle. For me, the past started that day I rolled off a boxcar in Rozette, Montana. Everything before that, I keep stored in a musty brown steamer trunk in the cellar of my mind.

Back at my place, I took a shower and commenced to wash down some Ellington with some beer. I met Duke Ellington once, years and years ago, when I was pretending to be a student at the University of Illinois. He'd done a concert, and afterward a pal of mine set up an interview for the student newspaper. My pal did the interviewing. I did the listening. Ellington had changed from his tuxedo into khaki slacks and a couple of sweaters. Even then, he was elegant, sophisticated from pomaded hair to polished black loafers. My pal asked a few stupid questions and Ellington was polite and I kept on listening. When the interview was over, Ellington sat at the piano and just fiddled around for maybe half an hour while the rest of the band broke down the set. That half hour, listening to Ellington go off alone inside the music, was better than any of the earlier concert. He was a man who didn't dream of house payments. Or live in two rooms at the top of a house full of yesterdays and cats.

Music made the beer sit better in my stomach, while the beer livened up my ears. A nice match. When Al Hibbler slid into "Do Nothing Till You Hear From Me," I closed that old steamer trunk, picked up the phone, and called Janice Bowie. She answered on the second ring. We exchanged a few sweet nothings about the night before, then I asked her if she wanted to go downtown for a while.

"We'll listen to some tunes at Angel's, make some sensational eye contact. Stuff like that. Then I'll ask a guy I know about a tattoo."

"You really know how to show a girl a good time."

"Spare no expense, I always say. How about it?"

She said I should pick her up in an hour. She'd spent the afternoon explaining Neanderthals and it would be a relief to step up to Cro-Magnon, if only for a few fleeting hours.

"Great," I said. "And remember, I *do* love you madly."

"What?"

"Never mind." I hung up the phone and considered another beer, but decided against it. Angel's can be a pretty high octane joint, and it's usually wise to start out the night with a little room to spare in your tank.

Chapter 6

I've heard people say that Pastor Roscoe Beckett belongs in the penitentiary. Mostly it's cops you hear say that. On the other hand, I've heard people who aren't cops say he should be hitting his guitar licks on stage in New York. Truth is, the Pastor has done both. Twenty years ago he was riding high, preaching the blues, when a woman in Philadelphia laid him low.

"Beat out a tune on my hand with a hammer," the Pastor told me when we first met. That was about ten years back, and at the time I was stuffing him in the backseat of a police car. He'd staggered onto the stage out at Tinker Creek and ripped a guitar off the shoulder of some kid with a green Mohawk haircut. Such an outrageous display of good taste had gotten him arrested, and nearly gotten him killed during the riot he started.

"Name was Dorine," he said. He was tall, and fat even then. He had straight black hair that hung past his shoulders. He covered his hair with a black beret, and wore a hand-painted silk tie knotted under a half dozen chins. "Dorine, Dorine, why you got to be so mean?" He sang that all the way to jail.

The next day, I passed through the station to pick up a paycheck, and met the Pastor on his way out. I was surprised he could remember his own name, much less me.

"Ah, the po-lice man," he said. He had the worst case of bad breath on record in the twentieth century.

"You don't look like your belly will starve," I said. "But maybe your head could use some breakfast."

"Ah, the charity of strangers."

"I threw your ass in jail once and I'd do it again. I don't think that qualifies me as a stranger."

We walked out of the police station and across the alley to the Cloverleaf, Nails Hogan's bar and grill for cops and anybody else on the skids.

"So who's Dorine?" I asked after he'd touched up his hangover with some coffee.

"I talked about Dorine, eh?"

"'Dorine, Dorine, why you got to be so mean.'"

The Pastor chuckled. "You're right, then. You ain't no stranger. Dorine, Dorine, well now, let me see."

Before she remodeled his hand—his left hand, the one he used to chord—Dorine was the Pastor's main squeeze. That is *main* as opposed to *exclusive* squeeze. It was the difference in those two degrees of expectation that finally cost Pastor Roscoe Beckett his career as a blues guitarist and a year in the Philadelphia lockup.

"I was asleep, see, passed out on the floor with this gal, I think her name was Kathy . . . Cassie . . . Cora . . . some shit like that, who knows, man? Anyway, next thing I know there's this big goddamn . . . *crash,* and before the meaning of that *noise* can penetrate my alcohol-soaked *brain* and I can say, whoa, shit, it's Dorine, and, like, *do* something, it's *bam, bam, bam,* and I got a *hand* looks like something you wouldn't even feed a motherfuckin' *shark.*"

The year in the lockup fell on him because before Dorine could control her rage well enough to do something rational, like hit him in the head, he used the good hand he had left to break her jaw.

"It was clearly a case of self-defense, man." Pastor Roscoe Beckett tied into a slice of ham, dipping it in biscuit gravy on the way to his mouth. "But that judge, he took one look at this"—Beckett slapped his belly, which swelled like a dirigible under a blue pinstripe vest—"took a look at that, then took a look at that skinny little Dorine with her mouth all wired *shut*—best thing ever happened to her goddamn *mouth*—I watched that judge take it all in and I knew it wouldn't have mattered if she'd tried to blow me up with goddamn *dynamite,* man, I heard the big door close right then and there. *Screeeeech . . . Boom . . . goodbye!"*

His hand eventually healed well enough that he could play. He could squeeze the blues out of a big old Gibson hollow body so well that most people would figure he was just about as good as a man could get. But the Pastor knew better. He knew how good the *before* edition of himself sounded, and he wasn't the least bit fooled by the *after*. He spent maybe half a dozen years on the road, then fell to earth in Rozette not long before I arrested him.

"You know, man, I was bitter, I mean *bitter*, for a long, *long* time," he said that morning in the Cloverleaf. "But after a while, I just said, well, man, fuck it, and headed out here into the wilderness, where you see me before you today. Seed cast upon stones. That's the blues."

I became a disciple. After a few weeks, I persuaded Pastor Roscoe Beckett that second-rate blues was better than no blues at all. He argued that having a gimpy hand put him over the edge, because being white was all the handicap any man could bear when it came to preaching blues. I managed to get him a job tending bar at Angel's, where I could listen to decent bands, bands without guys sporting Mohawks and mascara. After a few weeks, the Pastor started doing a set while the main band took a break. It wasn't long before he was an authentic attraction. He could have moved on, moved up, I guess, but Timmy Sullivan, who owned Angel's, got busted in the cocaine trade, and rather than sign the bar over to his attorney for fees, he sold it to Pastor Roscoe Beckett on good terms. Now, Pastor Roscoe Beckett is a genuine citizen. I remain a disciple, but since I'm a cop I can't exactly sit at his right hand. Still, I try not to stray too far down the table.

Janice was sitting on the front step when I pulled up in front of her house. Even though Halloween was past, a pair of jack-o-lanterns still burned on either side of her porch. The moon was not far past full and the air was still and warm, with a sharp, dusty tang of fall that had me driving with the window partway down. Janice waved as she walked toward my pickup truck. She wore blue jeans tucked into tall boots, and a beige wool poncho with dark figures that looked Aztec.

"No police car tonight?" Janice scooted onto the seat and slammed the door.

"My personal chariot." I found myself hoping that the inside of my truck didn't smell like motor oil and stale beer. I've had my old blue Chevy since the days of marital bliss with Big Al,

who told me a dozen years ago that the truck was too much of
a junker than to bother taking. Without knowing it, she'd
given me some good advice. Always keep an outfit that your
old lady thinks isn't worth ripping off. That way, you at least
come out of your divorce with a ride. "Just a tuneup and some
detail work and it's as good as new," I told Janice.

"Trust me, Banks," Janice said, "they wouldn't even use this
heap in the movies for Godzilla to step on. Now tell me what's
going on."

As I drove back into town, I told Janice about the dead end
day Hanrahan and I had endured in the pursuit of our arrow.
Tonight, I was on the prowl for some better luck with the
tattoo on Linda Leeds's backside.

"My students tell me Angel's is a dive," Janice said.

"It is." I turned off the side road that leads up the small
canyon where Janice lived and headed toward downtown on
South Defoe. "The armpit of the civilized world. You'll love
it."

When I first knew Angel's, it was a kind of intimate
post-sixties apocalyptic family affair. But since the Pastor
started holding Meeting, the joint is wall-to-wall people. I
tried to explain to Janice Bowie about Angel's and me as we
climbed the cement steps that led up to Rankin Street from the
parking lot down along the river.

"Last night," I said, "you asked about the scar on my throat."

"You said it was an award for being Chump of the Year." She
smiled and took my arm. "Then, before I could get you to
explain, things got out of control and I forgot about it."

"Fallout from the sixties," I said. "Call it the Wilted Flower
Syndrome. I go in a place like Angel's and hear that music, see
those people, smell the dope and patchouli oil, and it's like a
time warp." I told her about being young and believing in a
certain way the world should operate, and I told her about hot
summer nights and lying in your own blood.

"I'll have to give you one thing, Banks," Janice said. We
hopped the curb and jaywalked through the traffic. "When you
get almost murdered, you sure hold a grudge."

"You're goddamned right." I slapped the hood of a Firebird

that flashed by without a hint of slowing down. The brake lights popped on and I took a deep breath and got ready to shout back at the driver, but the silver car sped on. "Always take your grudges seriously, sweetheart. They'll hold you up when everything else lets you down."

The smoke was a wall, music the passage. I showed the doorman my badge instead of a cover charge and we made our way on inside, past a pair of keno machines on the left and a pool table on the right. I crowded up to the bar long enough to get a pair of beers from the bartender, who was walking around under a Fistful of Dollars hat. When I handed Janice her beer, she tried to say something, but the music was deafening and when I leaned toward her and she shouted, I still couldn't hear, so I took her by the arm and squeezed between a pair of reptiles in leather and we wound our way through the crowded tables toward the far end of a cramped stage, near the back door. My lungs were already starting to burn from the smoke.

The big man himself sat on a stool under a cone of red light. Over the years, he'd added a couple of sidemen, a tall skinny kids on bass and an old guy who looked like a midget behind a set of drums. The drums and bass kept nudging the Pastor along as he played and sang, stroking that big old Gibson until it growled and pleaded like his voice.

I looked over the crowd. I didn't see anybody I knew from the old days. What I mean is, I didn't see Marian Tawney.

The crowd clapped and stomped and every now and then, the Pastor opened his hooded eyes for just a moment and smiled ever so slightly behind his black beard, which dripped with sweat. He had on a baggy black tuxedo, with a red scarf tied loosely around his thick neck, black high-top tennis shoes, and, as always, a black beret. A gold cross dangled from his left ear. For a good twenty minutes he kept at it, plowing a deep, straight furrow of need through a rich black field of heartbreak. Finally, his eyes feinted in my direction and his head dipped almost imperceptibly. A few moments later, he slid from the stool and started into a desperate riff, then turned quickly to his sidemen, jumped as high in the air as a three-hundred-pound man can jump, and tore off the guitar line in mid-phrase. Perfect.

The full house was screaming for more when the Pastor waved and blew them a kiss and I pulled Janice behind me out the back door, into the alley.

"Testimony," I said. I drained off the last of my beer and threw the bottle in a dumpster.

"He's the best kept secret in town." Janice leaned against a blue Toyota that was parked near the door. We were standing under a rough carport. There was a streetlight in the alley proper, but it was dark under the corrugated tin roof. On the wall across the alley, somebody had scrawled a swastika and the words *Raygun Sux*, and next to that was the crude sketch of a nude woman and more literature: *Rad Fems 2*. Maybe the sixties weren't dead at that. Above the din of voices from inside, I heard a bottle clank across the floor. The odor of vomit wafted up the alley.

"He's no secret," I said. "You just travel in different orbits."

"I'm not as stuffy as you think."

"No, Professor, I guess you're not."

A man in a long GI surplus overcoat staggered through the door, walked around the Toyota, and began to urinate.

"Nice going, slick," I said.

"Go fuck yourself," the man said.

I started around the car after him, but Janice grabbed my coat and pulled me back. "To each his own orbit."

"Asshole," I said.

"Yeah, fuck you, too," the man snarled, then passed out and fell ahead in his own water.

"Maybe he'll get fixed by a bunch of stampeding Rad Fems," I said.

"Who's that, Jim?"

I looked back and saw Pastor Roscoe Beckett standing in the doorway. I nodded toward the heap of clothes on the ground. "That semiextinct species over there."

The Pastor laughed and shook his head. "How's it goin', Jim?" He calls everybody Jim, saying the name long and slow, *Jiiiuum*, like honey.

I introduced the Pastor to Janice. "Darlin'," the Pastor said. He took her hand and caressed and kissed it, before letting it slip away like an orchid placed gently on a slow dark river.

"Do this lady a favor," the Pastor said, "and don't marry her, Jim."

My marital history has been the subject of more talk than Communism in Rozette, Montana.

"Pastor," I said, "you ever get any enemy women you need married, just let me know."

"Ah, Jim. I was never arrested by anybody more accommo-datin' than you. Now what is it that's on your mind?" He took a long thin cigar from the inside breast pocket of his jacket.

"Tattoos. Not the public shops. The guys working at home."

"Skulls, snakes, or naked women?" The tip of the cigar glowed against the Pastor's black beard. Smoke braided into the air.

"Dragons."

"This about that gal you dug out of the park?"

I looked at Janice. "The man's a genius."

"Hey, Jim, Jim." Beckett's eyes flashed as he drew on the cigar and the tip brightened. "I just like to know if I'm dealin' with a consumer or a killer. That's all."

"She had a dragon on her left cheek—"

"You mean—"

"Yeah, her bottom cheek. I want to know who might have put it there."

"There's four shops in town, you know that?"

"Right."

The Pastor had three other guys in mind. Guys doing serious work, not the straight pin and India ink jobs that come out of the penitentiary. I handed him a pocket notebook and pen. When he handed it back, I had three names. Wattie Roebuck, Ed Ballinger, and a guy named Hendershot. Under Roebuck and Ballinger he had written an address.

"This guy Hendershot, I don't know how you could find him," Beckett said.

"You know him?"

"No, hell no. I know Roebuck because he sometimes drinks in here. He's the one told me about Ed Ballinger being in this line of work. I just heard Hendershot's name once. I got all this one afternoon when me and Roebuck were having this serious discussion about art."

"Anybody else?"

"I would think so. I never made a list, you understand. Nobody ever asked before."

Beckett smiled at Janice, then dropped his cigar and ground it out with his heel. "You think one of these guys took her off?"

"Beats me," I said. "You know them. What do you think?"

"Sex murder?"

"We don't know. Doesn't feel like it, though. And she's all in one piece. That make a difference?"

"Nah." Beckett shrugged. "Just curious." He thought for a moment, then rolled his shoulders. "Hell, I don't know, Jim. It ain't like I really *know* any of these guys. They could do a hundred gals, be news to me. I only know to tell you about 'em because of I hear so much talk around here."

"What made you figure it was the girl from the park?"

"That make a difference?"

"Roscoe, I'm too tired to play word games."

The Pastor laughed and clapped me on the back, nearly knocking me down. "Me, too, Jim. Me, too. Nah, I don't know nothing you ought to hear. Just a guess, you dig? You never come see me in the nighttime about nickel-dime bullshit, man. No, Jim, I just figured it must be that lady, get you kicking over my rock like this."

"Keep it under your beret, you dig?"

"See you around, Jim." We shook hands. He took Janice's hand and kissed it again. "You, too, Jim." Then he slipped away back inside the bar.

I stood there looking after him as he made his way back to the stage. Janice started inside, too, but I caught her arm.

"No more music?" she asked.

I shook my head. Seeing the Pastor usually picks me up, but for some reason that night, I felt irritable. It hadn't taken any more than one pass through Angel's to start me thinking too much about Marian Tawney. I heard Roscoe lay into his guitar again, and instantly I saw her dancing all those years back. I got an acrid whiff of cigarette smoke and smelled the smoke from the cigarette she'd smoked not long ago in my car. Someone in the crowd started to clap, and I heard that dead sonofabitch Hudson's baby smacking at her breast.

"Let's get the hell out of here," I said. I led her out from under the carport, past the man snoring in his own pee. We turned right down the alley, and after a short walk, came out on Defoe, where we took another right, heading for the stairway down to the river. When we stepped clear of the buildings and onto Rankin, the wind jolted us. It was a cold wind, colder than seemed to fit an early November night.

"This goddamn wind," I said as we ducked back behind the shelter of the building across the street, a down-at-the-heels men's store. A pair of headless torsos in the display windows invited the world to come and browse. "Coldest goddamn street in town."

"Someday the wind will blow all this away." Janice took my arm and leaned her head against my shoulder.

"Fat chance," I said.

"Yes it will. Scour it all away. It's just a matter of time."

Chapter 7

I know our town isn't really big enough to be called a city, but we call it a city anyway. The City. *Inside the City*, as opposed to out in the County. Seventy thousand people are jammed into this valley—I almost called it *our* valley—which was once a Pleistocene lake. The mountainsides are covered with a thin layer of coarse, loose sediments. Some of those same mountainsides are also covered with subdivisions, where people have tried to move out of smog and into class. Geologists say the weight of all that construction eventually will cause the sediments to slip away from the underlying bedrock. When that happens, whole neighborhoods will slide into rubble. Talus with a price tag. Thousands of people will want the government to fix their disasters. A new batch of geologists will apply for federal grants to study what went wrong. The zoning office will promise tough new rules. Real estate types will scream about government spending, the city's antibusiness attitude, and freedom. Deceased Republicans will spin like dervishes in their graves. Displaced victims will settle their insurance claims and buy more houses on some other mountainside. Liberals will worry. Those of us who remain Pleistocenian in our outlook will continue to trudge along our way. The process is as easy and sure as gravity.

And then, as Janice said, the wind will blow it all away.

"I like the lights on the river," I said. I kissed the back of her neck. "At least the view outside is a hell of a lot better than inside." Somewhere down in that gloom, Pastor Roscoe Beckett continued his evening testimony.

"The streetlights give everything an amber tint."

"Streetlights and smog. I think the smog adds a nice touch. A little twentieth-century authenticity." There were three

Ellington records still on the turntable. I added some Glenn
Miller and turned on the power. A moment later, we were
boarding "The A Train."

"I like your apartment." Janice was making a very self-
conscious attempt to be convincing. I hadn't wanted to bring
her to my penthouse, located high atop the Hollingshead
Arms. I figure, why tempt fate by showing a woman that your
home life consists almost entirely of a kitchenette, a Hide-
A-Bed, old phonograph records, and a terrific view of a two-bit
noncity choking to death on its own exhaust?

"Your hair smells good," I said. Maybe if I kept the
conversation moving, she wouldn't take time to look around
more closely.

"You should have a dog," she said. "Men living alone should
always have a dog."

"You've confused this dump with a farm." I kissed the back
of her neck again. "Besides, Miss Hollingshead has been
known to have seizures at the mere mention of the word *dog*."

"Then you should move someplace where you could keep a
dog." She turned around and put her arms around my neck.

"And give up this view?" I kissed her.

"Sacrifices must be made." She kissed me back. "The A
Train" pulled in at the station and "Satin Doll" got on board.

"If this were a better life," I said, moving from the first to the
second button of her blouse, "all of our sacrifices would be past
tense."

"We'll just have to struggle." She finished the last button on
my shirt, then pulled the shirt off my shoulders.

The perspiration dried on my chest and I began to chill. I
was glad now that we'd come to my place. This way, I wouldn't
have to get up and go home. I wouldn't have to get up and walk
any damned dog, either. For a moment, I felt selfish, thinking
such thoughts. It didn't take long, though, before I settled for
simply feeling good.

"I'm going to die," Janice said.

"What will the police think of that?"

"Tell them you burned me down."

"I can't tell them. I'll be dead, too. Hanrahan will have to figure it out on his own. He's got four kids. He shouldn't have any trouble."

"Won't you be embarrassed, having your best friend look at you in bed, naked with a strange lady?"

"You aren't a stranger. He's exhumed a body with you, remember? Besides, it's nothing to me. You're forgetting I'm dead, too. Don't worry, he'll understand. The smile on my face. That'll be his first clue. Now Blieker, if Blieker found us, that's something else. You don't know Sam Blieker, my other partner. He's depraved. God knows what he would think."

Janice lay on her side in the crook of my arm and drew large circles on my chest with her fingertip.

"Cupid," I said.

"What's that?"

"Cupid. That chubby little bastard with the bow and arrow. That's what he did to her." She was circling the sharpened nail of her index finger around my solar plexus. "Drilled her in the heart like Cupid." I reached up and held her hand still. I felt my neck beginning to tense up. I closed my eyes and tried to relax again.

"It sounds to me, Detective, like you are in severe need of treatment."

"Is that a prescription, Dr. Bowie?"

"It is."

I smiled and looked over at her. Her eyes were closed. She snuggled closer under my arm. I kissed her eyes and pulled a blanket over us.

"I think we've discovered a cure," I said. The record changed and one of the Glenn Miller sides dropped onto the turntable. "Stardust." "Tuxedo Junction" after that. Midway through "Blues in My Heart," I felt sleep start to tug, like cement blocks tied to my ankles. Then the Miller band moved into "Stormy Weather" and Janice stirred again.

"I like this music," she said. "This song. It makes me think of cigarettes and empty glasses with rings of red lipstick on the nightstand. London flats and nights that might have to last forever. Love made quickly and desperately in the face of great danger."

"A time when everybody knew the right thing to do."

"And now we don't?"

"Do you?"

Janice propped herself on an elbow and gave me a disgusted look. "Sex is weird."

"Maybe we still know the right thing to do," I said. "It just gets harder to do it."

"That's closer," Janice said.

"But not the big cigar."

"The right thing was never easy. Not now, not then. It just *seems* easy when you remember it, especially when you're talking about a cultural and not a personal memory. That's because we know how the past turned out, and even if it turned out bad, that's still less fearful than an unknown present or future. That's why primitive cultures always set their most important memories to music. We sing and dance around the fire at night," she said quietly, "because that's always gotten us through the darkness before."

"So you think we're still primitive."

"Take off your tuxedo and turn out the light . . . I'll show you primitive."

"Heavy stuff . . . heavy, *heavy* stuff," I said. "Is it a sign of middle age when sex makes you feel profound?"

"It's the best I could do," she said, "with my brain half-paralyzed by passion. Sex isn't always weird."

"No, " I said. "Sometimes sex is just fun."

"Absolutely." She kissed me, then lay back on my shoulder. "So tell me, are you any closer to knowing who killed the girl?"

"We'll have better luck tomorrow. With this list of guys from the Pastor." I didn't like the taste of telling Janice we were still nowhere. "It would help if we just knew who she was."

"That's a tough break."

"Lots of things are tough breaks." I sounded harsh, even to myself. Janice started to pull away, but I caught her up and told her I was sorry. I was trying not to think about birthday parties and first dates, fevered phone calls and slumber parties with the giggles, all the monumental discoveries on file in all the synapses that suddenly quit when some bastard short-circuited Linda's life with that ugly little arrow.

"It feels funny," I said, "not knowing who she is. Without a name, it's like she never had a life. So I catch myself making up a life for her, trying at least to give her back something. I figure she had a boyfriend in high school, a nice kid who played baseball and worked at a golf course in the summer. She'd hang on his arm after ballgames, and in the summertime they'd watch bad movies at the drive-in and neck. They were going to get married, but he was older and he went off to school to become something important, a doctor, maybe, and he fell in love with somebody else. She worked in a department store, and she never got over this guy. So she withdrew all the money out of her savings account, money she had all the way back to when she baby-sat for the people down the block, and went off on a trip, trying to get her bearings. Now she's dead and alone in the middle of nowhere. Her people are worried because they don't know where she is, what's happened to her. Don't even know how to start trying to find out. And nobody out here knows who she is . . . nobody except me."

Neither of us said anything for a while. I heard a distant siren, some cop in a hurry. I hoped what he found was not felonious and brutal. Too many times I hear sirens late at night, and the next thing I hear is my telephone. That night, though, the siren was followed only by the soft scratch of arborvitae against the house. Sometimes in the summer, I can open my window and, if it's very quiet, I can hear the river. But we were a long way from summer.

"I've got a confession," Janice said.

"I've taken lots of those. What's on your mind?"

"I feel silly talking about it."

"But you'll feel better if you confess," I said. "Everybody does. Trust me."

"I'm pretty good at academic detachment. But I keep thinking about the coyote and her hand . . . what used to be her hand and all the rest of her and it's like she's . . . I don't know . . . "

"Meat," I finished. "Like she's meat."

I pulled Janice closer and held her tight. Her head lay on my chest. I tucked the blanket under her chin.

"I can hear your heart," Janice said.

"Heart like a drum." I closed my eyes and let my head settle deeper into the pillow. When the wind sweeps you away, you must learn to love wind.

Chapter 8

After all that deep talk about sex and death, Janice and I both fell asleep, which is the state at which one usually arrives after excessive sophistry. I remember crashing wide awake at about six o'clock. Dawn was still thirty or forty minutes away. In the startlingly bright moonlight, I lay watching the slow, forgetful rise and fall of Janice's back as she breathed. There were freckles on her shoulders. I closed my eyes, hoping for a few more moments of renegade sleep, but the players were already starting to play inside my head. I kept seeing the red, blue, and yellow dragon, kept hearing one of the tattoo artists—I couldn't tell which one—kept hearing him say over and over, *Yes, hell yes, I knew her name, her name was* . . .

Her name was what?

Nobody in my dreams had an answer.

So I slipped out of my bed and started a pot of coffee before heading for the shower. I tried to be quiet, but Janice was up and dressed by the time I'd shaved. She stood at the window, looking demurely down at the river, while I pulled on jeans and a comfortable old blue Pendleton shirt.

Neither Janice nor I said much, just enough to iron out the morning's logistical details. After a second cup of coffee, I slipped into a shoulder holster and then an old brown leather flight jacket and handed her the Aztec poncho and we left. Neither of us had much more to say on the drive to her place at the edge of town. It was just daybreak, a stinging November morning with frost and few leaves left on the trees.

"I'll see you tonight," I said. From her drive you can look out over town. There were gasps of woodsmoke as early risers fed their stoves. "If that's okay with you."

"And why wouldn't that be okay?" Her voice was sharp enough to cut diamonds.

"I don't know *why*. All I know is you've been acting snakebit since we got up."

"Since *we* got up."

"Right."

She pursed her lips and puffed out her cheeks and drummed her fingers on her knee. "I'm sorry. I'm not behaving very well."

"You don't have to be sorry for that. Unless you don't trust me enough to tell me what's going on. Then you should be sorry."

She frowned at me a moment, then held out a hand. "Look, Banks, you're a half-decent guy. I came on to you the other night at my house. No regrets. Not a single one. And last night was notably above average."

I took her hand. "You're all heart, Doc."

She smiled. "Sometimes, you know, you wake up and you're not the same person you were when you went to sleep."

"Stampeded?"

"Maybe. I'm not an old maid, but I'm not used to waking up someplace else . . . with somebody. Anyway, it's my problem, not yours. All you did was seriously turn my head."

I kissed the back of her hand. "I like the Janice who sat with me on her couch and talked about nothing special. And I like the Janice I introduced to my pal Roscoe Beckett. If the Janice I know needs to pull back a bit, that's fine. Whatever. I can't—won't—be something different for you. Works both ways."

She managed a tight smile and a quick nod. "Be careful today?"

"Always," I said.

"And about these tattoo places you're going to visit. I looked all over you last night and couldn't find one single tattoo. I don't want to find any tonight."

"Never."

Janice slammed the truck door. I watched her into the house and then drove off, listening to the familiar squeaks and rattles in my truck.

No matter how long I've lived here, mornings in western

Montana always strike me as startling and rare. I grew up in the Midwest, on flatlands where the sun in the morning appears all at once, without subtlety, like a huge eye glaring at you from the east. Morning in the mountains is different. Here, morning is a series of flirtatious glances, first off the slopes far across the valley, where there will often be pockets of fog hanging in the small tight pine and cedar canyons. And now a closer brush against cottonwoods along the river, then with maples and ash in town proper, pure light always moving east, cutting back toward the sun, now striking the top two or three stories of the taller buildings downtown, then the street and finally the first graze off the riffles in the Holt where it broadens out across a gravel bar just downstream from the Defoe Street Bridge. Mornings here are a tap on the shoulder. They make it easy to live in our town, make it easy to forget that there are children here, who last night wanted nothing more than to pass through the dark hours without hearing a foot on the stair, a hand on the door. Mornings like this make it easy to forget that permanent darkness underground, where some of us wait forever to be found.

"I always wanted one of those naked women," Red Hanrahan said. "The kind that does the hootchy-kootchy when you flex your bicep." He held up the photo of Linda Leeds's dragon and studied it in the light. It was nearly noon and we'd been to the four established tattoo parlors, the kind that operate as regular businesses. So far, nobody had owned up to the work of art in question.

"I met this guy once, a real asshole," I said. "Had a dotted line across his throat, then an arrow pointing up from the words 'Cut Here.'"

"Sounds like good advice to me," Hanrahan said.

"Yeah. But he was still walking around. Some days you just can't find anybody who'll follow instructions."

Wattie Roebuck, the first of the in-home tattoo artists on Roscoe Beckett's list, lived in a one-room cabin at the Big Pine Motel. The Big Pine was probably a classy joint back in the days when you needed three spare tires and a route from the

Chicago Motor Club to drive across America. The court, laid out in four rows of individual cabins, sits in a tall grove of cottonwoods along the Holt, just upstream from the defunct Corso lumber mill. Each cabin consists of a bedroom, kitchenette, and bath. They're made of white stucco, and paneled inside with knotty pine. Pretty ritzy numbers back in 1940. Today, calling the place a slum would be generous. The prevailing odor is a blend of burned Polish sausage and onions, stale garbage, and dog shit. You could conduct trench warfare from the potholes in the dirt lot. Hanrahan is convinced that if you ever dug the joint up, you'd find as many dead bodies as live ones, enough stories to populate the Naked City.

"I think you missed a hole back there." Hanrahan rubbed the side of his head, which had just bounced off the window. "Let's park this heap and walk."

"You don't think we need rappeling gear to do this road on foot?"

"I'll risk it."

"What about wild dogs?"

"Just stop the fucking car."

I stopped the car. We struck out, and found Roebuck's crib three cabins ahead.

Wattie Roebuck could stand in the rain and not get wet. He had about a dozen long black hairs straggling from the top of his bald head. His face looked like the bones were slowly shrinking away, leaving the skin to hang in sagging folds. He was barely over five feet tall. He could have been in his mid-thirties, or he could have been sixty. He looked like a man who'd dug his way out of several graves, and had several more ahead of him. He could have used a bath, too.

"Whadya want?" Roebuck whined from behind the ratty screen door. I showed him my badge. "Why ya all the time comin' 'round pickin' on me for?"

"You got it wrong, Watty. I never picked on you till now."

"Yeah, sure, well, goddamn." Roebuck mopped his lips with his sleeve. It took several seconds for gravity to regain control of his face. "So what is it?"

"We're trying to find a guy that gave a girl a tattoo," Hanrahan said.

"We heard you do tattoos," I said.

"So what?" Roebuck said.

"So we want to know if you did this job here."

Hanrahan showed Roebuck the photograph. His slippery eyes flicked over it, then up at me.

"What if I did?"

"Did you?" Hanrahan said.

"Ain't sayin' I did, ain't sayin' I didn't. Not yet. What's in it for me?"

"Wattie," I said, "how come you're being such a prick about this?"

"It's my nature." Roebuck's tongue flirted over his lips. "Now, like I was saying, what's in it for me?"

"What's in it, Wattie," I said, "is this here dragon was found on a dead girl's keester. Right now, we just want to know who the girl is. The only thing that might make me and Red here think that the guy did the *tattoo* is the same guy did *the girl* is if that guy is too goddman stupid—or too goddamn *guilty*—to answer a couple of simple questions. That about cover it, Red?" I'd been waltzing with creeps all day. My feet were getting tired.

"You got it, Leo."

"That ain't my work." Roebuck sounded like he might get whiplash of the tongue. Again, he dragged a sleeve across his lips. The skin of his jowls wobbled.

"You know whose it is?" I asked. I'd asked the same question of the four people we'd already talked to, so I was surprised when Roebuck shook his head, then kept at it until I thought I'd have to reach out and grab his face to make him stop.

"What about Ed Ballinger? We heard he was doing tattoos out of a trailer on the west end. Maybe it could be Ballinger."

"Nah, nah. Guys that do tattoos, see, they get like these little trademarks. Take this dragon you got here. I might do a dragon, sure, and Marvin Pulaski, he does dragons, too, down to that shop he's got on the Strip. Me, though, I'd do the colors different. And Marvin, he does a lot longer tail, twistier on the end. More dramatic, see. Same with all the guys around here, one way or another. Anyway, it ain't Ed Ballinger. Guy's dead. Been dead half a year. You look at that picture you got there, that dragon's still not all the way healed up. It ain't been there no six months. Course, I got no way of knowing when the picture was taken. I ain't got a crystal ball, you understand. I just figure you ain't been sittin' on the picture six months, waitin' for it to hatch."

"Your generosity makes me numb, Wattie," Hanrahan said. His piggy eyes gleamed. "No, seriously, I'm moved. "

"Thanks," Roebuck said.

"How about a guy named Hendershot?" I asked. "I heard something about him, too."

Roebuck shook his head. "Joint. Been in the joint longer than Ballinger's been dead.

"Now . . . " Roebuck picked at a tooth with the nail of his little finger—"now, I *seen* a dragon like that once."

"What?"

"I said . . . I *seen* . . . a tattoo . . . like that . . . once. You got a toothpick on you?"

"Where?" I resisted an impulse to jerk Roebuck out of his dirty socks.

"On a guy down to Angel's Bar one day."

"What's his name?"

"Beats me." Roebuck was sucking on his teeth again. If he didn't level off soon, I was going to fix his teeth. All of them.

"You know where we can find him?" Red Hanrahan took a step closer and leaned into Roebuck just slightly. Not enough to intimidate him, you understand. But it was only fair that Mr. Roebuck understand the urgency of the situation, so that he could make informed decisions about the course of our conversation.

"Don't stop talking on my account," Hanrahan said.

Roebuck left his teeth alone and swallowed. "Said he lived upstairs. You know, one of them apartments over Angel's."

"I tell you, Wattie," I said, "let's make a deal here. You just tell us what you know about that tattoo and that guy, and we'll try not to get excited, okay?"

"This was a couple of months back. I was at Angel's, like I said. Knockin' back some shooters."

According to Roebuck, he had been in the bar for about an hour when a man sat down across the corner from him and asked for a beer. It was while he was drinking that Roebuck noticed the tattoo.

"On the back of his left hand, see." Roebuck held out his own hand.

"What'd he look like?"

"Kind of a dark blond guy."

"How's he wear his hair?"

"Short. Real short."

"Age?"

"Late twenties, I'd say, just for a guess."

"Height?"

"How's that?"

"Height . . . his height, Wattie. Jesus Christ, feels like I've got to blast this stuff out of you with dynamite."

"Average."

"Average what?"

"Height. His height was average. You asked about his height, didn't you?"

I glanced at Hanrahan, who looked back at me.

"Built real good, too," Roebuck volunteered. "Like he could probably kick your ass."

"Thanks. I'll bear that in mind. You think his tattoo was the same as this?"

"That's what I said, ain't it."

"But how can you tell it's the same?" Hanrahan asked.

"You mean, a dragon's a dragon, right?" Roebuck said, beginning to smirk. "That what you're saying?"

"That's what I'm saying."

"Well, it ain't. You got that picture there? You look at that while I tell you about this guy's dragon. See how the head's cocked back kind of funny, and the tongue looks bigger than it ought to be? Nobody in his right mind makes a dragon tongue that big."

I looked at the photo. "You're sure?" I said.

"For Chrissake, I'm an artist. Why the hell you think I was talking to the guy? He's just sitting there, this big blond piece of cheese growing mold, and I see the tattoo and I say, 'That's unique, my friend, where you go to get a dragon like that?'"

"And he said?"

"Nothing. He just drops this look on me, like *thud*, drains off his beer and leaves, like I had bad breath or something."

I hated to hurt Wattie Roebuck's feelings about his breath. "You seen him since?"

"No."

"But you said he lives—"

"Yeah, upstairs, I know. It's like this. After the guy leaves, I say to nobody in particular, I say, 'Who the fuck is that?' and some gal at the bar, she says she don't know, but she thinks his name's White, thinks he lives upstairs."

"And that's it?" I said.

"That, my friend, is it. You find this guy, you'll know it. Just check out the tattoo. A real piece of shit. But don't tell him I said that. He ain't the kind of guy who'll make a positive response to a little honest criticism, if you know what I mean."

"White," I said.

"The very one," Wattie Roebuck said. With that, Roebuck slammed the door in our faces. An instant later, he jerked the door open again. "Matter of fact, don't tell him you even talked to me." The door nearly came off its hinges when he closed it the second time.

"A mystery guy with a tattoo," Hanarahan said. "I love it."

"Karma." I kicked a crushed beer can out of the way. A low black dog slipped out from behind a ragged two-tone green car seat that leaned against one of the cabins. The dog trotted over to the beer can, sniffed it, then gave Hanrahan and me a curious look. A hungry look.

"Karma," Hanrahan snorted. "You believe in that Chinese horseshit?"

"Why not. Maybe it's my karma to believe it, your karma not to believe it."

"Karma. A bunch of shit thought up by a bunch of fat bald Chinamen I bet don't even believe in sin. What kind of religion is it doesn't believe in sin? You've been watching too many Bruce Lee movies." Hanrahan closed his door and stretched his legs against the fire wall. I started the car and backed into an empty space between two cabins. "Keep it up and next thing, you'll be trying those fancy leg kicks, giving yourself a hernia."

"Not me, pal." I turned east, back down the strip toward

town. "Karma's one thing, but in a pinch, I say whack a guy with the nearest blunt instrument."

Hanrahan grunted. "Butte Bushido, eh. Now that's a line of thinking I can grasp. My grandpa, he came over on the boat, you know."

I knew.

"Grew up and got old and died in the Butte mines, back in the days when a job was a privilege and *union* was a word you said only if you didn't mind getting your brains jarred loose. But hell, you know all that."

I knew all that.

"Nothing like Butte in the old days. Nothing ever again. Twenty below zero and mass in a musty church. Lunchboxes. Steam drifting out of the tunnels. Small houses and big families. Landslides. Saints. And good old-fashioned *sin*." He looked at me and winked. "Now that's Anaconda Company karma for you. That's a karma I can get a handle on."

Ah yes, sin. There must be sin. How else are we to appreciate the cozy white cabin under giant cottonwoods beside the green river? What else, if not a firm grasp of sin, could draw us ahead of the sun into the wilderness, off on an eternal honeymoon with no weapons save a roadster full of maps and dreams, and the solace of a good meal and a night at the Big Pine Motel under our belts? Ah, the road. Ah, sentimentality and sin. Ah yes, tomorrow.

The sign on the street-level door next to Angel's advertised a modeling and escort service, which I knew was no longer there. I knew the business was gone because Hanrahan and I had busted the owner a couple of years ago for taking photographs of an eleven-year old girl in a garter belt. I hadn't noticed the street noise until Hanrahan and I stepped into the rancid silence of the stairway. The wooden steps told their life story as we climbed up to the landing, where three unmarked doors waited like choices on a TV game show for the down and out. Hanrahan shrugged and picked the middle door to bang his knuckles against. I was about to try the one on the right, when I heard shuffling footsteps, followed by the chatter of several locks wagging their tongues inside the woodwork. The door inched open and an old woman smiled out at us.

Her smile didn't take long to fade. "What is it?" she said. "I thought you were my daughter."

"I'm Detective Banks, from the police." I held out my ID card and badge and gave her a long moment to study them. "This is Detective Hanrahan."

"I thought you were my daughter. She drops in from time to time," said the woman. "She lives in Spokane and drops in on me now and then."

"I see," I said. Spokane is nearly three hundred miles away.

The door crept a little wider. "Maureen's an entertainer. A singer. Maureen Meehan. But that's just her stage name. Ada, that's her real name. Ada Meehan, after her father's mother. I saw her once on the *Mike Douglas Show* from Las Vegas, but she has a steady singing job in Spokane, so she doesn't have to travel around like before. That's much better for her and she's close enough she can drop in sometimes. Whenever she wants."

Hanrahan nodded. "We're from the police, ma'am," he reminded her.

Her face folded against itself like crinkled paper at the edge of a fire. "Something's happened to Maureen."

"No . . . " Hanrahan said.

"What's happened?"

"Nothing." I forced a smile. "Maureen's fine. We're just trying to find your neighbor. Mr. White. The young man with real short blond hair. That's all. Can you tell us which apartment he lives in."

"Oh, that one there." She pointed to the door on my left. "But he's not home. Has Mr. White done something wrong?" She brushed her fingertips against her cheek, then touched Hanrahan's arm just above the elbow.

"We just want to talk to him," Hanrahan said.

"He's not in trouble," I said. When the cops ask, it always means trouble. And everybody knows that when the cops say there's no trouble, it's a lie.

"We just want to talk to him," Hanrahan said again.

"Fisher White," she said.

"Yes, ma'am." I felt like Joe Friday, standing like that in an apartment door with Hanrahan, trying to put a rudder to a conversation.

"He gives me money," she said. "To help out, he says. But I don't need the money, so I send it to Maureen in Spokane. That's my daughter, you know."

"Sure."

"She's a singer."

I nodded. "Is Mr. White ever around during the day?"

"Oh, he's here all the time . . . except when he's gone."

"I see." If I still smoked, I would have lit one up right there.

"Do you have an attorney?" Hanrahan said.

I kicked him in the leg.

"What?" Mrs. Meehan frowned, and glanced down at Hanrahan's leg.

"Nothing." Hanrahan avoided my eyes.

"Are you making fun of me, young man? Is he making fun of me?"

"No . . . I'm sorry."

"It's a failure of his upbringing," I said.

"I should say." She frowned again, then smiled up at me.

"And this is Mr. White's apartment?" I nodded toward the door she had pointed out. Reality was somewhere, if I could just put my finger on it.

"That's the one. Right behind you." She pointed over my shoulder, taking the opportunity to scowl once more at Red Hanrahan.

"We'll stop back later," Hanrahan said.

"That would be fine," said Mrs. Meehan. The skin on her face wrinkled, looking like a wadded-up note you'd smoothed out to be sure you really understood what it said. She was smiling at me. "You should try to help your friend here. Goodbye." Abruptly, she pushed the door closed, then a quartet of locks sang their curtain call.

We waited on the landing until her footsteps faded deeper into her apartment. I imagined that her rooms smelled of vinegar, a burned oven, and too many years, too many Christmases knowing Maureen Meehan was on the road. Entertaining. For a moment, we both stood and stared at Mrs. Meehan's door, but I don't know why.

Then I stepped to the door of Fisher White's room, just to

be sure. I knocked and waited. Nothing. I knocked again. Still, no answer.

Mrs. Meehan's door opened again.

"I told you he wasn't home."

"We have to check," I said.

"But you can believe me," she said. "I know everything that goes on around here. Everything." Then she closed the door again. The old woman was right. That meant she would know exactly when we left. She'd know every noise in the building—they were the only children she had left.

"Leave a card?" Hanrahan asked.

I'd already taken a business card from my wallet.

"Might as well, with the old lady. I'm sure we're no secret."

I scribbled a note on the back, asking White to give me a call, then wedged the card between the door and jamb. Then we headed back down the stairs. Each step sang a new verse in the heartbreak blues.

By the end of the day, I was nearly caught up with my paperwork. Hanrahan was in the last stages of organizing his notes from our contacts with Wattie Roebuck and Mrs. Meehan before we put a wrap on things for the day. Six hours of legwork had brought us down to the name of a guy who might know something. Fisher White. That was our hook for Monday morning. Hanrahan and I had talked about working through the weekend and decided against it. The girl in the park had been dead for nearly a couple of weeks, and none of our leads was exactly sizzling. I managed to beat my work ethic into submission, and decided that a couple of days of enforced detachment would be a good investment for both me and Hanrahan.

I don't know what Red Hanrahan's plans were for the weekend, but I decided to go antelope hunting. I had a permit on the ranch of a friend of mine over on the east slope of the mountains, just south of Cascade, Montana. Getting out of town would do me good. When I called Janice and asked if I could stampede her into going along, she said that the trip would do her good, too.

Hanrahan and I were on our way out, when Vic Fanning

called us into his office. His desk was bare, except for a telephone, a clean legal pad and an elkhorn deskset that held two pens.

"This guy White," Fanning said. His blue pinstripe jacket hung from a wooden hanger on a hook behind his high-back chair. The sleeves of his white shirt were creased. "Fisher White. What's the deal with him?"

"*Fisher* White?" Hanrahan said.

Hanrahan looked at me and I looked at Hanrahan and then Hanrahan said, "The tattoo. A guy tells us White may have one like it."

"You sure of that?" Fanning sat so straight he could have been tied to his chair. I remember him from his days in Uniform Patrol. He never drove over the speed limit.

"We can't be sure till we ask him," I said.

"I'll handle that for you," Fanning said.

"What's that supposed to mean?" I said.

"It means stay off him. I'll get your question answered."

"And how will you do that?" Hanrahan asked.

"In my own way."

"You care to explain that?"

"No."

"Just like that," I said.

"Just like that." Fanning got up and put on his jacket. "I'll have an answer for you Monday morning." He turned off the light in his office and crowded through the door past Hanrahan and me. "Good night."

We stood there in the dark. I heard Fanning cough twice from the stairwell, and then he was gone.

"So it's *Fisher* White," Hanrahan said. "How do you suppose Fanning knew his first name?"

"I'm sorry, Red, but you've mistaken my unerring instincts for genuine psychic powers. I don't know."

"That's great, just great. A captain who knows about our snitches before we even meet them."

"Maybe it's him who's clairvoyant."

"Right, sure. That's what it is. I'll tell you what it is, Leo." Hanrahan followed me out and slammed the door behind us. "It's a curse. The Curse of the Goddamn Dragon Lady."

Chapter 9

So there we are, Hanrahan and me, left with an empty chair in Fanning's dark office while Fanning sashays off to home and hearth after ripping us off for the only lead we've got in a homicide investigation. Vic Fanning. I love it. The thing you have to remember about Fanning is that all the time he's using one hand to keep you in your place, he has the other up testing the wind. I was feeling a draft and it was time to do some testing of my own.

"So who the hell is this Fisher White guy?" I asked Hanrahan as I drove him home.

"Faster than a speeding bullet, I guess. Guy's got some kind of squeeze, that's for sure. I'm still bleeding."

"Do me a favor?" I said. "Stick around the house tonight?"

"What favor? Only place I ever go is the grocery store and work. Asking me to stay home is like asking the Pope not to get married."

Hanrahan didn't say anything for a while, but I could tell by the nature of his silence, the way he kept shifting his legs and looking away from me out the window, that he knew I was up to something. Finally, when I stopped outside his house he asked me if I was going to clue him in, or if I was going to play this thing the same as Fanning.

"You always get pissed when I tell you I'm going to do these things," I said.

"It's part of my job to get pissed at you."

"And it's part of my job to keep you from being an accomplice."

"Bullshit."

"Bullshit, yourself."

"Look, Leo, I don't know why you're making a production out of this. You're going to surveil White's apartment."

"What makes you think that?"

"For Christ's sake, Leo. How long we worked together? Four, five years? You think I don't know your moves by now? Hell, what makes you think I wouldn't surveil the place myself?"

"You think Fanning is involved in this?"

"No, hell no. But it's obvious that somebody sucked him in. It's just as obvious that we'd want to know who . . . and why."

"So can I take that as a yes? You'll be around home?"

"Why don't I just go along?"

"Because you've got longer to retire. Because you want to be a sergeant. Because you've got a house full of people who like having you around at night. Because I might need somebody I can trust to spell me later."

"Because there's no overtime in it," Hanrahan said. He gathered up his notebook.

"Hard to put in for overtime when you're double-dealing your captain."

"So watch yourself," Hanrahan said. "And let me know."

I dropped Red off, then drove back to the station and collected up a pair of binoculars and a large metal case of camera gear. Then I headed for the Rankin strip.

The buildings on the south side of Rankin in the 100 block are all two-story. From the back, though, they appear to be three-story, with the basements opening into the parking lot. The buildings all house businesses on the first floor, and most have apartments on the second. Through the years, a web of wooden stairways and landings has been spun from ground to roof. I started up. It was less than thirty minutes since Fanning mugged us when I stopped on a rickety landing crowded with lawn chairs, a rusty charcoal grill, and drooping clothesline. I caught my breath for a moment, then knocked on Pastor Roscoe Beckett's door.

"Hey, Jim." The Pastor didn't ask me if I wanted to come in.

He just looked at my baggage, threw open the door, and made way.

"Didn't know you was married again, Jim." He pointed to the case and smiled, probably thinking that slipping around with Janice the night before had gotten me chucked out of still another woman's house. The Pastor had on baggy blue slacks and a blue and gold dashiki. His black hair was pulled into a stubby que. The tiny gold cross dangled from his ear.

"I know how it looks, Roscoe." I lugged the case into his living room, which fronted Rankin Street halfway down the block and across the street from the stairway door to Fisher White's place. "But I'm not breaking up with another wife. I'm working."

Roscoe Beckett shrugged. "Hell, Jim, I always thought it was the same thing."

I separated the blinds and looked to my left, down the street toward White's. From the Pastor's apartment, I could see Fisher White's windows, but because of the angle, I couldn't see inside. I'd have to settle for photos of anybody who used the stairway door.

"I know you won't tell me nothin'," Beckett said. "But if you're gonna invade my humble home, I wish you'd at least tell me if you're working something at my place of business."

"No."

I looked at my watch. It was nearly six o'clock. I'd lose the light in about an hour. Even so, Rankin was a bright street and I had film that should be sufficient. I took out a pair of 7 X 50mm Nikon binoculars and focused them on the stairway door. I could nearly read the writing on a parking meter at the curb directly in front of the door.

"Sometimes you can be a real asshole, Jim," Pastor Roscoe Beckett said.

"Thanks," I said. I opened the case and set up a tripod, then attached a 600mm lens to the body of a 35mm Minolta and mounted the camera on the tripod. When I focused on the rusty handle of the door to the stairway, the door nearly filled the frame. "Now what makes you think I'm an asshole?"

"Let's say I got a good sense of smell."

"You're right. I surrender. I stink. Where's the phone?" I turned away from the window for the first time and looked around the room. It was a nice room. The walls were covered in red and gold cathouse brocade. There were a sofa with rounded lines and two matching chairs, the three pieces done in red velvet with gold fringe around the bottoms and lion's foot legs. Behind the sofa hung a huge painting of some naked women lying around under some trees. There was also a baby grand piano, which sat like a big black lily pad across the room from the sofa.

"This place looks like a whorehouse," I said.

"You said that the last time you were here. How many years is it now? I think you're just trying to flatter me."

"I don't know about that."

"Lotta things you don't know. You throw a guy in jail, buy him coffee for ten years, you start thinking you know all there is to know about him. Glad you could stop by for a visit. Come on in. Make yourself to home."

"Nice picture." I pointed to the naked women above the sofa.

Roscoe Beckett smiled. "Rubens. Not a half bad reproduction. Women almost as fat as me. Rubens, you know, he *loved* to paint flesh. He had a workshop studio. Lots of apprentices. Everybody did a certain part of the paintings. Kind of assembly-line art. But that Rubens, he was the boss, he always saved the skin for himself. I bought that during my Red period."

"And just when was that?"

"Couple of weeks right after I bought Angel's. But before I took up serious guitar again and went back into my Blue period, where I presently reside."

"Sorry I busted in like I did. I should've called first. I was in a hurry."

"I already said you was an asshole and you agreed. Case closed. Phone's in the hall. So's the bathroom. You look like a man gonna be here long enough sooner or later he'll need to take a leak. You want some coffee, Jim?"

"This place smells like fried chicken."

"That's cause the joint downstairs done sold two million fried chickens. Cream or sugar?"

"Black." I scooted one of the red chairs across the room,

parked it in front of the window, adjusted the tripod, and settled in.

"Don't mind me. Make yourself to home."

"Thanks," I said. "I have."

Traffic on Rankin picked up momentarily as a few after-work stragglers started for home. There was a steady stream of bodies past White's door, but nobody stopped. Nobody came out. I felt something hot against the back of my hand. Coffee.

"It's that dead girl," I said finally, after burning my lips and tongue on the coffee. "A dead girl, a tattoo, and an official order that's like a bone in my throat."

"You got yourself a regular Triple Crown," the Pastor said. He eased himself onto the sofa with a thunderous sigh.

"Hanrahan calls it the Curse of the Dragon Lady. On account of she's got a dragon tattooed on her butt." I heard myself laughing and looked at Pastor Roscoe Beckett, who wasn't laughing at all. "Somebody stripped her naked and shot a hole in her heart. Then dumped her in the ground and didn't even throw on enough dirt to keep the animals out. And then some sonofabitch who's supposed to be on my side tells me to back off."

"Settle down, Jim, take a load off. You'll live longer."

"She wasn't much more than a kid, Roscoe." I laid my head against the back of the chair and closed my eyes. In a moment, the room began to spin and I sat up again. Ever since we'd exhumed the body—even during those times with Janice—my mind had been going a hundred miles an hour, racing details. Now, the details had begun to recede and I was left standing alone in a dark place, looking down at the body of a beautiful girl reduced to carion. "Twenty-two fucking years old and I don't even know her name."

"Somebody dies, Jim, somebody always grieves. That grievin', sometime she's a piece of cake."

"This the gospel here, Pastor?"

"All gospel, Jim. All gospel, you go to the right church."

The coffee had cooled enough to drink. I crossed my legs and leaned to my right, toward the window. Shadows lengthened toward me up Rankin. Scraps of paper and leaves skittered along the sidewalk. A pair of scooters rumbled down the street in my direction, then cut across against traffic and up onto the sidewalk, where the drivers shut down and got off. They both wore leather chaps and had straight brown hair parted in the middle and reaching below their shoulders. Both had beards. And when they turned around, I could see that both wore Bandidos colors, too, which made them nearly indistinguishable from this distance. I don't know why, but for some reason nearly all the bikers I run into have long straight brown hair and beards and distant eyes, a look that always reminds me of Jesus dying.

After a swell that lasted perhaps twenty minutes, the traffic began to fade. A few moments later, streetlights flickered on and I could feel the window vibrate as the wind picked up.

"What time you go to work tonight?" I asked Pastor Roscoe Beckett.

"You forget. I'm the boss. I go when I feel like it. Leastways, tonight I go when I feel like it. Why? You feel a resurrection comin' on? Need somebody to officiate?"

I shook my head. At the moment, having been born once was plenty for me. "Fisher White," I said.

"Yeah?"

"He's a guy lives over the bar."

"I don't have anything to do with that. I just rent the downstairs."

"Guy about six feet tall. Blond hair cut real short. About twenty-five, twenty-six. That guy you gave me, Wattie Roebuck, he turned us on to White. He sound familiar?"

"He the one done killed that girl?"

"I don't know. I don't think so." I was evasive with the Pastor partly out of habit; good detectives always hold something back. This time, though, my own ignorance was both authentic and alarming.

"Why don't you pull that other chair over," I said, nodding toward the chair that matched the one in which I sat.

"You mean help the po-lice," Beckett said.

"I mean help me."

"Right. Help the po-lice. You make out like you're my friend, my great pal. You smile and talk nice and shake my hand and introduce me to your lady friend. But cut through all that shit, Jim, you're still The Man. Never walked your side of the street. I might shout over once in a while, maybe even meet you at the center line, but I never *crossed over*. Other night outside the bar, that was the first time you ever asked me for anything. We talked a lot down the years, but you never *asked* for nothin' before. I been thinking a lot about that. Not sure I like the way it felt."

"Roscoe, the vermin ate parts of her down to the bone."

"Vermin eat us all, Jim. Just a matter of time."

"I know. Yeah, I know it." I was talking perhaps more to myself than to the Pastor. I'd spent years studying the way people die. There was no reason for this to be any worse than the others. "Guess I'm just tired."

"Don't give me that *fatigue*, man. You *like* this shit, crawling around inside people's graves."

"You think so?"

"Man, I *know* so. When's the last time you tried climbing out? Huh-uh, man. You like it down there in the muck. Same as me. Put us together, you got harmony."

"Roscoe, you're full of shit."

"Sometimes I am and sometimes I'm not. I'm telling you you *like* it. Hell, I don't know if you're down in the dumps because that chick bein' dead and eat up *really* bothers you, or if you just upset because it's *supposed* to bother you and way down deep, where you *supposed* to feel stuff like this, it *don't*."

"You are full of shit."

"Be nice if I was, wouldn't it? But I ain't." He held up his left hand and flexed the mangled fingers. "That's one lesson I got *beat* into me."

"Pain rules."

"It's dependable, Jim." He coughed and laughed deep in his chest and tugged at his beard. "Dependable."

The room darkened and several times I felt myself start to nod off. I heard a radiator start to knock and hiss. It was warm. I pulled off my jacket and dropped it on the floor, then settled back in the deep chair.

"You ever think you'd get this old?" The Pastor's voice sounded deep and far, much farther than the distance across his narrow room.

"I feel like I've always been this old. Hell, I know what you mean. What right do I have in the matter? You know? She was nothing to me. Nothing to the world, even. My God, think of the horror out there every day, all through history. An arrow through the heart. That's a pretty easy ticket to get punched, when you think about the alternatives."

"The alternatives," Pastor Roscoe Beckett said. His voice hung on that last word and I waited, expecting him to say something more. Instead, he hauled himself out of the sofa and crossed the room to the piano and took a seat.

Except for the amber streetlights, the street was dark now. I was so tired, stoop shouldered, bare bones on cement tired, that I couldn't look anymore. I lay the binoculars in my lap for a moment and rested my head back against the chair. Behind me, I heard Pastor Roscoe Beckett start to work on the piano, wandering through a distant blues.

I woke up when Pastor Roscoe Beckett kicked my foot. I glanced at my watch. I'd been asleep nearly two hours.

"You ain't missed anything. I been watching," said Roscoe Beckett. "But lookie here now." He handed me the binoculars and pointed west, past Angel's. "Check out that tan Chevy in the next block, the one there in the parking lot."

The car was parked under a light in the lot at Hartsell and Rankin. A four-door Impala with a small radio antenna clipped to the trunk lid. An official-looking car. And behind the wheel sat an extremely official-looking man. It was Roger Quill, one of the local FBI people. I could see a pair of legs on the passenger side, but I couldn't put a face with the legs. I was getting happier by leaps and bounds.

"About an hour ago, Fisher White comes strolling down the street—"

"I thought you didn't know White."

"That's not what I said. I mean, I don't *know* him, just know who he is. Don't confuse things. Now White, he just about gets to the door, when that big tan car comes swooping up out of the east and pulls over to the curb. I don't know where it came from. I figure the guy was watching from down the street, waiting for White. White, he ducks in that big tan ride and away they go. All that happened too fast for me to wake you. So I just been watching. Car pulled in that lot about five minutes ago. I figure we wait and see who gets out."

"I thought you didn't go in for helping the *po-lice*." I sharpened the focus on the binoculars and steadied them by bracing my elbows on the arm of the chair. My mouth tasted like hell.

"Fuck it, man, it ain't *my* fault she was only twenty-two. Everybody at least ought to have a name, somethin' that says you was here. This White dude, maybe he give you something at least to carve on the stone."

I'd been watching for maybe two or three minutes when a man got out of the tan Impala. The man had short blond hair.

"Take a look." I handed the binoculars to Roscoe Beckett, who was standing behind me. "Tell me who you see."

"That there, son, is Mr. Fisher White. In the flesh." He handed back the binoculars. "Been in the bar a few times. Never says anything. Just around. Doesn't strike me as a very nice young man."

"Roebuck says he's got a tattoo on the back of his hand. Left hand."

"I wouldn't know about that . . . never looked that close."

I began snapping photos as White walked back toward Angel's. He had a tall, loose-jointed gait and a reckless tilt to his mouth. His hair wasn't just short, it was brush cut. He wore black Frisco jeans and a brown canvas coat with the collar turned up. When he got to his stairway door, he stopped and turned, leaned his back against the building, and folded his arms across his chest. I couldn't see the back of either hand. I snapped half a dozen more frames on the Minolta, praying that the light was adequate.

As White stood there, Roger Quill pulled out of the parking lot, turned east on Rankin, and drove slowly by. I took more pictures.

White watched the car pass, and after it was gone, he rubbed the palms of his hands on his hips. There was a dark smear on the back of his left hand. Then he stuck his hands in his coat pockets and walked back toward the lot from which he'd just come. When he got to the end of the block, he turned right on Hartsell and walked out of sight.

"That what you needed?" Roscoe Beckett asked.

I stood and worked the kinks out of my back and legs. The Pastor scratched his cheek and gave his large head a shake.

"That's it." I started to break down the camera gear. "That guy in the tan car, he's FBI. For some reason, he's keeping White under wraps. I never like having a package around unless I know what's inside."

"You got a bad line of work, Jim." Roscoe Beckett went into the kitchen and came back with a bottle of Moosehead.

"You going to offer me a beer?" I snapped shut the second metal case and set it next to the first by the door.

"Screw you. You're on duty."

"Thanks." I walked down the hall to the telephone.

"Anytime."

I called Red Hanrahan and told him about White and Quill. I told him I was shutting down and there was no need for him to hang around on pins and needles. In the background, I heard Barbara, his wife, shouting at me that he couldn't leave the house.

"Tell Barb," I said, "too short a lead makes a snarling dog."

Hanrahan laughed. We both knew that Barb put up with worse hours for a dozen years than most spouses would endure for more than a couple of paydays.

"I told her that last night," Hanrahan said. "Just before I bit her. Then she beat me with a rolled-up newspaper."

"See you Monday." I hung up and thanked Roscoe Beckett again for allowing me to trespass, and for keeping watch while I nodded off. He decided to leave with me and head across to check out the business at Angel's. By the time we got to the bottom of the stairs, he was breathing heavily and mumbling.

"Don't let the bogeyman get you now, Jim," the Pastor wheezed. Without looking back, he headed for the alley leading up to Rankin at the end of the block.

"I got bogeyman insurance," I called after him. "I'm on my way over to see her now."

Janice twisted the cap on the bottle of Johnny Walker and set it on the floor beside the couch, out of reach.

"Tell me another story," I said. She had been talking about her doctoral research on the Washington coast. I sat beside her on the couch, eyeing the empty spot on the coffee table where the Johnny Walker had been. I needed another drink like I needed a brain tumor. The room was dark, save the fire in the wood stove, which she was again burning with the door open, giving the air a smoldering tang. "Tell me a story about General Custer."

"What?" She gave me an odd look, the kind of look you see on people's faces when they pass our local transvestite flower vendor, that guy who spends all summer downtown at the corner of Rankin and Defoe, peddling daisies and Psalms.

"General Custer. Don't you know any archaeological stories about him?"

"No."

"I do. I found an arrowhead once. At the battlefield south of Billings. You ever been there?"

"Yes."

"Well, I've been there too, and I found an arrowhead. Went walking once, east of that road that runs from the Custer monument south to Reno's hill. Found it laying on the ground one spring not long after a big rain."

"Did you turn it over to the Park Service?"

"Bullshit." I looked at her. "Got it back at my place. Packed up in a box someplace with some other junk."

"Was it broad or narrow?"

"Broad, I think. Why?"

"Arrowheads made for hunting animals were narrow. So they could be pulled out easily and reused. The ones made for killing men were broad. Much harder to remove."

"Let me tell you," I said, "in a pinch, they'd use either one."

"I suppose so."

"I *know* so . . . not because they're Indians, but because they're people . . . I thought you didn't know any Custer stories."

"That's not a Custer story." Janice put her arm around my shoulder. "That's a Native American story."

"You mean an Indian story."

"Native American."

"You're right. Cops. We're all racists." I stretched my legs under the coffee table and kicked off my boots. "So tell me another anthroplo . . . anthlo . . . an-thro-po-logi-cal . . . anthropological story." I stared at the bottle of Johnny Walker and knew I was looking cross-eyed.

"Most of the stories I know are old stories. Stories about extinct cultures."

"Cavemen."

"Not exactly. But old."

"Amazing," I said. I slid away from her slightly, then lay my head in her lap and kicked my feet over the far end of the couch. "I know a great cave story myself." I looked up at her. Her black hair devoured the firelight. The room seemed to flicker and spin. I closed my eyes and listened again to the river.

"Why don't you tell me your cave story, then?"

"It's a great story," I said. "All about drawings left by an ancient culture inside a cave." But first, I needed another drink. "I need another drink," I said. "No drink, no cave story."

Janice handed me the Johnny Walker. I tipped my head forward and took a hit from the bottle.

"That's better," I said. The small hot globe of scotch settled deeper into my gut. Gravity. Bottle gravity. Bottle ballast. Keeps you on an even keel. "Now I can hear it better."

"Hear what?"

"The river."

It was during my first summer in Detectives, I told her. July. I was working with Vic Fanning, who was a sergeant back then. Several residents near the Mission Street Bridge, on the east edge of town, had called to complain about a bad smell coming from under the bridge. A real bad smell. Fanning took me along to hold his coat while he investigated.

A levee runs under the bridge and along the top of the levee there is a bicycle path. There is a piling at the water's edge, just below the levee, and from the levee, a gravel slope rises at a very slight angle to a cement retaining wall, where the bridge is anchored to the bank.

"It felt cool and damp under the bridge, out of the sun," I said. "It was about noon, and with a real high sky. No clouds. Sun glinting off the water. And the smell. That was as bad as everybody said."

There were ferns and willows growing at the base of the piling. Swastikas, drawings of marijuana leaves, and the names of lovers were painted on the piling, as well as on the retaining wall.

And the smell, that penetrating, sweet odor of summer death.

The footing was poor from the start and got worse as the bank steepened near the wall. Near the center of the retaining wall, someone had spray painted a verse:

> suffer the little children
> unto me, the prince,
> the savior
> the river
> of death

The verse ended just above the ground and under the word *death* lay a black book. That's what I was after, the book, a book like a Bible, and when I reached down to pick it up, my foot seemed to sink slightly in the gravel, then slide away. I gabbed the book as I fell onto my side. The stench was overpowering. As I skidded down the slope, my hip and knee and elbow gouged away the gravel.

"When I looked down, I saw a lock of hair stuck to a piece of gravel."

"Another dead girl?" Janice smoothed the hair back from my face. Her hand felt cool and dry.

I shook my head. "Boy. A ten-year-old boy. Turns out he'd been missing about a month. From Spokane. And I was right about the book. It was a Bible. All the pages stuck together with blood. The kid's blood."

We didn't take on an archaeologist to lift that body. We never found the killer, either. We worked differently in those days. Fanning decided that with a body this dead, we really had to get busy. He got an Instamatic from the car and snapped a few pictures. Then he called for a coroner from the Sheriff's Office and said it was his problem to get the body out. Let us know if they found any evidence. We had a homicide to solve, which meant we had places to go and people to see.

Not even Fanning would be that sloppy today.

" . . . never found the killer," I said. I was losing the match with booze and sleep.

"Lots of killers are never found."

"And lots of families and lots of cops lose lots of sleep. I know."

"I'm sorry. I guess that doesn't help."

"You don't have to be sorry. But you're right. It doesn't help." I thought about all my homicides through the years, from the Spokane kid under the bridge, through Sky King Hudson, and now Linda Leeds. "Trilobites," I said, finally.

"What?"

"Trilobites. Murders, that's what murders are like. Trilobites."

Trilobites are small, extinct anthropods, that lived from two hundred and twenty-five to five hundred and fifty million years ago. Some four thousand species developed, but they all remained unusually similar. The trilobites died and very fine sediments settled around their shells and the sediments turned into shale. Cleave a lucky piece of shale, and there you have a fossilized trilobite, which looks like a large, shiny black waterbug turned to stone. That's the way murders are. Your life settles around them like sediment, but they're always there, waiting for just the right stroke of a hammer.

I took several deep breaths. An instant later, I heard someone snore, and realized it was me. I turned onto my side and noticed that Janice was gone. There was a blanket over me. I opened my eyes for a moment and stared at the fire, now embers. *Suffer the little children . . . river of death.* Suffer us all.

I don't know what woke me first, my bladder, or the bull trying to gore a hole in my head from inside out. The room was cold and dark. It was nearly four A.M. I thought about going up and getting into bed with Janice, but quickly changed my mind. If she wanted me there, she would have taken me.

So I found my way to the bathroom, found the way back to my boots, found the way out, and after only a little trial and error, found the way home to my perch atop Miss Leona Hollingshead's mansion, where I lay down on the floor and passed out, a state of blessed anesthesia that kept me out of harm's way for a little while longer.

Chapter 10

We crested a small rise and I looked back at the ridge line, which extended southwest like a horse's leg into the main body of mountains. I handed my rifle to Janice and boosted myself onto an outcropping. Had the ridge been a true horse's leg, the shelf of flaking limestone would have been the hoof. I raised my head just above the skyline and the wind pounded my face, as though the mountain were trying to kick us free.

"See anything?" Janice leaned into the leeward tuck of rock. She had to raise her voice above the wind.

I motioned with my hand for her to be quiet. We hadn't come across any deer along the ridge top, and there wasn't a chance in hell any antelope would hear her, not with the wind and the altitude we'd reached above the long pasture below. It was just a matter of principle, that's all. You're supposed to keep your mouth shut when you hunt, so I motioned for her to shut her mouth. Simple as that.

Just over the rocks, the mountain fell away in maybe half a dozen steep tiers of scrub pine and juniper. The wind was sharp with sage. There is sagebrush everywhere in that part of the country. The antelope eat the sage and they taste like sage when you eat them. That's why nobody likes eating antelope much, people say. Because of the taste. Even when you jerk the hides off them right away, they still taste like sage. But the sage smelled good on the wind and I was glad to be away from Rozette.

Needless to say, the Friday night surveillance at Pastor Roscoe Beckett's, followed by my not-so-shocking lack of control at Janice's, had been cause for a change of plans. I didn't return to life until just after noon yesterday—Saturday—so our weekend was cut nearly in half. We drove to the ranch late Saturday afternoon and set up a camp near the sheep barns at the base of the long hill we hunted Sunday. There was water from a live spring, but no wood. Janice said she didn't mind running a cold camp, as long as it was only for one night. I was afraid we were pushing it, attempting something with as much potential for disaster as a hunting trip. I knew she hadn't come expecting gun bearers and horses, but it was a relief to learn that in the heat department, body heat was sufficient.

"Cold camps build character," she said as we took on a feed of Hormel chili straight from the can. Not much of a meal to zip together your sleeping bags on.

I looked over my shoulder at Janice. She'd leaned both rifles against the rocks and now she was drawing the hood of her orange sweatshirt closer around her face. A few strands of black hair fluttered across her eyes in the wind and she batted them away. I looked back. Hard to my left, the mountains fell away completely. Time was, from this spot you could see the smokestack above the smelter at Black Eagle. That's over forty miles away, across the Missouri River from Great Falls. Then whatever company owned the thing dropped it like a brick tree and all you could see now was flat. The wind sharpened and I squinted as tears smudged from the corners of my eyes along my temples. I slid back from the rocks and squatted next to Janice, who had taken an apple from one of the bellows pockets on the leg of her baggy green fatigue pants.

"This is it." I lay a hand along the inside of Janice's thigh and took a deep breath. The barns were about two miles back the way we'd come, near the imaginary horse's flank. We'd climbed straight up along the fence line, then worked out the top, halfheartedly looking for deer among the rocks and sparse trees. Working that way, we had passed above the large antelope herd that always grazes the lower pasture. Now we would drop down just under the crest of the ridge, not far from the line of cliffs that bracketed the upper reach of pasture, drop down and work our way back to the barns.

"We'll have to watch it," I said. "Antelope like to post a sentry, so when you're hunting, lots of times you come up on a lone animal and you've got to be careful, because usually the one you see first, he's just looking out for the others. The whole herd'll spook before you ever see them. Once they get their legs under them, you're out of luck."

"I'm walked out and we've hardly started." Janice still didn't understand why we hadn't scouted the pasture from the road, which ran along the base of the hill. We'd had a tough climb, and now we had even more walking. She still wanted to believe that we could have spotted the herd from the road and hiked directly to it.

"We'll rest a while." I put a chew of loose tobacco in my left cheek and spit once, off to the side away from Janice. Janice scowled. What the hell. It's not like we were married. I looked at my watch. It wasn't quite noon.

"We don't even know if they're down there."

"They're there. I told you. I've hunted this country for ten years. There's always antelope in this pasture." The pasture, though, is three sections, almost two thousand acres, which amounted to a considerable search.

"If we'd come up from the road—"

"They see you. I told you that. I told you you've got to come right up on them because they watch far off and if they see you start, they book and you end up chasing the sons of bitches all over hell."

"I need to pee." She handed me the .270 Remington I'd loaned her for the hunt, and headed for an outcropping of lichen-covered rock.

Luckily, her complaints were only perfunctory. Her years of fieldwork had made her good outdoors. She'd turned out to be good with my job, too, not all wrapped up in police mythology. Sometimes, I wonder if I'm not more disturbed by her work than she is by mine. I'm not used to sleeping with somebody who goes by the handle, "Doctor." Professionally, she is at least somewhat interested in that point in the dust when monkeys became men. My work, on the other hand, too often indicates that primates are primates, no matter how big the gap between their knuckles and the ground.

Janice was behind the outcropping for a moment and then we were off, across high pasture just below the rocks along the ridge. We both had deer tags, but antelope permits must be applied for by the middle of June, so I was the only one who could legally take an antelope. I had decided, though, that

Janice should go ahead and shoot. She'd never hunted before and she had this notion about wanting to know what it was like, taking life to feed yourself. The whole thing sounded pretty pointy-headed to me; my conception of death is well beyond the abstract.

"There's more cover here than you think," I said, making a rippling motion with my hand. "The country rolls and it only takes a five- or six-foot dip to hide a bunch of antelope. So we could walk up on them anytime."

"The Indians used to draw them in by waving a flag. They're that curious. At least that's what I've read."

"You may have read it," I whispered, "but I've never seen it."

"There's more to life than what you see," she shot back, softly.

"And more than what you read." I adjusted the rifle sling on my shoulder and walked on.

Miles ahead, tan and green hills arced against the mountainous belly and brisket of the horse. The mountainsides there are black with timber, laced with clouds that seemed to defy the otherwise tall, clear sky. We could have been hunting elk in that country. I've killed lots of elk there, where you walk across windy slopes, then duck into deep, still stands of lodgepole and spruce quiet as rooms in a vacant mansion. But for Janice's first time out, it was easier to try for deer and antelope. Easier country, easier kills. The same as with cases.

Cases.

Before leaving town, I'd read Robert Tolliver's piece in the *Free Independent* about our two active homicides. He'd speculated about a connection between the deaths of Hudson and the unidentified girl from Leeds Park. Tolliver had ended up hanging the speculation on Vic Fanning, who had been foolish enough to use the occasion to stump for a larger budget for the Police Department. Some guy over in Noxon, Montana, also used the homicides as a soapbox from which to rant about the right of all taxpaying Americans of the white persuasion to bear arms. He'd ended his letter to the editor with that great turn of heartland rhetoric: THINK ABOUT IT! Well, I thought about it, all right. And I decided that if I was suffering any guilt about ducking out of the investigation for a couple of days, then I was quite wrong.

I smiled at myself, thinking in cop terms out here where I'd come to escape all that. There was a time when I could separate my work life from my life in general. I had my life, and then I had the things that happened to me on the job. That was true even when I was undercover way back at the start, when work meant inventing a kind of life. Then work and life started to join, but for a while I could see it happening and still keep work at the station. At first, I tried to avoid talking to my friends—even my wives—about work because I didn't want them to think I was showing off, trying to be a TV cop. Then I wanted to tell them what it was like, but explanations eluded me. And after I became a detective, I *couldn't* tell them what it was like—really like—because they had no right to know. Not some kind of warped macho-cop right to know shit, no kind of theatrical-code garbage like that. It's just a matter of privacy, my privacy and the privacy of my victims. The privacy of a common grave, I sometimes believe, a privacy that Janice now shared, thanks to Leeds Park.

"You tired?" I put my hand on Janice's shoulder, offering to pull up.

She shook her head. "It's only when you take me straight uphill. I'm not a goat."

"You know what NASA decided was the best four-legged companion for a man in space over a long period of time?"

"You better not tell me an antelope."

"Two women."

"Aren't we clever today."

"Actually, it's a goat. You said goat and made me think of that."

"I'd be happier if you said I made you think of two women." She nudged me with her hip and we kept walking.

There are physically easier ways to hunt antelope. It isn't unusual to find guys who hunt antelope out of pickup trucks, hazing them across the pastures until they pull up within range or the animals tire or box themselves into a fence corner. Antelope don't jump fences and once you get them cornered, it's like fishing with dynamite in a well-stocked pond. I've hunted antelope like that only once, years ago, with my friend

Ben Huddleston, whose family owns the ranch. We went wild, flock shooting into a frantic herd. One of us finally broke the back of a fawn. I'd shot seven times.

"There's ways to do things," Ben had said. I knew what my friend meant as Ben stared off at something on the horizon while he stood on the fawn's head and the fawn kicked and bled to death from the gash Ben had put in his throat.

Janice asked, "Are you afraid of losing?"

"The case, you mean? Use all your time and energy building on a house. Get the guy and you've got this house that you can come back and visit and admire all the rooms. Don't get him, and one day you walk through a door and you're outside and this door's locked behind you. Nothing out there but cold and rain and no place to go."

"You'll work this one out."

"You think so."

"So do you."

"What's that supposed to mean?"

"Means you're a good detective and you know it."

"So?"

"So it's good you do your swaggering inside your own head."

"Humble egomaniac," I said. "That's the definition of a good detective."

I remembered waking the night before and pulling Janice close and looking up at the black and silver sky and as I watched, I felt all disconnected, broken up into a million parts that were really only one part and when I drew in the cold air slowly and held it till it warmed and then let it go, it was as though I fanned out all across that silver and black sky, and then I closed my eyes and breathed again and fell back asleep.

We kept walking. It felt good to remember breathing the sky that way. It's good to be able to accommodate your memories. It's good to have memories that you welcome back. Later that night, with Janice's head in my lap as I drove home through the Sun River country, I would remember the antelope like this:

We topped this little rise and there was a doe standing with her butt to us, staring off into the wind. We got down on our bellies then and started crawling and we must've crawled maybe fifty yards, stopping every few feet to catch our breath, before we could see down in this little crease, where there were half a dozen small does, probably yearlings, lying in the sun. I'd rather have had a buck, you know, but we only had the one day and the permit was for either sex.

So we got set.

It was only about a seventy-five-yard shot and the first time she shot I saw the bullet hit about three inches under the doe's neck. I had her shooting for the neck of the doe on the far right and maybe she should've been aiming for the chest because it was her first time. I don't know. Anyhow, she missed the first time and the does were on their feet right now. But they didn't run.

They didn't run for a long time, and Janice said, "What should I do?" and I said, "Shoot her again."

She missed again and that time I couldn't see where the round went, but the stupid antelope still didn't run. They saw us, all right, but instead of running, they started walking toward us. To see what the noise was, I guess, and Janice said, "Oh, my God," and I said, "For Christ's sake, shoot her again," which she did, but missed and they came a little closer.

Janice started to get up but I held her by the arm and told her to shoot once more, since by now I was afraid we were going to be the first people in history to get trampled by a handful of doe antelope. She shot and they came on ahead another ten yards. Hell, by then we should have scared them all to death.

I told her to shoot a fourth time and this time she said, "No, I can't do it, you should do it," so I lifted my rifle and found a doe in the crosshairs, settled the crosshairs on her brisket because by now they were walking straight at us, and it was like the whole world was hung up while that doe and I stared at each other, I guess both of us wondering what in the hell the other one wanted, and I shot and she kind of kicked up her back legs and I knew from that I hit her, and then they were all off and running. Ran and ran and ran. Ran like hell and I knew we'd never find her.

"She's hit!" I jumped up and took off after the antelope. The antelope crested the rise on the far side of the crease and were out of sight within seconds. I looked back once and saw Janice just a few steps behind and when we topped the far rise the antelope were there and we stopped and the antelope watched us.

Four does danced around a fifth, which lay on the ground. I brought my rifle up and waited for a clear shot at the downed animal. I held the crosshairs on her head but the other does kept bouncing through the trajectory. I felt my shooting hand tighten down.

"Look!" Janice whispered and touched my shoulder and at the same instant I saw the sixth doe from the corner of my eye. I looked away to my right. The sixth doe ran and I knew that she wasn't the one I had hit and by the time I swung back to the other five, they were running, too, headed for a coulee about two hundred yards away.

"God damn!" I slung the rifle on my shoulder. Janice started to run, but I held her back. "Let her go for now. The harder we chase, the farther they'll run. She's hurt. She'll stop nearby if we don't push her."

"You're sure she was hit?" Janice stayed beside me as I walked to the spot where the does had come to ground.

"I hit her." I walked slowly, trying to catch my breath.

"I'm sorry. I saw the one off by herself and I thought—"

"I thought the same thing. At first I thought they were protecting the one that was hit. Then I saw the other one and I thought they'd cut her loose because she was hurt. Then I didn't know. Then they were gone."

There was no blood on the ground. I could tell where the doe had lain by the slightly matted grass, but there was no blood. I'd lost sight of the herd when they folded into another crease in the mountainside between where Janice and I stood and the coulee.

"She'll be hell to find." There were no trees and the cropped brown grass rustled slightly in a wind much less severe down away from the summit. The slope puckered just enough to make an infinity of places to lie down unnoticed to die. "We'll just have to follow along best we can," I said.

"I guess I couldn't do it," Janice said. "That must be why I kept missing."

"Could be." What else could I say? I hadn't shot that well myself.

"Because they wouldn't run, you know? The first shot was

okay, I just missed. But when they started walking up to us . . . I kept thinking, like, they were just children."

"So now you've found out what you wanted to know?"

"You don't have to snap about it."

"I'm sorry."

"I've never done this before and I'm doing the best I can."

"I said I was sorry."

We walked a few steps farther and Janice hooked her free hand around my elbow. "Me, too. It's just . . . "

"Just what?" I stopped and leaned over and kissed her. "What's the matter?" Her eyes were large and brown, pale brown, almost hazel. Her face was raw from sun and wind and her nose was running and she wiped her nose with her sleeve. "Thank you," I said and kissed her again. "Now whatsa matter, baby?"

"Don't you try that *whatsa matter baby* crap on me, pal." Janice pulled away and I started to laugh and she laughed, too.

Then she stopped laughing. "I feel weird."

"Not half as weird as you'll feel tonight if we don't find that damned antelope. Come on."

For nearly three hours we combed the mountainside. It was as though one of the numberless creases had folded back upon itself and hidden the antelope away. We worked our way back and forth across the slope, first angling toward the summit, then gradually easing back down toward the road and our camp at the sheep barn.

"The gods of hunting are not happy," I said as we neared the truck. I thought abut the carnage I'd picked up after in the last few weeks. Now I'd added a wounded beast of the field to the list. What was it that Eddie Pfouts had told Red Hanrahan and me that day at the Antler? Something about well-placed shots and really wanting something to die?

"Gods are like that," Janice said.

"Is this the start of the cave story again?"

"They say Crazy Horse painted a red hand on his horse. For killing an enemy."

"I don't have a horse." And it wasn't me, I thought, who killed the sonofabitch. I was thinking of Hudson.

I checked the magazines on both rifles, then hung them in the rack in the back window of the cab. What I wanted to do before dark was to drive the length of the pasture and glass the slope. Maybe from below, we'd spot the animal.

In that country along the eastern slope of the mountains, where the Great Plains begin, sundown is a startling thing, so quick that it brings with it a sense of abrupt cold, even though the temperature might not begin to drop for several hours. As I drove eastbound, I felt a chill at my back and in the sky ahead to the east it was already night. I stopped every quarter of a mile and scanned the pasture through binoculars, but saw no antelope, either alive or dead. At the eastern boundary of the pasture, I turned around and headed back.

About half a mile from the sheep barn, we drove past a great hump that swelled uncharacteristically from the slope. About halfway down the hump, not fifty yards above the road, lay a large doe antelope. I could have sworn she wasn't there when we'd driven by fifteen minutes before.

"What does she want?" Janice rolled down her window and studied the antelope.

I shut off the motor and handed the binoculars to Janice.

"She looks very wise," Janice said, looking through the glasses.

"All antelope look wise. It's their large head and the coloring, the way they have those dark markings like mustaches and beards and thoughtful shadows."

"You're not going to shoot her?"

"No." I got out of the truck and the antelope quietly stood up. I crossed the grader ditch to the fence and the doe walked to the top of the hump and looked back at us, then started walking again and kept moving till she was out of sight. "Let's go." I climbed the fence and started up the right side of the hump.

"Don't you want the rifles?"

"Forget the rifles. Just come on." I didn't wait for her to catch up.

Behind the hump, the terrain fell away into a slight saddle, before rising up along the mountain. The mountainside ranged from bright tan along its western flank, to lavender near the hoof as the sun settled. The doe was gone.

"What do you think she wanted?"

I hadn't heard Janice pull up beside me. We were both winded.

"Who says she wanted anything?" I spend my life trying to attach meaning to the aberrations of people. I wasn't about to tackle the mysticism of animals. "How should I know? I didn't go up and light a fire and trace my hands."

We found the doe, dead, at the base of an umber shale outcropping above a thin creek. Her white belly looked almost pregnant. The soft white gave way to shades of tan along her flanks and back. Her eyes were dull. A swatch of black hair grinned under her jaw and a wad of masticated grass lay lodged in her mouth. She was sprawled on her left side and her body dammed the creek into a small pool that spilled around her head and rump.

"This isn't the same doe? The one from the road?"

"No." I climbed down the last tier of rocks. "That one moved too well. And there's too much water backed up for this one to have just lain down."

"Then that other doe . . . do you think she came to get us?"

"I told you, I don't know."

Janice jumped the creek and stood beside me. We each took a hind leg and dragged the doe out of the creek. The backwater cascaded over our feet.

"She's smaller than I thought," Janice said. "I could tell up above that they were small, but not this small."

"There's the entrance wound." I pointed to a small hole just behind the ribs on the animal's right side. I took her left front and rear legs and flopped the doe onto her right side. Her left ham was ragged and bloody, demolished by the bullet's exit. She was still warm, and had not yet started to stiffen up.

I said, "She must've veered left just as I shot. God knows how she ran this far.

"So tell me," I went on. "You're the expert on gods and old bones. You wanted to know what it was like. So how come do you believe we kept at it till we killed this antelope?"

"I was going to ask you," Janice said. She wiped her nose again on her sleeve.

I remembered all the days and nights I'd wished Sky King Hudson dead, all the situations I'd fantasized in which I killed him, proving once and for all that I was capable of avenging my deepest moment of fear. And when that death finally came, it was as though Hudson's corpse had simply fallen from the clouds and lain at my feet, with no more nor less meaning than the corpse of this poor stupid antelope. Protein, I thought. And then I started to laugh.

"Maybe I missed the punch line," Janice said.

"I didn't want to kill anything," I said finally. "Not today, I didn't."

"I shouldn't have asked you to shoot."

"No. It's my fault." I couldn't have laughed anymore even if I'd wanted. "If I wasn't willing, I shouldn't have come." I took out my knife and rolled the doe onto her back and lifted her chin to expose the throat.

"Let me have the knife," Janice said, bracing her leg against the doe's ribs. "Show me how to do this."

Chapter 11

"Don't you believe in answering your phone?" Hanrahan was out of breath from the stairs.

"What phone?"

"That's what I figured." Hanrahan kicked the door closed behind him. "I called here first, then called Janice's. She said you got back late last night. Said you killed an antelope. Where is it?" The corners of his nose curled as he looked around the room. "This place is a sewer. You still drunk? She said you got drunk somewhere along the line, too."

"What day is it?"

"Monday."

"Time?"

"About seven-thirty. In the morning."

"I quit being drunk somewhere Saturday."

I sat down on the edge of the Hide-A-Bed. Red Hanrahan stepped past me and over a stack of magazines, heading into the kitchen. I lay back on the bed and shut my eyes.

"A sewer," Hanrahan said again. "I told you not to get divorced the last time."

"You also told me not to get married."

"That was for the woman's sake. What was her name?"

"Deirdre."

"Right. Deirdre. That was for Deirdre's sake. She was a nice girl."

I heard the noise of dishes rattling and water running in the kitchen. My body, my brain, and my soul weren't equipped to accommodate anything louder than the boom and thud of my heart detonating sixty or seventy times a minute. Maybe I was getting too old to get drunk one day and climb mountains the next. Decisions, decisions.

"You got any orange juice?" Hanrahan called.

"This look like Florida to you?" I tried to go back to sleep.

"I talked to Fanning."

I tried harder to go back to sleep. For a few moments, the noise faded. Then Hanrahan kicked me in the foot and handed me a white mug of coffee.

"Help me up." I held out my free hand.

"Help yourself."

Hanrahan took his own coffee and wandered over to the living room window. Groaning, I sat up and turned and looked at his back.

"I hope you washed these cups," I said.

"I thought they were green cups," he said. "Then I picked one up and the green rubbed off."

"So what's on Fanning's mind this early in the day?"

"Fisher White. He's got a tattoo, but he doesn't know the girl. Not so much as a whisper of a lead. The rest of the tune is that we—that is the Rozette Police Department in general and Leo Banks and Red Hanrahan in particular—are to forget that Fisher White ever drew breath on God's earth. He wanted us to know that first thing, so we didn't escape and start in on White by mistake. I know you're hung over and deranged," Hanrahan said, "but what do you make of that?"

"What did you do over the weekend?"

"I watched *The Guns of Navarone* on TV." Hanrahan inspected his cup for signs of life and then took another sip of coffee. "You know, I didn't come over here just to drag your ass out of the gutter."

"What gutter?" I said. "I don't see any gutter."

"You're just not focusing your eyes right."

I tried to stand up, but my knees were wobbly and I sagged back onto the bed. I still don't know why I was being evasive and sarcastic with Hanrahan. Well, no, that's a lie. I was behaving like a moron because he was right. I've always lived under a tight rein, and lately I'd really given myself my head. Now I'd gone and collided with an Irishman from Butte, Montana, who knows what falling into a mine shaft is all about. That is to say, to fall into a mine shaft you first have to walk right up to where the mine shaft starts.

"All right," I said, "I surrender. Fisher White is hooked up with Roger Quill and the FBI."

"You know that for a fact?"

"I've got pictures." I told him the details of my surveillance Friday night. "It was after that I got drunk. Then we went out and killed the antelope. It's hanging in Janice's garage. So what did you do besides watch *The Guns of Navarone?*"

"Watched *The Magnificent Seven*. After that, Barbara and I went to bed and I tried to imagine she was a beautiful, dusky Mexican girl who whispered Spanish obscenities in my ear." Hanrahan pulled open the window and leaned out into the fresh air. "*No* sounds about the same in any language. Remind me to send the Pope some fan mail about this birth control thing." He turned back into the room. The expression on his face was sour. "So Fanning has contracted a dose of FBI fever."

"Been known to bring stronger men to their knees." I took a deep breath, swung out of bed, shuffled into the kitchen, and made another mug of instant coffee. When I got back in the living room, Hanrahan had folded up the bed and was sitting on the sofa. I sat down next to him.

"And it's Quill telling us to scram," Hanrahan said.

"That's about the size of it. Actually, he's telling Fanning to tell us to scram, and Fanning is buying into the whole thing, sight unseen."

"Well, that stinks, doesn't it?"

"You always had a great nose, Red."

I don't know what I found most irritating, Quill's condescension or Fanning's fawning response to it. So much for your little homicide, Quill seemed to be saying, but we're talking major league here. Now step aside, boys, you bother me.

Hanrahan slurped his coffee and looked at me, the sort of arch expression he affects whenever he's trying to goad me into making trouble for somebody. "You believe what Quill told Fanning? About White and the girl?"

"I don't know. I doubt if Quill would lie to Fanning, but I'm not thrilled about what White may have told Quill. You in the mood to get in trouble?"

"I feel like I've just been invited to the prom." Hanrahan finished his coffee. He cleared his throat and once more surveyed the room, which looked, God help me, like someplace where Sky King Hudson might live. "You still got running water in this joint?"

I did.

"Great. Why don't you go use it for a few minutes. Then we can cruise on down to work."

I took a deep breath and hobbled into the shower. Even if I didn't feel human, I wanted at least to look the part when I dropped my photos of White on Vic Fanning's desk. I wanted to look like Yul Brynner, riding into town on the sleekest horse in Mexico.

When we got to the station, I gave the surveillance film to Ardell Wings, who, after only minimal pleading, agreed to start on it right away. By nine o'clock, I still had not crossed paths with Fanning, who was closeted with the Chief talking about Important Things. Maybe Fanning figured that after delivering his urgent message to Hanrahan, he didn't want to talk to me either. I was anxious to talk to Fanning, but not before I had the photos of White in hand. There was bound to be a blowup once Fanning found out I'd gone behind his back, so I wanted my position to be as complete as possible, including a written report on the surveillance to go with the photos. Investigations are a detective's sculpture; reports and pictures are mortar and stone. I wanted to build a big, ugly Fisher White right in Vic Fanning's front yard. Of course, I wouldn't be telling Fanning something he didn't already know. The word to lay off White had to be coming down from the FBI in the person of Roger Quill. No, I was working toward a different kind of enlightenment. I wanted Fanning to remember I was more than just a ground pounder.

By mid-morning, I was still at my desk, typing. I had about another page left to compose, when I heard the office door open and close, followed by loud, official-sounding voices from out near Beth McCoy's desk. A moment later, Fanning stuck his head around the corner.

"Get Hanrahan," Fanning said, looking straight at me. Hanrahan was at his own desk not fifteen feet away. "Then get in my office. Now."

I frowned at Hanrahan after Fanning had turned away.

There is a window that opens from Fanning's office into the large bay where the rest of us work. I craned my neck to get a look inside Fanning's office, where a tall man stood with his arms crossed, glaring back at me. "Looks like an undertaker," I said to Hanrahan. "Or a fed."

"I hope Fanning is tame this morning." Hanrahan straightened some papers on his desk and together we headed for the captain's door.

"I heard that, Hanrahan." Fanning popped out to meet us. "You sons of bitches, this time you've really gone and jumped in fast water. Get in here."

Fanning stepped behind his desk and pointed Hanrahan and me into chairs. By then, the tall man was sitting in the corner to Fanning's right. He was gaunt, with severe Gary Cooper features. He held a large manila envelope in his lap. It turned out that he was a fed.

"This is Calvin Hoover," Fanning said. "He's with the Department of Defense."

"Calvin *Hoover*." Hanrahan started to smile.

"Detective," Hoover said, "I stopped being good natured about that more than ten years ago." Hoover had a tight, reedy voice, with an East Coast inflection. He wasn't smiling. His brushed salt-and-pepper hair looked bristly enough to scrub pots, and the hollows of his cheeks devoured light.

Fanning coughed and fingered the pulse in his throat, while he looked at his watch and counted under his breath. "Mr. Hoover has some information about your girl."

"Thank you, Captain," Hoover said. He straightened his tie. It was a maroon tie with small horses on it. It was quite similar to Fanning's, except that Fanning's was redder and the heads were ducks.

From the envelope on his lap, Hoover withdrew an eight-by-ten black-and-white studio portrait of a young woman and handed it to me. "Look familiar?"

Curiously, the girl in the photograph looked several years older than the one I'd lifted from the ground and taken to the morgue. Her hair was bright and feathery; I remembered hair that tugged at her forehead in a dull slab as Dr. Molyneaux washed her down with a clear plastic hose and the muddy water coursed down the gutters of the stainless steel table.

Death, it seemed, had accentuated her youth, obliterated that slightly jaded sparkle of a young woman who has only recently come to understand certain possibilities. There are no possibilities in the morgue. In the morgue, all smiles are the result of decay, and there is no need for bright lipstick, save to make the living feel better. I was not ready to see Linda Leeds smiling. Watch me now, buddy, that smile said. Just you watch. I won't let you down.

"Her name is Patricia Ryme," Hoover said. "Those were her prints you sent to the FBI lab."

"But you're Department of Defense," I said.

"Banks, let the man explain," Fanning said.

Hoover sniffed at me twice and explained. Patricia Ryme was the daughter of a man with whom DOD sometimes contracted to act as a middleman in certain . . . transactions. Because of the sensitive nature of those transactions, both DOD and the man preferred that he live quietly—that is to say, secretly—in Rozette, Montana, a place about as far removed from his business activities as he could get without leaving the lower forty-eight. Because of the nature of the association, DOD had a flag on the fingerprints of the man and his daughter in the FBI files. When the girl's prints turned up in the ID section's incoming mail, with my letter attached, somebody dropped a dime to Hoover's office.

"Just what office is that?" Hanrahan asked.

"I'm not at liberty to say."

"And the nature of this girl's father's transactions?"

"I'm not at liberty there, either."

"His address?"

Hoover shook his head. "Since you know the girl's name, I can tell you that her father's name is Jacob Ryme. Beyond that, I'm afraid information about him is classified. I can say, though, that I have made him aware of his daughter's death, and I have his consent to request that you refrain from any further investigation."

"Just like that," I said. "Just let her die and forget it."

Hoover canted his head to the right. An involuntary twitch played along the line between the left corner of his mouth and his left nostril. "I didn't say the incident would be forgotten. What I'm saying is that this is a jurisdictional matter. I'm saying it would be better for all concerned—for the country—if you let the matter be handled by others."

"Bullshit," I said. I know, I know—I should have been more diplomatic. But Hanrahan, Janice, and I had dug that girl out of the cold dark ground on Halloween with a regiment of ghosts everywhere you turned and I wasn't about to stand around and get hosed by any haircut from the nation's capital.

"And what's that supposed to mean?" Hoover studied his fingernails.

Hanrahan did his best to be helpful. "It's this stuff we have out in the boondocks, see, you stand behind a bull—"

"It means *bullshit*," I said.

Hoover shot a look at Fanning. "I would hope that the simple fact of my presence here is an indication to you, Detective, of the sensitivity of this matter. After all, I could simply have ignored the incident. Or held up the girl's identity." His voice was rubbery with pride. "Without my goodwill, you don't have any case at all. Then you can go back to looking like schmucks in your schmuck newspaper." His eyelids hooded momentarily as he looked from me to Hanrahan and back. "I came here having more respect for you people than that."

I was impressed. "You must be talking about our sense of duty and pride . . . love of country."

"I never understand why that's so hard to believe." For an instant, Hoover's face was like a small flame rippling in a draft.

"Then when the bull lifts his tail . . . ," Hanrahan said.

Fanning threw up his hand and whistled. "Here's the way it's going to be—"

"Captain, I don't think—" Hoover sat up straight and smoothed his tie. His face was extinguished.

"Here's the way it's going to be," Fanning said again. "DOD wants our cooperation in this business. Fair enough. We're just a bunch of two-bit cops in a two-bit town that's almost in Canada. Most of us out here call *pasta* spaghetti and when we eat too much of it we belch and fart."

"That seems a crude—" Hoover started.

"The thing is," Fanning went on, "this is the place where that girl got herself killed. You may have to answer to somebody with a bigger desk, but I have to answer to folks who go to work in the morning and watch TV at night and play softball on the weekend. People who'd blow up the goddamned planet before they'd get along with Arabs or Cubans. But they don't appreciate their public parks being turned into cemeteries. It scares them and it's rough on the landscaping. People get out of sorts . . . next thing you know, they don't want to give the cops a pay raise. And then the cops are unhappy and they stop working hard. They stop writing traffic tickets and the city's revenue goes down so we have to raise taxes . . . people complain because they're already paying so much taxes to fight Communism and here they've got dead young girls in their very own public parks."

Fanning shrugged and opened his palms to Hoover. "It's a bad situation . . . a vicious cycle."

"I still don't see how I can help. Not considering my mandate."

"You can help by trusting us," Fanning said. "You can show that trust by giving us the name and address of that girl's father. By letting us do our simple job in our own humble way."

"I'm sorry, I can't."

"But you see, that doesn't wash," Hanrahan said. "You've told us you talked to the man. Who would we know who would be interested in what he does with you people? He's just the father of a murder victim to us. If you've already discussed this with him, there's no reason *not* to talk to him."

"It's the unknown." Hoover tented his fingers under his chin. "For me, the operative risk is that you're an uncertain wind on a treacherous sea."

"No," I said. "The *risk* is what we'll uncover bumping around without some cooperation from you."

"Then I can take that to mean you won't break off the investigation?"

"That's exactly what it means," Fanning said.

Hoover's cheeks tightened and his lips thinned. "Very well. Fine. If that's the lay of things, then I suppose I can give you that much. But only on two conditions. First, that you not act on the information—that is, contact the man—for twenty-four hours. Second, that you contact him only through me."

Before I could say anything, Fanning drummed a pencil on his desk and said, "Done."

Hoover looked away from Fanning immediately, dismissing him. "I appreciate that, Captain. I'm sure you can understand that there are certain . . . arrangements that may be necessary."

Jacob Ryme was a retired Army officer, who lived west of town, not far off the highway up Smoketree Pass. Hoover gave us rough directions, and described a large log house along Pauley Creek, just off a gravel road running north from the highway.

Calvin Hoover stood and offered me his hand across Fanning's desk. His skin was soft, the grip firm and cool, like rigor mortis. "I think you've addressed all my concerns today, Detective . . . Banks. I'll let you get back to work on your homicide." He handed me Patricia Ryme's photograph. "You can keep that."

"What office are you with?" I asked as he turned toward Fanning's door.

Again, Hoover made what for him was a smile. "I thought you were too bright to need the national security speech," he said, then ditched the smile like bogus money.

"When can we expect to hear from you again?" I asked. The three of us trailed him through the outer office door.

"Ten o'clock tomorrow," he said over his shoulder. "Noon at the latest." Then he was gone.

"Quite an impressive fellow," Vic Fanning said, walking back into his office. "Out here all the way from Washington, D.C. I'll have to tell the chief about him."

"Yeah, a real thoughtful guy," Hanrahan said. With his index finger, he raked a spent chew from behind his lower lip and dropped it into Fanning's wastebasket.

"Jesus Christ, I wish you wouldn't do that," Fanning said.

"Yeah, sorry." Hanrahan reached into his hip pocket for his Copenhagen. "I was just so overwhelmed, I didn't know what I was doing. Jesus Christ, I'm sorry, Vic. It's not every day an authentic G-man comes to call. I just don't know the etiquette."

"Well, I'm damned glad you didn't do that while Hoover was still here."

"Oh, no. No. I wouldn't have dared." Hanrahan laughed and spit again. "The goddamn curse of the Goddamn Dragon Lady."

"I'm not sure we'll be able to work inside the confines of the deal you made with him," I said to Fanning.

Fanning leaned back in his chair and folded his arms over his tie with the ducks. "I don't want to find myself on the witness list for any congressional hearing." He busied himself with a stack of papers. Hanrahan and I went back to our desks.

"You didn't say anything about Fisher White and the FBI," Hanrahan said, after a minute.

"When you're in a small place with a cobra," I said, "concentrate on the cobra." I put Patricia Ryme's portrait in an envelope with the other photos from the investigation. Patricia Ryme. Giving her a name also gave her a life. "Let's get some lunch. And then let's go meet this Jacob Ryme guy."

"You trashing the deal with Hoover already?"

"Fuck Hoover," I said. "We've got things to do."

Chapter 12

"So what is it, Leo, you think this Ryme guy is a spy?" Hanrahan and I were on our way back across to the station from the Cloverleaf after having pork chop sandwiches for lunch.

"Spy," I said. "That has such an exotic ring to it."

"Kind of like . . . *Homicide Investigator*."

Spies and homicide dicks, I thought, our latest cultural cowboys. Our mission: to make the world safe for democracy, children, and unescorted women.

"Don't get too smug," I said. "We don't clear this case, people in this town will be spelling *homicide investigator* G-O-A-T."

We went in the side door of City Hall and walked past the court of Municipal Judge Walter Clay, a room that Thomas Cassidy has christened "The Grotto of Tears," then headed downstairs to the office.

"We'll tell Jacob Ryme what we know and show him the pictures of White." I couldn't see any need to be tricky with Ryme, and even if there were, sometimes straight ahead is the best deception.

We were on the way downstairs to our office when we met Lieutenant Frank Woodruff on his way up. Woodruff was carrying two large cases of evidence gear. He'd only been back at work for a day or so, and neither Hanrahan nor I had had time to talk to him.

Woodruff set the cases on the corner landing. "You guys know an old lady named Meehan?"

"That depends," Hanrahan said.

"This isn't the time," Woodruff said. "About twenty minutes ago, Patrol had a call about a noise disturbance upstairs over

Angel's. One of those apartments. They get there, it's this
Meehan woman. She tells them about loud noise in an
apartment rented to a guy name of Fisher White."

I glanced at Hanrahan and smiled. Red had the look of a man
who's just heard another stack of chips tumble into the pot.

Woodruff went on: "So Patrol gets there and this woman
tells them she thinks she heard gunshots. Nobody answers
White's door, it's unlocked, so they go in and find a body."

"White?" I asked.

Woodruff shook his head.

"Roebuck. Watson Roebuck. And this Meehan woman, she
mentions you guys were over there to see her. Yesterday.
What's the deal?"

"We were at Hogan's the last hour," Hanrahan said, laughing. "Getting outside some lunch. We got witnesses."

"Why do I feel relieved?" Woodruff said. Then he took
Hanrahan away from me to start on the new homicide. My job
was to stay with the girl from the park.

"And steer clear of Fanning," Woodruff said. "Somehow,
he's got himself mixed up with the federal government. He's
hot enough to torch off gasoline."

"I can explain," Hanrahan said.

"I was afraid of that." Woodruff picked up his load and
leaned ahead into the stairs.

Downstairs, Hanrahan gathered up his notebook and the
large aluminum case of photographic equipment, while I
collected my photos. At first, I felt like the last man left behind
to hold the pass, while the rest, more likely to survive, head off
to new adventures. The envelope of photographs felt heavier
in my hand. Alone, I began to feel even more responsible to
Patricia Ryme, whose acquaintance I had just made. Fortunately, I was able to shed that cross in about thirty seconds. It
ended when I realized that this was the first time since Sky
King Hudson's death that I was working alone. I liked working
with Hanrahan and Blieker, but . . . well . . . there's always something to be said for working alone. I think I was on
the verge of becoming a dangerous man.

Town fell away as I drove west on Rankin, which is the main
east/west arterial through Rozette. I passed St. Francis Hos-

pital, then the Big Pine Motel, where Watson Roebuck used to do tattoos before he was dead.

The scenery gave way to a string of car lots and trucking outfits. After four or five miles, I passed the airport, where the valley is at its widest part. In another three or four miles, the mountains narrowed again and the road, a highway now, made its first perceptible rise toward Smoketree Pass, still over twenty-five miles ahead. Just before a small bridge over a small creek, I turned right on a gravel road marked "Pauley Creek." A second sign, on the gravel road itself, said "Beware Logging Trucks Ahead."

Pauley Creek is good fossil country. There are plenty of logging roads, which cut through beds of limestone and shale. The ages range from Paleozoic through Jurassic and Cretaceous and into mid-Tertiary. These beds aren't nearly as interesting as those in eastern Montana, near Roundup and the Musselshell, where I want to go next summer. There, dinosaur bones turn up from time to time. Still, I've collected decent mollusks and snails, as well as a large number of leaf impressions from the road cuts in Pauley Creek.

Off to my left, as Hoover had described, sat a big old fallen-down barn and a new log house.

I followed the driveway to a cement pad near the house. I parked the car next to a four-wheel drive pickup, a black Ford short box with good wax job, smoked windows, and a roll bar. The two-story house sat at the end of a flagstone walk perhaps twenty yards from the driveway. There was a porch along the front of the house and a rottweiler dog on the porch. I watched the rottweiler for a while from the car, and decided I'd be perfectly happy if I walked away on both legs from my meeting with Jacob Ryme.

I got out and walked toward the house as though the dog were an old friend. The rottweiler sat at perfect attention near the door. I tiptoed onto the porch. The dog eyed me evenly, as an eagle might gauge the dive toward a spawning salmon. I was about to knock, when the door opened and a tall man in his fifties stepped out onto the porch. The dog didn't flinch.

"Yes?" The man closed the door behind him. He wore sharply pressed khaki slacks, and a camouflage safari jacket over a green commando sweater. "May I help you?"

"My name is Leo Banks. I'm a policeman."

The man had crisp, sandy hair and a smartly groomed beard. Although he was quite trim, the safari jacket and sweater helped hide a slight paunch that betrayed his age. I guessed that the beard was designed to detract from further betrayal in his face. His face flickered in what may have been either a smile or a grimace. It was impossible to tell behind the beard.

"Is this an official visit?"

"Yes," I said. "I'm afraid it is."

The man clasped his hands behind his back and nodded slowly. I expected to hear the rottweiler's claws on the porch floor at any moment.

"Jacob Ryme." He extended his right hand. The rottweiler still hadn't moved.

I took his hand, which was warm and solid. "I understand you were in the Army, Mr. Ryme."

"Yes." His smile was distinct now, perplexed. "Several armies, as a matter of fact." He was conceding me limited points for preparation. Now we both knew there was a game on.

The rottweiler took several steps after us, but stopped at the threshold, watching me with eyes that were far too casual.

Ryme ushered me into a warm room that appeared to be a combination den and office. A large desk sat in a double window that looked out upon a stand of alders along Pauley Creek. The wall to my right was nearly all stone, built around a large fireplace, where a fire rolled and snapped. Two tan leather sofas faced each other across a squat oak table in front of the fireplace. There was a mantel, which was crowded with framed photographs. On the wall above the photographs hung a crossed cavalry sword and an M-16 rifle.

"Interesting." I nodded toward the sword and the M-16. "I've never seen a statement quite like that."

"Yes, it is a statement." Ryme stood with his hands locked behind his back as he looked up at his trophies. "That's very perceptive of you. A statement of tradition shaped by necessity." He looked back at me and shrugged. "A poetic weakness, I suppose. Please sit down." He motioned me into one of the leather sofas, then seated himself in the other.

Something told me I should resist a guy who dealt in statements of tradition shaped by necessity.

Ryme cleared his throat. "What's on your mind, Mr. Banks?" For a man who had just learned of his daughter's death, he was remarkably at ease.

"I talked with Calvin Hoover today," I said.

"Yes?"

"From the Pentagon."

"Of course, I met a lot of men during my years in the Army. I don't believe Mr. Hoover was one of them."

"That figures," I said. That really figured.

"I beg your pardon?" If Hoover had been there at that moment, I would have fed him to Ryme's dog.

In one of the photos on the mantel, a girl in her teens cradled a shotgun in the crook of her arm as she knelt beside a dog and smiled at the camera. The dog was a Gordon setter. The girl was blond. She was the same girl whose photograph I carried in the notebook at my side.

I took out the photo Hoover had given me and handed it to Ryme.

"Calvin Hoover," I said. "From the Pentagon. In Washington, D.C."

For the first time since we'd met, Jacob Ryme's composure wavered.

"You really haven't talked to him, have you?" I said. "Hoover or anybody else."

"No." He didn't raise his eyes from the photo. "She's dead, isn't she." It wasn't a question.

"We found her last week."

"The girl from the park."

"I'm sorry."

"I read it in the paper and didn't think anything about it."

"Why is that?"

"Why—"

"Why didn't you think anything about it?"

"She was supposed to be on her way to school in Seattle. A week ago last Saturday."

"How was she traveling?"

"By air. I took her to the airport myself."

"Which airline?"

"Northwest."

"Did you see her get on the plane?"

"No, I was in the middle of a business engagement. I just drove her to the airport and came home. I helped her inside with her bags and then I left."

"Did anything seem . . . out of the ordinary to you?"

"Suspicious, you mean."

"That's right."

"No." He answered immediately. I wondered if he was answering the question for me, or simply validating an evaluation he'd made at the time he dropped off his daughter.

"I take it she was here on a temporary visit."

Ryme nodded.

"While she was here, was she seeing anybody?"

"No."

"No dates? What about visitors? Phone calls?"

Ryme dismissed those subjects sharply. "I'll save you the trouble, Detective. During her visit, there was nothing, as you put it, out of the ordinary." There was a finality in his tone that made me wonder whose immediate past was not open to inspection, Ryme's or his daughter's. But I wasn't sure if my curiosity was the result of Ryme's behavior, or of Calvin Hoover's.

As we talked through the afternoon, twilight came as the house fell into the shadow of the nearby mountains. I finally grew more comfortable with Ryme when he began to come across with more of his own story than I expected. He told me he'd been retired from the United States Army for about ten years. He was a full colonel. Airborn. Three tours in Southeast Asia in the sixties and early seventies.

I asked, "What about the rest of your family?"

"I lost my wife in 1975." He stared at the floor for a moment, then looked up. His eyes had a gleam. "I suppose that's the main reason why I left the Army. Patricia was our only child. When my wife passed away, Patricia was eight. I decided to retire within a year. That was in the mid-seventies."

Ryme stood, and put two sticks of wood on the fire.

"You miss the military life?"

Ryme watched the sticks catch fire. "Since resigning my commission, I've kept many of my contacts. It's been both lucrative and useful, as I'm sure this . . . Hoover? . . .

could tell you. The rest of it is mostly an attitude. You take that with you anywhere you go."

I said that it must have been difficult for Patricia, having a military father who kept his attitude, but mostly, I ventured, kept his contacts, and put them all together under clandestine circumstances. "More difficult than the Army, I'd think." You never know how much line a fish will take until you toss out the bait.

"Possibly." Ryme stroked his beard and returned to the sofa. "Of course, those were circumstances I could not foresee at the time I retired. Both the financial circumstances, and the . . . ah . . . the strategic circumstances of my ventures." He clasped his hands between his knees, then opened them like the jaws of a trap. "I'm sorry, but I really can't discuss my affairs in any great detail. And I can't see what possible interest they might be to you, beyond a certain morbid curiosity."

"Somebody murdered your daughter," I said. "Maybe your past is the key."

"Are you implying . . . "

"I'm not implying you're involved in anything criminal," I said.

"You say that," Ryme said, "as though I should be relieved to hear it." He brushed both sides of his mustache with the back of an index finger, an indignant mannerism that annoyed me. At a time like this, what did Jacob Ryme's dignity have to do with anything at all?

I hardened my voice slightly, hoping to lean on Ryme's dignity. "Didn't it seem odd not to have heard from your daughter since she left?"

"I raised her to be self-reliant. Part of that means you then have to respect one's ability to get along. She would have called me when she was ready. That might have been a few days, or a few weeks."

This guy had enough composure to be in politics.

"What time did you drop her at the airport?"

"It was about two o'clock in the afternoon."

"Can you remember exactly?"

"No."

"Did you have a way to contact her in Seattle?"

"Yes."

"Have you tried to call her?"

"No . . . well, several times, but it wasn't anything important."

"Where was she going to live in Seattle?"

"I don't know. I mean, I know, but it's written down somewhere over on my desk."

"We can get that later." I leaned back in the sofa and gave him a moment. Then I said, "What about a tattoo? She had a fairly new tattoo. Do you know where she might have had it done?"

"A tattoo? Patricia?"

"A small dragon. Done recently. On her hip."

Ryme's face tightened. "A dragon, you said?"

"A dragon." I fished through the envelope of photos and brought out a closeup of the creature itself. I handed it over to Ryme.

"My God." It was as though his eyes were snared in the faint blue veins of the dragon's wings. "Over ten years."

"What about ten years?"

Ryme looked up with the same kind of sleepy aggression I'd seen in the rottweiler's eyes. "What?"

"Ten years. You said something about ten years?"

"My daughter is dead."

He said it as if, for the first time, it was real. I reached across and tapped the photo of the dragon, which he still held. "This thing brought a look to your face. It was a look I didn't like."

"So many dangers," he said. "Countless dangers. Too many to figure . . . this."

"Figure what?"

"Detective, you've told me the elements of something you couldn't measure."

Abruptly, Ryme dropped the photo on the seat beside his thigh. "So I have two choices. One is that I can go along with you. Once I do that, then you will take whatever action you're able to take. You seem like a competent sort. Who knows, maybe you'll make an arrest. Maybe the person responsible will even be convicted. And then what? Prison? Parole?

Rehabilitation? Outstanding. And just who rehabilitates my daughter?"

"I can't argue that with you. In a case like this, nobody wins." I was using my best coffin-side manner.

"Maybe. Or let's say I deal with this myself."

"How? Take the guy off, cash in some revenge?"

"Exactly."

"And if you fail?"

"Impossible. I win just by trying."

I felt my jaws start to clamp down. "Let's knock this shit off, okay? I hear that kind of talk everyday and I can tell you right now it's crap. Somebody broke the law here and it's my job to do everything I can to settle it. You may have the information I need to do that. But you, no, you want to pull this kind of shit. Well, I can tell you right now, pal, you've put your tit in a ringer and I'm going to sit right here and squeeze till you come across."

So much for subtlety and compassion. I haven't let go with such a blast since the day Linda Westhammer followed me into the men's room, harping about sexism and seniority.

"You can't treat me this way." Jacob Ryme was working hard at getting his back up.

"The hell I can't. I'm doing it right now."

"This is outrageous!" Ryme was on his feet reaching for me. I stopped him with a fistful of photographs.

"*This* is an *outrage*. This is how she looks right now, downtown under a dirty sheet on a gurney in a big walk-in cooler at the morgue."

When Ryme made no offer to accept the pictures, I stabbed at his belly with them. He took the dozen photographs. He did not, however, look at any of them.

"You fuck with me," I whispered, "and I guarantee you'll follow the guy who killed your daughter right down the toilet. I don't give a rat's ass who you are."

Ryme held the photos at his side and turned away. "I can imagine well enough what she looks like."

"It's not the same," I said. "*It is not the same*." I could have hit him over the head for making such cruelty necessary.

Finally, as though in slow motion, Ryme leafed through the photographs. When he was done, they slipped from his fingers and scattered at his feet. "No." His voice was ragged. "It's not the same."

"She got that way because somebody shot her through the heart with a stupid little arrow. I was there when Dr. Molyneaux dug that stupid little arrow out of what's left of her chest. Now, are you ready to get down to business?"

Thirty years of steel and starch hadn't gone for nothing. Ryme's voice snapped back to normal. "What is it you want to know?"

Over ten years. I wanted to know exactly what that meant. "What's so important about that tattoo?"

"Old age and treachery," Ryme finally said.

"How's that?"

"Old age and treachery will overcome youth and skill."

I was impressed. "I think I read that once on a T-shirt."

"That scar above your collar," Ryme said, "how did you come by that?"

"A guy cut me." A cheap way of saying, *None of your fucking business.*

"I trust you came out the better."

"He's dead." I didn't like the way my cheap answers were making me feel.

"Good." Ryme nodded his head sharply. "Excellent. There's a place in life for killing like that."

I felt uncomfortably warmed by Ryme's bravado. The scar on my throat burned and throbbed as it hadn't since that first night in the hospital after Hudson cut me, the night when I refused all pain medication, telling myself I didn't want to forget how close I'd come to heading up a funeral procession of police cars. The scar continued to surge and burn.

"Listen, my friend." Ryme bit the words off, using much the same tone he'd used on the rottweiler. "The world is full of undesirables. Decent people lose ground inch by inch every day. Then it falls to men like you and me to keep our finger on the scales. I've killed dozens of those kind. I'd kill dozens more, if I had the chance. Anybody who doesn't understand that has his head in the clouds."

Ryme settled back onto the leather sofa and raised his face toward the mementos strewn along his mantel. I could hear the wind draw at the chimney, livening the fire. Through the windows behind the desk, a flight of yellow leaves sprayed from the grove of alders along the creek.

"You didn't kill him, did you?" Ryme said at last.

"Kill who?"

"You know who I mean."

He meant the man who had cut my throat.

"No. He went to the penitentiary and when his time came he got out and then somebody else killed him."

"You didn't tell me that."

"You didn't ask. Anyway, it's none of your goddamned business." There, I felt better about cheap answers.

"But it is, you see." Ryme looked down from his trophies and stroked his mustache again. "There's something you don't understand here. You want me to cooperate, tell you everything I know about somebody, and then you'll go out and investigate him. You see this as a nice neat operation. I give you information and you write a report. What you don't understand is that the man you're looking for won't give you that option. This man wants me. He won't let you sidetrack him from that. I have to decide if I can risk you sidetracking me. I have to decide if you can pull your weight. This doesn't have anything to do with punishing him for murdering my daughter. It has to do with survival."

"That's fine." I gathered up the photographs from the floor where Ryme had dropped them. "You don't want to go along, that's up to you. This is America. You can go out and kill the guy if that's what you want to do. Or maybe he kills you instead. What is it you people say? Kill 'em all, let God sort 'em out? Well, in this case I'm God. I do the sorting. Right now, as far as I'm concerned, you're just another asshole. I can put you in prison or I can put you in a grave. Your choice."

By the time I finished my speech, I was at the door. Ryme stayed behind on the couch. I had the door halfway open when he said, "Caldwell. James Caldwell."

Chapter 13

Jacob Ryme and James Caldwell met at Fort Benning in 1976, when Ryme was the commander of an airborne unit. Caldwell was a squad leader in that unit, a nineteen-year-old kid from West Memphis, Arkansas.

At first, Ryme told me, Caldwell seemed like a born soldier, the kind of troop you might recommend for OCS, if it hadn't been for the war being over, leaving the Army a glut of young officers with combat experience and nowhere to put them. Caldwell excelled at everything. Weapons training. Hand to hand. Conditioning. Military bearing. Always wanted to be first in the door.

"You have to understand," Ryme said. "I was the colonel. Just the fact that I would take that kind of special notice of a squad leader—any squad leader—tells you something."

About six months into Ryme's command, something went wrong. With the exception of one man, Caldwell's squad was extraordinarily tight. The odd man out was a Latin kid from El Paso.

"Hector Montoya. Not a bad soldier," Ryme said, "according to his record and what people—some people—said later. Except Caldwell was always riding him for something. Petty stuff. His locker, or the condition of his uniform. It all came out later, of course, that Montoya was singled out. But nobody picked up on it at the time."

It was during a night training jump in July that Hector Montoya died.

Nobody was ever sure, Ryme told me, what happened. Caldwell was the jumpmaster that day, and Montoya was the last man in line. There was an apparent malfunction in Montoya's parachute, and he went in hard.

"What about his emergency chute?"

"Not deployed. But not surprising. The jump was at twelve hundred feet, which leaves a terribly short time for corrective action. It was reasoned that Montoya simply froze . . . did not respond in time."

"You say the malfunction was 'apparent,'" I said.

Ryme nodded. "There's a log book kept with each chute. There was no record of a problem with that chute. And the rigger who packed it had an outstanding record."

"What about witnesses? Other jumpers, the aircrew?"

"None," Ryme said. "The cockpit was isolated from the cargo area, and Caldwell and Montoya were the last men in the back of the plane."

There was no way to prove that Montoya's death was anything more than a tragic accident. There was an investigation, of course. The Army can suffer twenty percent casualties, and if twenty percent was predicted, then everybody takes a deep breath and goes on with his career. But individual, unplanned deaths are always investigated. It was during that investigation that Jacob Ryme began to have very bad feelings about James Caldwell.

"When you talked to people outside the squad, Montoya had the look of a good soldier," Ryme said. "But to Caldwell's people, he was dog meat."

While interviewing Caldwell, Ryme noticed that he had a dragon tattooed on the back of his left hand. When he checked further, he found that every man in the squad had the same tattoo. Every man, that is, except Hector Montoya. While it's not unusual for military units to settle on some emblem to set themselves apart, Ryme found it somewhat extraordinary that Caldwell had designed the tattoo himself, and executed each of them as well.

"I've seen the tattoo in your photographs many times," Ryme said.

"Did anybody ever come over? Talk to you? Anybody inside the squad?"

"Mark Dietz. He was the only squad member who ever said much of anything. And that was nothing, really. Nothing material. He said Caldwell had it in for Montoya. That's about it. The kind of thing that made you more suspicious, but offered no proof."

The talk didn't end with Dietz, but it didn't exactly go farther.

"There are four squads in a platoon," Ryme explained. "Even though nobody in Caldwell's squad had much to say, it wasn't long before the senior NCOs started coming to us, saying that there was a lot of reluctance among the other three squads to jump with Caldwell or any of his people."

"And your response?"

"There was no choice. I ordered the squad broken up. And had Caldwell transferred to a non-airborne unit."

I thought for a moment about what Ryme had told me. He hadn't accused Caldwell of any wrongdoing. And, Ryme's own response seemed to be that of any commander dealing with the effects of a bad accident and bad chemistry.

"You've told me the official version," I said. "Now, what do you think really happened?"

Ryme smiled, but it didn't erase the grim look on his face. "I think Hector Montoya was murdered."

"How?"

"Well, on the surface, it seems difficult. Really, though, it could be fairly simple. Remember, Caldwell and Montoya were completely alone. All Caldwell needed to do was subdue the other man—something that Caldwell was very capable of doing. Then, pop his chute inside the plane, jettison the body. Simple."

"Why?"

"God knows." Ryme crossed and uncrossed his legs, then shifted his hips. "It could have been racial, but there were three black men in the squad, too. I suspect it was more a matter of Montoya somehow resisting Caldwell's goals for the squad, whatever those goals were. Maybe he just didn't want a dragon on the back of his hand. Maybe Caldwell felt he needed an outsider to draw the others together and he arbitrarily settled on Hector Montoya. Maybe it was like that, just a decision of leadership."

A decision of leadership. I liked that. I was about to tell Ryme it was good to know America still had a few good men, when Ryme held out his hand, stopping me.

"I didn't say I agree. But it's a state of mind I can comprehend."

"Well, hell," I said, "even an ordinary guy like me can comprehend it. Comprehension is hardly the problem."

"Nobody ever said command can't grow corrupt."

"No. Nobody ever said that. Did you ever confront Caldwell with your suspicions?"

"Yes. I called him in just before he cleared the post."

"And what did he have to say?"

"Nothing. Nothing at all. He came to attention and smiled."

I stood up and walked to the fireplace and tried to warm myself. I was cold, though, from the inside out.

"You keep tabs on the men from that squad?"

Ryme laughed. "There were other questions of leadership involved. I resigned four months later. It's true, I resigned into a more lucrative and interesting line of work, but I still resigned. I do know that Caldwell finished out his hitch—less than a year—in a kitchen at Fort Bliss. As far as I know, the rest of the men just went their own way. Except for Mark Dietz. I heard Dietz died in 1978 in a boat explosion in Florida."

"How did you get that information?"

"A newspaper story. The clipping came in the mail, in an envelope postmarked Miami."

"You got that clipping while you were living here? In Rozette?"

"No, this was just after I resigned. A few months. I was living in Houston then. I've only lived here in Montana for about three years."

"Any idea what Caldwell is up to these days? Besides maybe murdering your daughter?"

Ryme's expression and manner gave up nothing. I might as well have been asking for a morning report on his troops.

"I heard his name once. In a conversation with some of my Latin American associates. It was a conversation about hiring soldiers."

"And did you—"

"I didn't say anything about the Montoya incident. The people who were having this conversation would have considered it a recommendation for the kind of work they were looking for. I wasn't inclined to do anything that might give Caldwell a leg up."

"And you didn't want them to know you knew Caldwell?"

"I am an intermediary. Who they put on their payroll is their business."

"Were you afraid of Caldwell finding you?"

Ryme gave me a cold look, which vanished in an instant. "Of course not."

"But you more or less punched his ticket. At least as far as the Army was concerned."

"Caldwell punched his own ticket."

"Was Caldwell a good jumper?"

"He was an expert jumper. As good as there is."

"Then he knew what he was doing."

"Exactly what he was doing."

I thought for a moment about what precisely it was that Caldwell had taken on, sliding as he had done down a thin line, while traveling at breakneck speed hundreds of feet off the ground. With the hope of accomplishing what? A heroic rescue, or the perfect homicide of an unwanted individual in the unit? Ryme had painted Caldwell as the kind of man who would be equally satisfied with either outcome.

"Would you agree," I said, "that Caldwell is a man of some daring and resolve? A guy with a memory?"

Ryme seemed mildly frustrated. "All right, Caldwell could have turned into a complication, sure. I live where I live because I don't like complications. They have to be removed. I've removed enough complications. It was easier this time to remove myself."

"But now . . . "

"That's right. Now I have a complication. And you have a complication."

"No. I have a suspect. If I have a complication, it's you."

The afternoon had turned to dusk and I was curious about what Red Hanrahan and Woodruff had put together in the apartment above Angel's. I went back to the sofa and pulled out the surveillance photos of Fisher White. I handed them to Ryme.

"Caldwell?"

"That's him." Ryme studied the pictures with analytical detachment. "Were these taken here in town?"

"I took them last Friday night."

"Where?"

"No. We have to decide some things before I take you any farther."

Ryme stood and walked to the window behind his desk. The wind had stiffened and it was spitting snow. Ryme placed the palm of his right hand on the glass for a moment, then touched his palm to his forehead.

"Cold," he said. "Winter soon. I always enjoy that. Coming back from the jungle to a Montana winter. The snow, it's like a bandage. Maybe that's because I never fought a battle in the snow. I always fought in rain and mud and heat. The snow is a great bandage."

I wondered if he would be that philosophical about snow drifting over his daughter's grave. I said, "What will you do when I leave here?"

"Leave with you."

"Who says I'll take you along?"

"You'll take me. You won't have any choice. Not after I tell you about the other surveillance. The one on this house." He turned. "I caught the flash of light off a lens one day. I went out the back way, hiked up the canyon, and circled around above where I'd seen the light." There was a road up the back side of the hill and he'd found a car there. There was man in the shelter of an outcropping.

"Caldwell?"

"No."

"You think I'm involved in that surveillance?"

"Of course not. But I think you may know who is." Ryme went to the table and searched through the Fisher White photos. He selected one and handed it to me. "That's the car."

He pointed out Roger Quill's tan Impala.

Chapter 14

Dry leaves rattled across the lawn, nipping at our legs as we walked toward my car. Above Bride's Canyon, the moon was wedged in a cloud bank. It had stopped snowing, but the wind still smelled like snow. I walked easier after Ryme shut the rottweiler in a kennel.

At the end of the walk, Ryme offered me his hand.

"I want to thank you," he said. "For not shutting me out."

I shook Ryme's hand. It seemed as though I could feel his bones through the skin. Maybe it was my own bones I felt.

"Let's say I shut you out," I said. "You'd have gone off on your own, maybe gotten me or somebody I care about hurt."

"That could happen yet." Ryme tossed his soft black bag into the backseat. "Having me under your thumb won't guarantee nobody gets hurt."

"I know." I started the car and pulled out of the drive. "All it guarantees is that you'll have to work harder to fuck us over if that's what you decide to do."

We spent five minutes at the drive-up window of a fast-food place, and by six-thirty I had us checked into a room at the Congress, the last authentic downtown hotel in Rozette. A narrow nine-story pile of brick and granite, the Congress rises like a donjon from the corner of McLean and Defoe, within easy walking distance of the train station. It's the kind of joint where you have to ask special for a private bath. Don't get me wrong, the Congress used to advertise itself honestly as the classiest hotel on the line between Minneapolis and Seattle. The German ambassador once stayed at the Congress. But that was back in the days when it was chic to take the train west and wrap yourself in a buffalo robe on the ride out to shoot the elk. Nowdays, the train station has been turned into a rat's nest of shops selling safari clothes, gourmet ice cream, high-tech kitchen gadgets, and a herd of books on how to make your body slender, your personality unique, and your whole life meaningful. The Congress, on the other hand, doesn't labor under the burden of being antique—it's just old. Ryme and I were the only occupants on the eighth floor.

Ryme rummaged through a bag of burgers and coffee while I phoned Fanning. The greasy burgers smelled at home in the room, which was done in faded pastels and art deco furniture. A print of some pink flamingos under pale green palms beside an ashen blue lagoon hung between the beds. The cigarette burns on the nightstand were like long brown chevrons.

"This is cute, Banks," Vic Fanning said. "I give my word to a federal agent and then you go right out and bend me over and load me up."

"There wasn't any choice, Vic."

"Don't feed me that shit, Banks, we always have choices. You could have done nothing. That's a choice. You could have talked to him and then waited till tomorrow and taken it up with your superior, which is me. That was a choice, too. You could have called me *before* you snatched—"

"Hoover pissed me off," I said.

"Oh, that's good. Wait, let me write that one down. *Hoover . . . pissed . . . me . . . off.*"

I closed my eyes and took a deep breath. "We're at the Congress," I said.

"Great choice. You got great taste in accommodations."

"Nobody would think to look for us here."

"Nobody would dare."

Ryme was at the window, chewing on a hamburger while he examined the fire escape. I told Fanning I didn't have time to talk and I needed a couple of detectives at the hotel to sit with Ryme through the night.

"He can't take care of himself?"

"That's not the point."

"You can't trust him."

"Just get me a couple of guys," I said, then hung up.

"Your boss?" Ryme unlaced his black Herman's Survivors and made himself comfortable in the middle of one of the two double beds. The mattress curled around him. He ran his hand over the pink chenille spread.

"My boss," I said. "Sometimes he tries to be an idiot."

"That's what they get paid for." Ryme seemed especially circumpsect, considering what had gone between us earlier in the day. No, he was more than circumspect. He was completely detached. With most people in these circumstances, I would have attributed such detachment to shock. We all hide from many things, and the most immediate place to hide is one's own mind. But except for the most fleeting lapses, Ryme's mood had been painstakingly even since he'd opened his door and decided to talk to me rather than feed me to that goddamned beast he called a dog. Now, I found myself staring at him as he methodically daubed catsup on his french fries. After several bites, Ryme looked up and caught me.

"Got a problem, Banks?"

"Just wondering, that's all."

"Yes?"

"Wondering if you give a rat's ass your daughter is dead. Little things like that."

"Because I'm not hysterical?"

"Not hysterical. But maybe at least a little distracted."

"Is there something I could do to prove to you I cared about Patricia?"

"If you have to ask, then I guess it doesn't really matter, does it?"

Ryme shrugged and stuck another french fry in his mouth. "I learned a long time ago not to care much about other people's misgivings. You should try it sometime, Banks. Life is much clearer that way."

I parted the curtains and looked out at the parking lot eight stories down. The snow had turned to rain. Small puddles sparkled on the asphalt. By concentrating on the window, I could see Ryme's reflection from the room behind me. I shifted focus and looked back outside. I realized we were only about two blocks from the White/Caldwell apartment upstairs over Angel's.

The eighth floor of the Congress is higher than most of downtown Rozette, Montana, where no architect has seriously tried to compete with the surrounding mountains. The roof-

tops below were dark mesas underlain by two glazed ribbons
of second-story windows and storefronts.

It's curious, the way streetlights divide the night into
segments. I remember walking the downtown beat one night
a long time back. It was about this time of year. I was walking
with Paul Culp. We kept hearing this clamor up in the sky and
we looked up and saw a flock of snow geese. Must have been
a thousand of them. Circling and circling over town. Culp said
after dark the geese confuse the lights of town with water. Said
they'd circle like that all night, and they did. Culp knew all
about things like that. Sometimes, I think he knew too much
about life outside town to waste his own life being a cop.

And there I was, in the company of Colonel Jacob Ryme,
U.S.A. Retired, a man whose life, both professional and
personal, proved only that the human race had little more to
look forward to than its own destruction. So why did I want
him to see us as men cast from a similar, if not common mold?
Why did I feel, despite my words, that I was courting his
favor? These were not comfortable questions. I think I liked
the man. I tried to slide open the window, but it was painted
shut.

Pastor Roscoe Beckett would tell me to tune up my ears, and
get on with things. He's not even a cowboy. Neither am I.

So what?

I'm not a saint, either.

Saints are a pain in the ass.

"I'm not—" I turned back into the room and stopped. Ryme
had pulled a blanket over himself and gone to sleep.

Thomas Cassidy flipped on the TV and made a couple of
quick circuits up and down the dial, before settling on an old
John Wayne movie. Linda Westhammer leaned against the
wall near the bathroom door and chewed on a toothpick. Her
black leather jacket crackled when she folded her arms. She
wore red stretch pants with stirrups and black high-top
Reeboks. Blond hair frizzed from her head like the last fraction
of a fuse.

"*Rio Grande*," Cassidy said. He slid the blue down jacket off his shoulders and sat on the edge of the bed next to Ryme's. "This is a real classic."

"Directed by John Ford," Jacob Ryme said.

"Right." Cassidy looked over at Ryme and nodded appreciatively. "Right."

When they arrived, I had talked briefly in the hall with Westhammer and Cassidy. I told them that Ryme was the father of the dead girl Hanrahan and I dug up out of the park, and that, for the moment at least, he was on our side. I told them he could leave anytime he wanted, but they were to discourage him as much as possible without breaking the law. And, they were to make sure nobody disturbed him in any way that might be detrimental to either Ryme's health or the health of the person doing the disturbing.

According to Cassidy, Wattie Roebuck, our unlamented tattoo expert, was dead from two gunshot wounds to the head. That was all Cassidy knew. He'd done background on Roebuck—"A real zero," Cassidy said, "nothing but a couple of pops for felony theft in Texas, no local family or history"— before being called to the scene to go with the body to the morgue.

"He doesn't know about Roebuck being dead," I said, nodding toward the door to our room. "I'd like to keep it that way for now."

"You think this Ryme guy is tied to that?"

I shook my head. "Roebuck put Hanrahan and me onto a guy looks real good for Ryme's daughter. Ryme knows this guy, his name's Caldwell, but he's been using the name Fisher White."

Westhammer's face brightened. "That's the same—"

"Right," I said. "The apartment where Roebuck bought it. I'm convinced this guy Ryme would like to do Caldwell."

Cassidy looked as troubled as Cassidy ever manages to look. "Ryme came right out and told you that?"

"He didn't have to. He's acting too leveled out to have anything else in mind. I don't want to help. Till I know more about the Roebuck thing, I don't know how much it might do for Ryme."

"Did you know," Ryme said now to Cassidy, "that in two of the John Ford cavalry films there's a character with the same name?"

"Tyree. He's a private in this one, and a sergeant in *She Wore a Yellow Ribbon*. You know, I've always wondered if they're supposed to be the same character, or if it's just a fluke, or maybe something that only people who know a lot about the movies are suppose to understand, like an inside joke or something."

"I don't know," Ryme said. "But they're both played by—"

"Ben Johnson."

"Amazing," Jacob Ryme said. "With a mind like that you'll make sergeant—"

"—in eight or nine years." Cassidy looked back at Ryme again and started to laugh. "You better sit down and watch this, Westhammer. This is a real classic."

I looked at my watch. It was just after seven o'clock. Thomas Cassidy and Linda Westhammer had made it to the Congress less than half an hour after I'd called Fanning.

Westhammer looked like she'd swallowed battery acid. "I had a date with a guy who promised to marry me."

Cassidy was impressed. "Or a reasonable facsimile of marriage. Fanning said get a partner. I tried Harold Hoopes first, but he had the flu. I'll probably catch it, just talking to his wife on the phone. If I don't catch a worse disease here tonight."

I told Cassidy to be sure that at least he or Linda stayed awake all night. Linda Westhammer yawned.

"I didn't search him, but he's probably got a gun." I watched Ryme for a reaction, but, as usual, none materialized. "Guys like him always have a gun or two."

"No strain," Cassidy said. "I brought along a manuscript to touch up. Judge Clay wants to see what I'm working on. I think he issued an order." I've been with Cassidy several times when Walter Clay has buttonholed him about this book-writing business.

"I promised Walter I'd murder six attorneys this week. He said six wasn't enough. He wants me to write a gothic romance about a housewife who has an affair with a vacuum cleaner salesman who's hung like a Shetland pony. He says it'll sell millions in the grocery stores of America. He says I'll be rich."

"I'd buy it," Linda Westhammer said. She peeled off her black leather jacket. Under it, she wore a black sweater with a huge pair of red lips on the front.

"Sure," Cassidy said, "but if I write it, I'll have no soul."

"Cassidy, you're fucked up," Linda Westhammer said. There were tiny beads of sweat on her forehead. When she lay her jacket on the floor, I heard a faint thud. Her gun, I figured.

"I'd consider it a personal favor," I said to Ryme, "you didn't murder these two in their sleep."

Just then, John Wayne grabbed up Maureen O'Hara and kissed her on the mouth. Cassidy gave Linda Westhammer a sidelong glance. She hadn't moved from her post by the bathroom door.

"Stick it up your ass, Cassidy," Westhammer said. She stepped to the radiator beside Ryme's bed and kicked it and I got the hell out of there.

Chapter 15

"If the poor bastard had stuck with talking to us instead of trying his hand with that guy he went to visit, he maybe would of lived another couple of days." Hanrahan looked to his left at Sam Blieker, who was nursing the tail end of a Camel.

Blieker nodded and coughed. The last four or five years, he's taken up one of those low tar and nicotine brands. When he works a murder, though, he always backslides to real cigarettes.

I sat down behind my desk and put my feet up. The office had that sense of peace that only transpires after the business day, when the Detective Division shuts down and there are no incoming phone calls, no typewriters tattling away about our failures, no poor miserable people walking in to have their lives restored.

Hanrahan was on the edge of his chair with his elbows on his desk, the fingers on his right hand drumming against the fingers of his left. This is the pose he always assumes when he's just fallen into a big job and is ready to start talking things through. Blieker, who was wearing his blue suit, sat rumpled and intractable, a scowl fading off into the white tundra of his high forehead.

"Where's Woodruff?" I asked.

"Just left," Hanrahan said. "It was his turn to deal with the newspeople. I heard he needed a chair and a whip. We're about to pull the plug, too. We sealed the apartment, put out an attempt to locate on Fisher White."

"You going to arrest him tonight?"

"We were just deciding that," Blieker said.

I looked at Hanrahan. "The Meehan woman do it for you?"

"She puts White in the apartment just before noon. He

stopped off and asked her if anybody'd been around looking for him. No noise on the stairs or anything else to indicate he left after that. Nothing at all, till just after one o'clock, when she hears a guy come up and knock on White's door. A few minutes later, she hears some banging around, shouts, shit like that. Then what she thinks could be a shot, but muffled. Then somebody goes tearing down the stairs and she calls 9-1-1. By the time the cops get there, White is in the wind."

"The shouting," I said, "she say what it was about?"

"Money, she thought," Blieker said. "But she's not real sure. And maybe something about a warning."

"Both ends against the middle?" I said.

Blieker drew on his cigarette and savored the smoke as he exhaled. "Why not? Roebuck checks his finances and decides that telling White the cops are onto him is a good investment. White agrees, but pays him off instead with a bullet."

"You got a plan to find White?" I asked.

Blieker stretched his shoulders and crossed his legs. "Not really. Right now, we're just winging it." Blieker lit another cigarette.

Wattie Roebuck's days of winging it were gone. He'd had his wings clipped by a press contact wound to the back of the head. With press contact wounds, all of the gases from the burned gunpowder are vented into the tissue against which the muzzle is pressed, a process that tears the tissue away from the wound in a pattern known as starring. There was one piece of spent brass found near the body. 9mm Winchester Western. But there was no exit wound, so no bullet had been recovered yet. That meant we wouldn't confirm the caliber until a bullet—either whole or in pieces—was recovered at autopsy, and the diameter of the entrance wounds could be more accurately measured after the wound was cleaned and the surrounding area shaved. There was a long chance that the 9mm brass was coincidental, and with press contact wounds, even a .22 can turn a head into a very ugly thing. Press contact wounds are also relatively quiet; the body makes a great silencer.

"I'm surprised the Meehan woman heard anything," Blieker said.

"I think she's the kind of woman who listens very hard," I said. Hanrahan agreed.

As soon as the coroner had pronounced Wattie Roebuck, Woodruff ordered the apartment sealed until they could get a search warrant. Then, with paper in hand, they processed the apartment for evidence before giving it a good toss.

"This is the part you'll like," Hanrahan said. "We found this funny little thing that shoots arrows. Real short arrows. It's a kind of slingshot thing, that you hold in one hand and brace against your wrist. It has a compound action that uses surgical tubing. Do anything for you?"

"The girl," I said.

"Yes, the girl." Hanrahan looked at Blieker and asked him for a cigarette, then waved him off.

"Time was, you'd walk a mile for a Camel." Blieker lit one cigarette from another.

"Walked out," Hanrahan said. Then, to me: "And how was your day in the country? I just want you to know, I got forty diseases, going through Fisher White's garbage and Wattie Roebuck's blood."

I told them the Jacob Ryme story. That is, I told them the essential elements of the Jacob Ryme story, the identification of his daughter, the tie with Fisher White, who was really a nasty piece of work named James Caldwell, and the decision to put Ryme on ice at the Congress, where, I hoped, Cassidy and Westhammer were still alive and keeping an eye on him. I spared them all that stuff about rainy nights and alienated detectives, the emotional drek.

"Why the lock on Ryme?" Blieker asked.

"He's not a man you can trust to let things take their course—take *our* course."

"A crackpot?" Hanrahan asked.

"No. Not at all. If he was a crackpot, I'd have left him alone. What he is, he's a guy who could promise a solution and make good on it. Guy could cut out your heart slick as a surgeon, then smile and say it was a good way to drop a few pounds."

"And he's going along with you? A guy like that?" Blieker gave me that look he always gives you, that look when he cocks his head forward and arches his brows and balances his black glasses, when he's wearing them, in a furrow on his forehead.

He wasn't wearing his glasses that night. He didn't need them to see we were on a fast track.

"I didn't say I'd made a convert of him," I said. "I think he's just hanging around to see what happens. He stays close, he stands to have more information that might help him if he decides to take Caldwell himself."

Blieker was grumpy. "Everybody says that shit, says he wants to get the guy himself."

"Trust me, Sam. Ryme can take a flyer whenever he wants. I'm telling you it's in our best interest to make sure he doesn't want."

Hanrahan sat back behind his desk. "So what do we do, Sergeant?"

"Well," Blieker said, "I think we should talk to Mr. Caldwell, give him a chance to tell his side of the story."

"If we can find him," I said.

"That's right," Blieker said. "And in the meantime, if Uniform Patrol happens to come across Mr. Caldwell, I think they should arrest the sonofabitch and throw his ass in jail. Until we give him a chance to talk his way out of all this."

At about eight o'clock, Hanrahan ran a sheet of paper in his typewriter and we spent ten minutes putting together a briefing sheet on Ryme and Roebuck homicides. Then we attached one of the surveillance photos of Caldwell to the sheet and Hanrahan took it upstairs to deliver to the Uniform Patrol Shift commander. Tomorrow, Blieker would combine and summarize our work and take it to the county attorney for an arrest warrant. For tonight, though, there was sufficient probable cause to arrest Caldwell on sight.

Blieker seemed even more worn down than I would have expected, and I thought I knew the reason why.

"Must be our lucky day," I said as we were getting ready to lock up. "You're still walking around with the Hudson thing uncleared, now you get this one to hang around your neck. A matched set."

Blieker could still manage a little cheer. "I convinced Woodruff to put his name on this one. These days, everybody gets his own homicide. I may have to give the next one to Cassidy, just to keep him from going to the union with a grievance. By the way, that reminds me. There was a call for

you. Just before you showed up. A woman named Marian
Tawney. Says she talked to you before about Hudson. Said she
wants to talk to you again." Blieker buttoned his brown
overcoat and pulled the office door closed. "Wants you to stop
by her house." On the stairs, he handed me a slip of paper with
an address. I already knew the address, but I took the paper
anyway.

"I'm a little troubled, Leo," Blieker said. "I don't think I saw
this woman's name in any of your reports."

"It's personal," I said. He hadn't been involved when
Hudson cut me, so I had to tell him who Marian Tawney was.

By the time we got upstairs, Hanrahan had already left. The
station was quiet, except for the woman who sat behind
inch-thick Plexiglas at the twenty-four-hour desk. Blieker
nodded goodbye and flipped up the collar of his overcoat.

I was almost in my car before Blieker stopped me. "So. You
going to go see this Tawney woman?"

"I'm not sure."

"You know what she wants?"

"No."

"Bullshit, you don't. Even I can figure out what she wants,
she wants to *see* you. You know that, same as I do."

"See *me*. The man who would not die." I shrugged and
looked past Blieker down the alley past the limpid green door
of the Cloverleaf and on above to the west face of Hollow
Ridge. Even at night, the dull white above the snow line
reflected the ambient light from the city.

"You're a grown man. You can do what you like."

"Maybe she has some information about the shooting. You
could use a little information, you ask me."

"You believe that?"

"Maybe."

"I guess that means you're more fucked up than I thought.
Take my advice, go home. Put on some Benny Goodman,
some Dizzy Gillespie. Put on some tunes, open a can of
beer, just one, and drink it and take a good pee and go to bed.
Those things, things like with that Tawney woman, you never
get those things back. The way you felt, I mean."

"What do you mean, the way I felt."

"Don't bullshit me, Leo. Why else wasn't her name in your

reports? See, you can always get close . . . but now you
know what it means, all of it. You know too fucking much. Just
go home."

And call Janice, I thought. I should call Janice and tell her
I'm alive and I want to see her again, need to see her soon to
talk late into the night about ancient drawings and antelope
and rivers.

"I've nearly lost my mind," I said, "following that kind of
goddamned advice."

"Maybe. But you still have a mind to lose."

There is a certain way that your footsteps sound when you
turn up the sidewalk to a woman's door at night, isn't there? I
mean, you wear the same shoes you've worn all day, the
sidewalk is just ordinary cement. You're still the same slightly
heavy guy who has trudged through one more slightly heavy
day. Yet there's something, a kind of anxious, light-footed
precision in your steps . . . *go back* . . . *go on* . . . *go
back* . . . *go*.

And when you knock, isn't it as though you are calling
someone away from her life?

"I wasn't sure you'd come," Marian said. Her voice was low.
The wedge of light cast on the narrow porch widened as she let
me in. "The baby's asleep."

"I'm sorry. Maybe I should have called first."

"No, this is fine. I wanted to see you. But I didn't want to do
it down where you work."

"You're right. It's a bad place to talk. At least the things I
think you want to talk about. About that night I saw you in the
alley. And before."

"And before," she said. "Mostly about the *and before*, I
think." She wore a floor-length white cotton caftan with dark
blue pinstripes. Her feet were bare and her nipples shone
through the fabric. Her dark hair, long and shining, was pulled
back and held in place by combs decorated with brass figures
that looked Egyptian. She was wearing gold wire frame
glasses. She opened her mouth, about to say something, then
stopped and turned away. "Would you like some tea?"

I said I would and she told me to sit down on an antique
daybed stacked with bright red and gold pillows.

The house was tiny, almost as small as my apartment. Across

the room, nearly within arm's reach, sat a TV and stereo on a set of shelves made of stained planks stacked on old bricks. Just to the left of the shelves there was a closed door, which I assumed was the bedroom, where the baby slept. A large fig tree in a black and orange pot filled the front window. The kitchen was to my right, through a door covered with a beaded curtain. On the wall behind me hung a color poster of John Lennon. There was a copy of *Ms.* magazine folded open beside me on the daybed.

I heard the beaded curtain rattle and looked up. Marian Tawney handed me a brown hand-thrown mug. Hers was nearly identical.

"You make these?" I said, indicating the mug.

She smiled and set her mug on an end table. She closed the magazine and put it on the table, too, and then she took off her glasses and lay them on the magazine. She raised her arms. The loose cuffs slid up her forearms.

"These are the hands of a klutz," she said.

The long, slender fingers didn't look like they belonged to a klutz.

"A friend of mine from the center, that's the day-care center where I work, she's a potter."

I sipped the tea. It tasted smoky.

"It's called Lapsang souchong," she said. Her voice sounded like the tea tasted.

I tried not to think felonious thoughts about her hands and hair, the caftan settled loosely over her legs, her bare feet tucked beneath her as she settled back into the pillows.

"The tea," I said. "It doesn't taste like strawberries."

"What?"

"Nothing. An inside joke." I cleared my throat and wiped the back of my hand over my forehead. The room was warm and I wanted to take off my coat, but I was still wearing a gun and I didn't know quite what to do about that.

"What was it on your mind?" I said.

That troubled look tightened her face again. Her eyes stopped the involuntary, aimless wandering that people's eyes do when things are on an even keel.

I settled back and waited for the words to start. "I knew all along"—her eyes jumped directly to mine—"knew there was something that night you were afraid of. And I knew it wasn't me. Most people in your spot would have been afraid of me . . . but not you."

"I guess that's a compliment." She tried to smile and shifted her weight on the couch. "When I was a kid—"

"This isn't going to go away."

"I read stories to the kids at the center—"

"You're not listening. Not to me, not to yourself."

She took another sip of tea. "No. Not listening at all. I wanted to tell you that night in the car, but I was too afraid. I decided that maybe you'd find out what happened and I wouldn't have to risk anything, maybe even risk my baby."

"We all want that. Sometimes we just can't get it."

"It was okay, I could even live with you not finding who killed him. It wasn't like he was a saint." She rocked slightly with a bitter laugh. "I'm better off without him around. And this is the only way to make sure he isn't around."

I remembered my comment about driving a stake through Sky King Hudson's heart. Her voice made me feel like a man holding a hammer.

"Then I read all that stuff in the paper . . . oh, Christ."

I tried to recall Robert Tolliver's stories about Hudson. They seemed fairly innocuous, then and now. Convicted cop-stabber buys farm, authorities investigate.

"I'd close my eyes at night and all I could see was her face, like there was a soft light shining on it, and then the dirt falling—"

"What?"

"The dirt . . . dirt falling. It was like I could feel the ground pressing in around me."

"What the hell are you talking about?"

"The girl in the park. Patricia Ryme. I'm afraid somebody will find out and kill me. She's my friend . . . she was."

I felt my own eyes stop their normal, aimless wandering. I wanted to grab Marian Tawney by the shoulders and shake the story out of her. This, however, is not a sound interview technique; people don't place their trust in detectives who appear to be lunatics. I took a deep breath and forced myself to relax enough to encourage her to talk.

"Why don't you start at some point where you can ease into things?"

She found her cigarettes on the table. The match was steady in her fingers. "For a long time after that day with you and Sky, I drank a lot . . . a *lot* . . . did lots of drugs. I can say that, can't I?"

"Say whatever you want. That's why I came, isn't it? To hear what you've got to say."

"And then I moved to Seattle. That's where I met Patricia. I tended bar. Did some modeling. But not—"

"I understand."

"No, I mean it, no funny stuff. Just regular modeling. But that didn't seem to fit with who I was."

Marian Tawney found out who she was when she fell in with some radical types who drank at one of the bars where she worked. Political talk became a balm for substance abuse.

"What kind of politics?" I asked.

"Latin America, mostly. Third World self-determination. That kind of shit." It wasn't really the politics that bound her. Rather, she felt anchored by people who seemed to have something on their minds besides personal gain. Then, about three years ago, Patricia Ryme began to come around with these people.

"From the start," Marian said, "she seemed to have the inside line on something. Nobody knew much about her. She was younger than most of us. Very bright. Determined in a way that could be intimidating, especially in somebody that young. From the start, I took her for somebody with a secret. It turns out I was right."

I thought about the rubble of papers on my desk, where I'd left Hoover's photo of this striking young woman, the same woman whose photographs I'd seen beneath a sword and automatic rifle on Jacob Ryme's mantel. Did Marian Tawney ever learn Patricia Ryme's secret?

"I guess I should have been flattered that she'd trust me," Marian said. "Of course, she might have told me just because it was a coincidence that I was from Rozette and she knew she'd need help."

"She convinced you to come back?"

"About eighteen months ago. She said she needed a place to stay when she came to visit him."

"Her father?"

Marian started to flare, but then it passed. "I don't suppose you'd tell me how you knew that." Her tone said that she was used to being left behind at the edge of secrets. I didn't have the heart to answer.

"And did she come here? To Rozette?"

"Three times. At least, three times that I knew of. I didn't know she was here this last time . . . the time she was killed."

"Why couldn't she stay with her father?"

"I never knew that. But I always felt like it was more his idea than hers."

I wondered if this was an indication that Ryme's life was, for whatever reason, even more secretive than Hoover had implied.

"And the secret," I said, "you said she had a secret."

"Money."

While politics was a balm for Marian Tawney, it became a passion for Patricia Ryme. She associated with people who were deeply involved in funneling resources to leftist groups in Latin America. She said that she had access to money. Significant money. But the source always remained clouded. When she convinced Marian to move back to Rozette, she also convinced her to tell people that the move was strictly personal, not something done at Patricia Ryme's behest.

"But you seem to be saying that she trusted you. Why not tell you the whole business?"

"I also said she was very bright. Maybe she could just read people." Marian stopped, and I knew that she was thinking back to the day she'd snitched me off to Hudson. "Or maybe she just figured I'd be safer if I didn't know it all."

"Her father?" I asked. "Was he the source?"

"I never knew this for sure. I mean, she never came right out and said so. But God knows I've spent enough time around drug dealers to know how spooky shit goes down. Who else, if not her father?"

"And she thought this was something just the two of you could pull off?"

Marian shook her head. "There was somebody else involved. Some guy. But I never knew who."

"You think maybe this guy killed her?" I made a mental note to come back the next day with a picture of James Caldwell.

"I don't know. If I was sure, maybe it wouldn't have taken me so long to come to you."

"And what does this have to do with Hudson?"

"Hudson was Hudson," she said.

"An asshole."

"An asshole who had my number."

When he got out of prison, it didn't take Hudson long to start slipping around to Marian Tawney's place. One night, he came across some letters from Patricia Ryme. From them, he learned just enough to know that there was money in the wind. Marian knew that there was no shortage of people who would run up the flag over Hudson's death, and that this information made for slim pickings as far as tying his murder to Patricia Ryme's. But like she'd said, she's been around enough to know how shit happens. Enough to keep herself and her baby metaphorically underground, before they got there for real.

"What makes you think you can trust me, I won't give you up?"

She looked down at her lap and thought. "I'm not sure. I mean when I'm alone here, just me and the baby, it's important for me to talk to you. But now you're here, I get the shakes."

"I never held a grudge, if that's what's bothering you."

"No. No, I was never worried about that. I was never afraid of what you might think."

"I never hated you."

"That's not it, either. You'd have come back on your own if you hated me. I guess I just believed that if you wouldn't come after me for what I did back then, it meant there was something about you that could be trusted."

"Is this the *and before* you wanted to talk about?" I was afraid to say more. Most of things I knew to say at that point were dangerous. I remembered her touch. It was a touch that remained, fifteen years later, incomplete.

She laughed. "It isn't that easy. You know it's not." She started to drink more tea, but her mug was empty. "I always had an impulse to take care of people. Like you, that day you were hurt. And Patricia. My son. The kids at the day-care. Hudson had that figured right down the line and turned it all into bullshit. For so long, I saw and felt everything in terms of Hudson. Now, with him dead, for the first time I see things in terms of myself."

"So what is it you see?"

"I see me holding your face between my hands, your blood all over my legs. You know how hot a person's blood is? When there's a lot of it? I never knew that."

"Yes."

"I wanted to wrap myself around you and make you better."

"That's what you did." I took her hand and held it to the scar on my throat. "Like that. You were perfect."

She pulled her hand back. "It wasn't enough. You know it wasn't." She leaned closer and kissed the scar. Without saying anything else, she pulled my coat off my shoulders. I slipped out of the shoulder holster, then put my hand behind her head and pulled her closer. She unbuttoned my shirt.

"And this," I said, "is this your way of taking care of me?"

"No." Her face was serious and she kissed me. "This is taking care of *us*."

I lay back on the pillows and pulled her with me, sliding the caftan up around her shoulders.

Perhaps an hour later, I felt Marian start awake and then I heard the baby crying in the other room. Without saying anything, she stood and looked at the closed door. Her breasts were round and flushed and her hair had fallen free of the brass combs. There were red smudges on her back where I had held her. Standing, I could see that she had a mother's hips, not fat, but full from giving birth.

She slipped into the caftan and stepped to the bedroom door, then looked back quickly at me before going in.

Marian closed the door behind her and for a moment I lay listening, trying to hear her talking to her baby. I couldn't hear anything, though, so I sat up and dressed. I was just pulling on my boots when Marian came out with her baby.

"This is Richard." She carried him on the point of her hip.

"Richard Tawney." The baby looked up and pulled his mother's hair as she spoke.

"Not Richard Hudson," I said, wishing I hadn't.

"No. Never. Mr. Richard Tawney."

He was a good-looking boy, with light brown hair and deep brown eyes. I took his right hand and shook it. "Mr. Tawney, it's a true pleasure," I said. He giggled and pulled Marian's hair again. For the first time since I'd arrived, I felt like an intruder.

"I think I should go. You have an important job here."

"I hope you don't think this, tonight . . ."

"Someday," I said, "when we're old and this is all over—"

"No." She put her fingertips on my lips. "It's over now. Please."

"I understand." I put on my coat and looped the shoulder holster over my forearm. "I'll try my best to find out what happened to your friend. And I won't give you up. I promise." I wondered if we'd been settling a debt or sealing a bargain, and decided that I didn't want to know. I kissed her lightly. Then I kissed Mr. Richard Tawney. Then I left.

Sometimes, you know, your footsteps leaving a woman's house don't sound nearly the same as they did going in.

It was less than half a mile from Marian Tawney's place to my apartment on Eau Claire Street. In the moments it took me to make the drive, it started to rain again, a deliberate late autumn rain that had a settled-in feel to it. Perhaps the snow line would inch a little closer to town. I parked and gathered up my gun and walked slowly up the outside stairway through the rain.

Inside, I opened a beer and put on some Creedence Clearwater, just like Sam Blieker had suggested. I had the instructions down, but not the timing. I stood in my living room window, looking down at the river, listening to the rain nick at the window and watching the water cascade down the glass in a slow, dark sheet to the sash.

Janice. I should call Janice. But it was late, both on the clock and inside my head. Sooner or later, I would call her. What I would say, though, was something else. If I told her about Marian Tawney, would that be the end of things? Or would a silent lie be worse? Even with three marital DOAs under my belt, I didn't have a good answer to that one.

I was still standing in the window, big as life, when the first bullet crashed through the glass and smacked into the ceiling behind me.

I dove onto the Hide-A-Bed, crawled to the door, and switched off the light.

Then I crawled to the end table and jerked my gun out of the holster.

Back at the window, I took a quick peak out the lower left corner.

I saw two muzzle flashes from the gazebo, just before what was left of the glass disintegrated. Again, I heard the bullets lodge in the ceiling, but I never heard the shots.

I rolled over the bed, then made my way into the kitchen and out that door into the interior stairwell, where I nearly gagged in air that smelled like the inside of a tomb for cats. I took the steps three and four at a time, then slipped out the front door, crept around the west edge of the house, and started making my way along the row of arborvitae toward the gazebo.

The rain ticked softly on the green-black shrubbery and threatened to turn to ice at any moment. My footsteps felt quiet, yet sounded deafening on a brief stretch of wet gravel. The sharp gust of a bullet, followed by a dreadful rattling in the branches just above my head, sent me diving for the levee just a few steps ahead. The ground stammered slightly as two or three rounds slammed into the wet grass near my chest.

Gripping my gun, I scrambled up the levee, then skidded over the crest and banged my left shoulder and hip onto the large bare rocks on the other side. I doubled over from the pain, like a cat hugging its victim, then forced my left shoulder open and began working my way blindly down the levee, toward the gazebo. The rain felt like a thousand small teeth biting my face and neck.

"Yo, Banks!"

From the voice, I could tell that the gazebo was almost directly across the levee.

"Banks!"

I didn't answer. I kept my eyes along the top of the levee, expecting at any instant to see him come over the top. I crept on past the gazebo, then worked my way up to the top of the levee. I clamped the .357 tightly between my hands, then swung up, gun first, for a glance at the gazebo.

Nothing.

I dropped back quickly.

"Now, that was a dangerous thing, Leo." The voice came from the arborvitae, the same hedge I'd used for cover. "But you can relax, Banks, I just wanted to give you a message."

"Yeah, what's that?" I looked behind me, upstream. I wasn't far from a large clump of willows. The rain had dissolved into a fine mist and a heavy wall of fog was edging downriver.

"What's the message, Caldwell?" As soon as I spoke I moved for the willows and the fog.

"Ryme. You tell that motherfucker this, tell him I enjoyed it all. All of it."

"What's that supposed to mean?" I didn't like broadcasting my position, but I wanted to keep Caldwell talking.

"Means what it means. Means I like my work."

I eased my way into the willows and used their cover to cross back over the levee. The fog was starting to settle around me.

"Means I plan to stay busy." Now the voice came from near the levee where I'd first crossed.

The wet, matted leaves slipped under my knees as I crawled to the edge of the willows and looked out across the yard, past the gazebo. The fog was so heavy I could barely make out the arborvitae. My forearms were sticky with mud. I noticed the smell of the wet ground. It smelled like dirt we'd removed from Patricia Ryme's grave.

"Next time you see him, you just tell him that. Tell him I'll keep practicing till I've done him, too."

I heard a soft grunt from the hedge, followed by a bullet clipping through the willows to my right, where I'd been the last time I spoke.

By now, the fog obliterated everything, the house, the gazebo and river, the lights of the surrounding town. Yet I felt helpless, pinpointed inside a wet, platinum blond bubble that reflected all light, while revealing nothing.

"Tell him I want him, Banks. You tell him that and you

remember it, too. You got something I want." A high, shrill burst of laughter, colder than the air itself, seemed to erupt from the fog all around me. Then absolute silence.

After a long while, I was aware of a rapid dull chatter and realized that it was the chatter of my own teeth. I waited a while longer, then made my first tentative move back through the willows.

I spent nearly twenty minutes making my way back to my apartment. I worked my way out the back side of the willows, then around the far side of the neighboring house. Then I went a block to the south before finally approaching the front door of the Hollingshead place. The outside stairway looked clear, but I wanted to check the inside, so I went up that way. There was no sign of Caldwell.

Inside, I searched my apartment before locking myself in. I called 9-1-1 to report the shots and have them dispatch Patrol to the area to look for Caldwell. That was perfunctory, though. Twenty minutes. He could be miles away. I hung up the phone, then peeled off my wet clothes and stood in the shower until the hot water ran out.

Now, in bed under all the blankets I owned, I tried to make sense of what had happened, while listening absently as Creedence Clearwater ran through the jungle.

If Caldwell knew that I had Ryme, that meant two things. It meant that he'd been watching us when we left Ryme's house. It also meant that he'd somehow identified me. I'm not in the phone book, so that had to mean that he'd followed me home, maybe that night, maybe sometime before.

And he knew my name.

If he wanted me to deliver a message to Ryme, then he probably didn't know where Ryme was that night. I thought about warning Cassidy and Westhammer, but decided against it. A warning might set off some sort of activity at the Congress, activity that might only serve to tip Caldwell. Besides, if Caldwell already knew where Ryme was and wanted him tonight, he'd have taken him.

I looked at the cardboard I'd taped over the shot-out window, then up at the three nicely grouped bullet holes staring down from the ceiling. Clearly, Caldwell didn't want me dead, either. Not yet. Just scared enough to make his point.

He'd done a good job.

And what, exactly, was his point?

Tell him I enjoyed it . . . all of it . . . I like my work.

I took those statements to be admissions that Caldwell had certainly killed Patricia Ryme, and probably Wattie Roebuck, too.

Means I plan to stay busy . . . till I've done him, too.

Meant trouble.

My day had been long enough without getting shot at. It had started with an anonymous dead girl and no prospects. Then Calvin Hoover had put a name with the face and now Patricia Ryme had a history, too. I tried to reconcile what Marian Tawney had told me about Patricia Ryme's clandestine ways with my sense of what she was. It's easy, sometimes, to transfuse the dead with innocence. Hell, in my murkier moments it took an act of will to remind myself that the man I'd watched die pitifully that night in St. Francis was the same man who had tried very earnestly to put me in the same spot. How could my poor girl from the park be a thief?

At any rate, the package looked like it was coming together. Now I knew who was busy killing people in our little town, and I knew why he was doing it. I even had Sky King Hudson thrown into the bargain. All I needed now was a man in jail, before I had any more in the morgue.

I closed my eyes, then opened then again and stared up at my ceiling. Some guys get to lie in bed with a beautiful woman and look up at mirrors. Me, I get to look at bullet holes and go to sleep alone.

Chapter 16

Before I left for work the next morning, I took the small evidence kit from the trunk of my unmarked car. I dug three bullets out of my ceiling. You could have covered all three holes with a coffee cup. Then, I had a look around Miss Leona Hollingshead's backyard. The rain had blurred any footprints that might have been made the night before by Caldwell. But from three locations, I did find a total of seven pieces of spent brass. Nice shiny Winchester 9mm brass. I sealed each in a small glassine envelope, as I had the three bullets, for lab comparison with the ballistic evidence from the Roebuck and Hudson homicides.

Hanrahan was standing in his front window, watching, when I pulled up at his house. While driving to the station, I told him about my information from Marian Tawney, and about my little tête-à-tête with Caldwell down by the river. I didn't tell him that Marian and I had also settled an old score.

"You've got a good story," Hanrahan said. His red hair was still wild and sleep-tossed. He rode with his hands jammed deep in the pockets of his gray goose down coat. "How much of it can you get by a jury?"

"You've been spending too much time with Jack Tracer," I said. "You're starting to think like a lawyer."

Hanrahan laughed. "Proof? We don't need no stinking proof!"

"Damned right. We're making the world a better place. We're the last honest men."

"So we like this James Caldwell, eh?"

"We do."

"And we're going to march right into Vic Fanning's office and drop this whole number on the feds."

"We're not."

"We're not?"

"Look at our choice of feds. It's not like we're just unloading a case."

"No shit. This Hoover guy looks like he drinks blood. And Quill, hell's fire, he's just one step removed from going around smelling bicycle seats." Hanrahan lifted a hand and wiped the condensation from the window. "We will harvest no crime before its time."

When Red Hanrahan and I got to the station, Roger Quill was standing around inside a blue blazer and gray slacks waiting for us. Calvin Hoover was standing around with him. They were doing their standing around in Vic Fanning's office, and Fanning was standing around right in the middle of it all. Quill had a manila envelope under his arm.

I looked at Hanrahan. "Our week for greeting feds bearing manila envelopes."

"I feel like a kid just got off his bike," Hanrahan said. "Sniff sniff." He went ahead to our desks to check on Ryme, Cassidy, and Westhammer. I took the point into Fanning's office and closed the door after me.

Quill pulled perhaps a dozen eight-by-ten photographs from the ominous envelope. They were grainy surveillance photos of Jacob Ryme and me as we walked from the door of Ryme's house to my car.

"Tell me a story," Roger Quill said. He rubbed at a razor burn under his collar.

"Me, too," Fanning chimed in.

Hoover covered his mouth and coughed. I don't know what he'd done the night before, but whatever it was had managed to deepen the hollows under his cheekbones.

"Why do you want to know?" I asked.

"Is there some reason you don't want to tell me?" Quill spoke in a flat tone. The tone all federal investigators use when they talk about things that affect the future of mankind.

I leafed through the photos again, then dropped them on Fanning's desk.

"What happened to our arrangement?" Hoover asked.

Quill looked at Hoover. "What arrangement?"

Then Hoover asked, "Where's Colonel Ryme?"

Quill cut that one off. "*Colonel* Ryme?"

Hoover didn't miss a beat. "Haven't you ever heard of national security?"

Quill turned back to me. "Or interfering with a federal investigation?"

Hoover looked at Quill. "What investigation?"

I was about to get whiplash from all this looking around, when Fanning's phone broke the vicious cycle. The call was for me. It was Hanrahan.

"Your boy Bogarted last night."

"How do you know?"

"Linda Westhammer just walked in the door with a cup of coffee and bags under her eyes. You want to hear it from her?"

"Not now."

"Don't want to talk, right?"

"Right."

"Well, it's really pretty simple. About five o'clock this morning, Ryme says he wants to get some breakfast. So they take him to one of those new joints out on the Strip. About halfway through his chili-cheese omelette, Ryme excuses himself to go to the can. That's the last they see of him.

"So Miss America and Captain Wonderful, they start hot-footing around the neighborhood, figuring they'll spot the guy, but not really knowing what they'll do with him when they find him. Unfortunately, the finding him part is a bridge they do not get the chance to cross."

"That it?"

"Almost. After a while, they get the bright idea that he's still got stuff back at the Congress. So Cassidy goes back there, where he is now, in case Ryme shows up, and Linda comes over here to give us the good news. You want me in there with you now?"

I did. A few seconds after I hung up the phone, Hanrahan brought our own manila envelope into the office.

"Well?" Hoover said. He said it like a man who wasn't used to having his conversations interrupted by phone calls for other people.

"We're waiting," said Quill.

I looked at Hoover, then Quill. "What team did Babe Ruth play for?"

Quill threw up his hands. "I don't fucking believe this shit."

"Gentlemen," Fanning cut in, "is this really necessary?"

"You asking me or them?" I said.

"Banks," Fanning said wearily, "just answer the question."

"Which one?"

I took out the photos I'd taken of Fisher White/James Caldwell. I dealt the photos to Hoover, Quill, and Fanning. "This is a guy calls himself Fisher White."

"What's that supposed to mean? 'Calls himself Fisher White.'"

"He's your informant," I told Quill. "You mean you don't know?"

"Who says he's my informant?" The look Quill gave Fanning answered his own question. "I thought you *talked* to this guy." Quill jerked a thumb in my direction.

"Wasn't that you," I said, "dropped him off last Friday down on Rankin? There." I pointed to the tan Impala in one of the photos. "Isn't that your car? Same car Caldwell got out of a few minutes earlier down the block? But hell, I don't know. Maybe this guy Caldwell, he's your brother-in-law and you were just talking to him about hanging some sheetrock in your basement this weekend. Whoever he is, next time you see him, ask him if he owns a nine millimeter pistol. Ask him what he's doing with that little gizmo Woodruff and Hanrahan found in his apartment. The one that shoots arrows like we found in Patricia Ryme. And as long as you've got him in a talkative mood, ask him how come he's taken up shooting at me in the middle of the fucking night."

Quill's shoulders stiffened. He looked like he was about to ask for a cigarette and a blindfold. "I think, Banks, you'd better stop fucking around, do some explaining."

"I concur," Hoover said.

Fanning snarled. I think he wanted me to explain, too.

So I did some serious explaining.

Once you knew all the players, it didn't take a brain surgeon to figure out that James Caldwell was working from a plan to destroy Jacob Ryme. First, Ryme's daughter is out to score some money from her father. She ends up dead at the same time that Caldwell happens to be taking his meals in our fair city. Then, our only lead to her death, Wattie the schmuck

Roebuck, gets himself ventilated in Caldwell's apartment. And for dessert, Caldwell pops a few caps at me to make sure I get the message that he would like to open direct negotiations with Jacob Ryme. Now what, pray tell, was the Bureau's interest in James Caldwell? I looked at Roger Quill for some clarification.

"He was giving us this Ryme guy." Quill circled Fanning's desk, loosening his tie as he walked.

"Us?" From the breast pocket of his jacket, Hoover removed a black felt-tip pen and a small black leather notebook. "Could you define *us*, please."

"*Us* . . . the Bureau . . . " Quill stopped walking and looked at Hoover. "Me."

Hoover glanced up between notes. "Is that Q—U—I—L, or is it with a double L?"

"Hey, fuck you!" By now, Quill's tone had picked up some slight inflection.

I tried not to laugh at Quill's predicament. He'd gone out on a limb with an informant. It wasn't really his fault that the informant had all the marks of a homicidal maniac. Pretty tough luck for an aspiring special agent.

"Roger," I said, "maybe you should elaborate."

"Yeah," Hanrahan said. "What is it you guys call it? A situation report?"

About a month ago, Quill got a call from a guy who identified himself as Fisher White. White said he had some solid information on a man who was dealing in illegal arms. Quill said that was fine, why didn't Mr. White stop by the office someday and talk things over. No, White was scared. The guy was connected, connected but good, and White had developed a taste for earthly pleasures that he wasn't about to give up just to do Roger Quill a good turn. What White would do, he said, he would meet Quill alone in some public place, give him some corroboration. The meeting took place, and White gave Quill a packet of documents that included photocopies of letters to Ryme from people in D.C. and Latin America. There was nothing specific in the letters about arms deals, and Caldwell had blacked out all names. Still, there was something shadowy about the letters, as though important subjects were talked around in ways that only an insider would fully comprehend. Quill kept the documents and put them in his office safe, without passing word of the transaction up the line. He didn't know for sure what he had, but he knew he heard a clock ticking.

"You've got to understand," Quill said to Hoover, "we get information like this all the time. I just wanted to know a little more about what I had before I put Ryme in the system."

"What about Fisher White?" I asked.

Quill shrugged. "I ran the name, it came up dry. There was no way to know at the time the name was bogus."

Hoover wasn't impressed. "So you commit yourself to a surveillance? Without any kind of authorization? Without any kind of corroboration of what the informant told you?"

"But he came with corroboration, see? He had the documents."

"Which he undoubtedly stole," Hoover said.

"Big fucking deal." Quill's face looked like he'd just stepped in something warm and sticky on the sidewalk. "You think I'm going to sit still and get beefed by somebody like you about stealing a bunch of lousy fucking documents?"

"Don't be absurd." Hoover scratched the side of his nose, then made another scribble in his notebook. "What you're really telling us, Mr. Quill, you're telling us that all of this—the meetings, the surveillance on Ryme—this was just packaging. A way for you to market the White/Ryme connection to your superiors once you decided you had a salable product."

Quill straightened. "Some people might call it that. Others might say I was just doing good background."

"Without any sort of official check on Ryme."

"Sure, an official check. And what would that have got me? White said Ryme was connected. So I run him through the mill, what do I get? A blank wall? Another boot from the Bureau, this time maybe clear the fuck to Alaska? A dead informant? Who the fuck knows what you people would do."

Hoover sighed. "*You people*. I like that. Another conspiracy buff. Really, Mr. Quill, I would think the Bureau was above that kind of thinking."

Fanning shuffled some papers and cleared his throat. "So where do we go from here?"

At the moment, Quill didn't have an opinion. Hoover said we could start by giving Ryme back to him. Obviously, I didn't care much for the sound of that.

By noon, I had managed to make it clear to Hoover and Quill that Jacob Ryme wasn't a prisoner of the Rozette City Police Department. I didn't risk explaining the complete truth of that statement. What Ryme did from here on out was his own business. I'd put him under wraps only as a matter of protection and as a sort of coerced cooling-off period. This was a tough sell, though, considering that we refused to tell Hoover or Quill just where we had taken Jacob Ryme. For once, thank God, Vic Fanning went along.

"I hate to tell you guys," I said, "but having Caldwell shoot at me just to prove a point, that makes this thing less abstract than national security or federal investigations, any kind of horseshit like that."

Roger Quill looked like he'd taken a serious overdose of his own career. He'd snugged up his tie three times and the color around his eyes and ears was scary. Fanning kept shuffling through the photos, glancing now and then at Quill. Red Hanrahan was preoccupied with his own silence. Hoover looked at his watch and asked me what I proposed to do now. What I proposed was to find James Caldwell and throw his ass in jail.

"In this part of America," I said, "that's generally what we do with murderers."

"It's nearly two o'clock on the East Coast," Hoover said. "I've got to go make some calls before end of business in Washington."

Hoover proposed that we break for lunch and regroup at one-thirty. Hoover left first, with Quill close on his heels. But Fanning called Quill back.

Fanning reclined in his swivel chair, put his feet on his desk, and looked down his nose at Quill. "You been stationed here five years, Roger. How come you got cute with me now? You made me look like an asshole."

Quill might have been discussing last week's Redskins game with a pal back at Quantico. "Like you said, Vic, I've been here five years. You know how many times you got to change flights just to *get* to this fucking town? Jesus Christ."

Quill shook his head and followed after Hoover.

* * *

Janice wasn't making much headway with her BLT. We were too early for the lunch crowd at Roosa's Cafe, an eatery on Van Valkenburg Avenue, not far from the station. I'd convinced Janice to abandon her dreams of cream cheese and veggies in favor of some authentic Americana. Roosa's is the oldest continually operating cafe in town, older even than Nails Hogan's Cloverleaf. It's run now by Beulah Waggoner, who may be the town's oldest continually operating waitress.

"I don't know how you can eat those fries without catsup." I slid the red plastic squeeze bottle in Janice's direction.

"How does your body tolerate this . . . stuff?"

"Cholesterol. Vitamins for the working class." I took the last bite of my pork chop sandwich. "You'll feel better after some pie. They bake their own pies here, you know. Real pies, the kind with lard in the crust." I knew Janice well enough to know that she was troubled, and that she had settled on the contents of lunch as a neutral subject.

I toasted her with a glass of iced water and smiled. "You are what you eat." She studied my plate as though it were a character flaw.

Janice had read in the paper about the Roebuck homicide. She pointed out that the story was not especially flattering to the Police Department. No surprise. We had too many dead bodies popping up around town to be generating compliments. I told her about the identification of Patricia Ryme and my meeting with Jacob Ryme. I went on to tell her what I'd learned from Marian Tawney. I didn't tell her the rest of the Marian Tawney story. Three divorces had taught me better than that. Neither did I tell her about getting shot at. I had enough baggage without piling on her worry.

Finally, Janice set her plate aside and concentrated on her coffee. "The other day, you said it was like she was shot by Cupid."

"An arrow through the heart."

"Do you know the real story of Cupid? Cupid and Psyche, his lover?"

"No."

"Psyche was the youngest daughter of a king. She had no

husband, until one day she was drawn to a castle in the forest. There weren't any people in the castle, only voices, and at night her lover came to her, unseen. He warns her never to try and learn anything about him.

"Psyche's sisters are dying to know about her wonderful lover. Because she's never seen him, Psyche makes up a story. When she's caught in that lie, she sneaks a look at him during the night, and sees that he's Cupid, the god of love. She pricks her finger on one of his arrows and when that happens, she's startled. Cupid wakes up and gets angry and leaves her.

"Now, it turns out that Cupid is Venus's stepson, and she's jealous of Psyche. Once she gets her hands on Psyche, she puts her through all kinds of terrible tests, does this horrible number on her. But Psyche triumphs in the end. She marries Cupid and is made a goddess."

"Patricia Ryme didn't triumph," I said. "It's a nice story, but what's the connection?"

"Curiosity, that's all. She reached out for something and got her finger pricked."

"But hardly out of love," I said.

"Maybe, maybe not. There's always love of the cause."

"Please."

"Or love of James Caldwell. If what Marian Tawney told you is true, then it's possible that Caldwell was the second partner. Maybe the Ryme girl fell for Caldwell. She sounds like an intelligent woman, but God knows love is a cure for that. Maybe she trusted Caldwell too much—and learned too much at the same time."

"You ever been a cop?"

"No," she said, "and I never will be. I couldn't handle the diet."

"I'll bet you're even bothered by Jacob Ryme's story," I said. I mashed the last traces of gooseberry filling between the tines of my fork. "I'll bet you're wondering why he tried to fob this off as revenge bullshit, and didn't say anything about the money . . . if there really is money."

"Now you're teasing me."

"It's the gooseberries. They're tart and they always make you feel sassy." I set the heavy white plate aside and motioned to Beulah for more coffee.

"There's something else bothers me," I said. "This bozo Hoover. He shows up here with a story about having Patricia Ryme's fingerprints flagged at the FBI. First, how did her prints *get* with the FBI? She ever been arrested? If so, for what? But that's a little thing, which may have an answer. The big problem is the time. You watch TV, you think there's some big computer in the sky that spits our fingerprint IDs. But I've waited *months* to get confirmation of an ID on somebody, when I sent in his name, FBI file number, and a complete set of good prints rolled from living, cooperative fingers. But this time, I send in a wing and a prayer and what happens? A mystery man from the big city shows up here practically before the mail has time to get to D.C."

Janice held her hand over her coffee mug and shook Beulah off. "What significance do you attach to that?"

"I think it means Hoover knew by some other way to come out here. The fingerprint business is just a cover. Let's say he gets a call from somebody here, *then* checks the Bureau to see if we've made a fingerprint submission."

"What do your partners think of that?"

"I don't know yet. So far, we've all been preoccupied with the mechanics of what was going on around us. The dead bodies. The exotic military adventurer. Mister Big from D.C. The FBI. Surveillance. Mystery killer. Rock and Roll. All the cosmic forces. We haven't had time to talk about lying, cheating, and stealing, the more mundane elements of crime."

Janice reached across and, with her index finger, wiped a taste of gooseberries from my pie plate. She made a sour face and took a sip of water.

"I'm worried about you, too."

"Gooseberries aren't generally fatal."

"Smart-ass. You know what I mean. Just how many shots did he fire at you last night?"

"Seven. I think it was seven."

"And you aren't afraid he'll ambush you again?"

"No."

"You have evidence for that?"

"I'm here, aren't I?" I was thinking about the tight group of three bullet holes in my ceiling. "I've seen how the guy shoots."

Before I had time to digest the stupid bravado of that statement, the phone rang back near the cash register. I looked up out of habit, and sure enough, Beulah was waving me back. Wondering what in God's name could happen next, I excused myself and took the call.

"This Banks?"

"Right. Hello."

"*Leo* Banks, death investigator?"

"That you, Caldwell?"

"Leo, listen, I got to thinking, after our little talk last night by the river."

"I been thinking about that, too."

"Good. That's good. Because, see, I went to visit somebody this morning. A lady friend of yours. I found something I think you should look into."

Caldwell gave me Marian Tawney's address.

Then he hung up.

Before leaving Roosa's, I called Red Hanrahan at the station, explained what was happening, and asked him to meet me at Marian Tawney's. As I turned onto her street, I looked in the mirror and saw his car race up behind me.

The tiny brick house seemed isolated now from the rest of the neighborhood, that kind of psychological isolation always generated by disaster. I watched the wind play over the brown grass in the thin strip of lawn between the sidewalk and the wooden porch. I started down the walk.

The curtains were drawn, but the front door stood open two or three inches. I knocked on the door, then called out Marian's name several times. There was no answer. I nudged the door open with my toe.

She was sitting on the floor with her left foot curled under her right thigh. Her back rested against the front of the couch and her left arm sprawled across the cushion, while her head lay on her right shoulder; her face was nearly covered by that auburn hair.

The caftan was matted to her chest with blood, and a pool of blood spread across the floor around her hips. I took several steps into the room and knelt beside her. I felt her throat for a pulse. Her skin was cool and unyielding. Marian's eyes were open, staring into something beyond sight, dry beyond tears.

I looked up at Hanrahan. The darkness behind his eyes was as dark as the deepest mine in Butte. "I can't stay here, Red. I can't do this."

"But you were here." He spoke in a soft monotone, as though he were trying to be gentle with a wild animal.

"What's that supposed to mean?"

"Relax, for Chrissake. It means you know a certain time she was alive. It means you know what the place looked like when you left, what could be changed. Means you at least have to take a look at things. Means you can be a cop for a while, save you from thinking about what you're thinking about."

"There's a baby," I said. "Jesus Christ, she's got a kid somewhere." I looked up at Hanrahan, but I couldn't move. I couldn't be the one who found a baby, too. I looked toward the bedroom door. Before I could say anything more, Hanrahan stepped inside.

I made it to my feet and followed after Hanrahan. He was standing beside the crib.

"Asleep," Hanrahan whispered, catching me as I tried to push past him. "He's just asleep, Leo."

Past Hanrahan's shoulder I saw the small mound in the crib. He was on his stomach, facing the opposite wall. The blue and white crocheted blanket that covered him rose and fell almost imperceptibly. I was grateful that he would awaken soon, but sorry as hell that he would have to.

I went back into the living room and squatted down beside Marian Tawney. Besides the blood on the caftan, there were two damp stains over her breasts. Milk. I tried to lift her right arm and felt the resistance of partial rigor mortis. Like Red Hanrahan had suggested, I was trying to be a policeman. But when I thought of her body being moved, locked in that awkward, desperate position, a sculpture of death, all clinical detachment failed me.

I stood up and looked around. The room appeared just as it had when I left. I went to the door and checked the latch. No sign of forced entry. The TV and stereo were off.

Hanrahan had come back into the living room. "I left just before midnight," I said. "She was wearing the same caftan when I left. I was only in this room. I had a cup of tea. I don't see the cup."

I put my hands in my pockets and edged through the beaded curtain between the living room and the kitchen. It was a small kitchen, with red cabinets and blue tile behind the sink. There were two pottery mugs in the sink. I couldn't tell which was hers, which mine. Without touching the cups, I looked inside them, as though the arrangement of the dregs could tell me something. On the stove, I saw a sterilizer filled with bottles and nipples. I started to say something, but what was there to say?

Back in the living room, I decided to test my new resolve. There were no powder burns on the fabric that surrounded the three bullet holes on Marian Tawney's chest. I began a first, careful search for spent brass—9mm brass, to be precise. I was still looking, when I heard car doors slam. Outside, Sam Blieker and Frank Woodruff stood talking in the street. A moment later, they started down the sidewalk.

"When you post her," I said to Red Hanrahan, "you'll find out she had sex with somebody last night. That was me. If anybody wants blood and hair standards to prove it, get a court order."

"Jesus Christ, Leo," Hanrahan said. "How come you never told me that before?"

"Because it was none of your goddamn business before."

"And now it is."

"That's right. Now it is. Now it's your business, it's everybody's business, it's the whole fucking world's business. Go on, Red, haul her off to the morgue and turn her inside out . . . take lots of pictures. Son . . . sonofabitch." I felt dizzy. When I stopped talking, I was surprised to hear the boy crying in the other room and realized that I'd been shouting.

Red scratched the back of his head and looked like he was trying to think of something sensible and conciliatory. If he persisted in that foolishness, he was going to have to talk to my back, because I was walking out the door.

By the time Woodruff and Blieker figured out I was leaving and shouted after me, I was already in the car. Before I could get away, Sam Blieker jumped in front of the car and banged his fist on the hood.

"Don't talk to me, Sam."

"Leo, listen—"

"I mean it, Sam, just leave me the fuck alone."

"Shut your fuckin' mouth and listen!" He reached through the window and across my chest and shut the engine off. "There's two things you need to know."

"This better be goddamn fast."

"First, we got a call from Cassidy. Jacob Ryme showed up back at the Congress. He's there now."

"Big fucking deal."

"Second—now listen to me, Leo—this Bowie woman, Janice—Hanrahan said you had lunch today with her. Caldwell knew where you were having lunch with her. He knew to call you there."

"So?"

"So pull your head out of your ass. Hanrahan also told me this guy Caldwell is trying to muscle you. The way I see it, there's a chance he knew about Marian Tawney because you led him here. You understand what I'm saying?"

Now that Blieker had managed to puncture my rage and grief, I didn't waste any time congratulating him for being such an astute guy. Instead, I paid him back by driving with reasonable care until he was about six inches behind my back bumper. If he hadn't spent thirty seconds explaining the obvious, I'd have been thirty seconds closer to Janice.

"There will be two cops at your office in twenty minutes." The phone booth smelled of urine and the cord wasn't long enough to reach outside. "I want you to go with them and stay with them and do anything they tell you."

"I think you'd better explain." Janice's voice sounded almost clinical, the way it had sounded that afternoon when we found the dead antelope in the coulee.

"I don't have time. You don't have time. Not for all of it." I took a deep breath and tried to slow down. "There's a woman dead because of me and so you've got—"

"You think he'll try to kill me, too."

"He won't just try. If he knows about you, thinks he can get to me through you . . . you're finished. Now give me directions to your office. There's no goddamn time to fool around."

When she was done, I told her to lock her office door, stay away from the windows, and stay put. "Twenty minutes. Thomas Cassidy and Linda Westhammer. Make them slide their IDs under the door. Go with them and do what they say."

"I've got classes. I'll have to—"

"No, you don't. You don't do anything except what I just told you. Don't even answer the damn phone."

"When will I—"

"I'll let you know. Now do what I said." I hung up. For the next ten minutes, I drove around town, watching my back until I was satisfied I didn't have a tail. Then I parked two blocks from the Congress and walked the rest of the way. Upstairs, I didn't waste any more time with Cassidy and Westhammer than I had with Janice.

"Put her on ice," I said. "Hanrahan, Blieker, and Woodruff are at this address." I scribbled Marian Tawney's address on a slip of paper and handed it to Cassidy. "When you come to ground, call 9-1-1, have them give it to a uniform *over the phone*, and have him deliver the information to Blieker, Hanrahan, or Woodruff at the address I gave you. Where you're at, the phone number, don't let them put any of that shit over the air."

Cassidy pocketed the address. "You want us to call you here?"

"We'll be gone."

Chapter 17

Jacob Ryme was sitting at a small table in the window. He was looking out the window, and when I closed the door, he didn't turn around. I sat down in the rickety chair across the table from him. The rusty radiator at my left elbow put out more noise than heat. It sounded like the bowels of a submarine on the business end of a crash dive.

I sat with my arms folded until Ryme finally looked at me. "There are four people dead. A tattoo artist, your kid, a lady friend of mine, and an asshole. Now Caldwell says he wants you. He wants me to give you up. If I hear one more word of bullshit out of you, I'll do it."

"Where would you like me to start?"

"Why is it so important for you to die?" Caldwell's pursuit was murderous and methodical enough to leave little doubt that Ryme was meant to cap off the body count.

Ryme shifted in the chair and looked out the window again, through the rusted iron bars of the fire escape. "A man is walking in the forest," he said, "and he comes across a track. A deer track. Because the man is a hunter he follows that track.

"He follows the track for a long way, all through the morning and on into the afternoon, follows it up a winding canyon. Then, late in the afternoon, it starts to rain and he loses the track. The forest gets heavier and it keeps on raining and then it starts to get dark. Not only has he lost the deer track, he's lost his own track, too, can't find his way back out of the canyon.

"The hunter knows it's getting late, so he tries a shortcut, tries to climb up out of the canyon. But the rocks are steep and slick from the rain and he falls, losing his rifle. Now all he has is a knife.

"Then, when it's nearly dark, he hears a noise. Just on the other side of a thicket. He hesitates, but because he's a hunter, he heads into the thicket. Very quietly. Then, near the edge of a clearing, he gets his first whiff of blood. He knows better. Only now he's a *hungry* hunter, so he moves ahead. The light is poor. He has to get very close.

"It's a bear. With his snout buried in the belly of the deer. It's a very small deer, and a very large bear. The bear is preoccupied with the deer, so the hunter is able to sneak up behind him and slice off a small piece of meat. A piece so small that the bear would never even miss it.

"Just as the hunter draws back into the thicket, the bear looks around and sees him. In that instant, the hunter knows that the deer won't be enough for the bear. Not nearly enough."

"And Caldwell," I said. "He's the bear?"

Ryme looked over at me and smiled. "Jimmy Caldwell, he's *one claw* on the bear."

"And the teeth?" I was starting to think like a detective again. "Calvin Hoover?"

Ryme smiled again and shrugged. "Maybe. Maybe just another claw. I know you thought I was lying, but I really don't know any Calvin Hoover. At least not by that name."

"But when I talked to you that first day at your house, you hit on Hoover."

"Not on Hoover. On a man out here from D.C. I'm not an idiot. I haven't survived by being an idiot. A fool, maybe. An idiot, no. Never."

"And your business activities?"

"I'm what you might call retired. Or trying to be retired."

Four years ago, Ryme was living in Houston. Since resigning from the Army, he'd been supplementing his pension by working for an export firm. He took a lot of trips, exchanged a lot of sealed envelopes for a lot of cash.

"A bagman," I said.

Ryme laughed, still looking out the window. "The Mafia has bagmen. The government has consultants."

Toward the end, Ryme had begun to sour on his line of work. He wasn't suffering an attack of moral or political scruples, he was just tired of living on the dodge. His mistake was that he didn't keep those misgivings to himself, which tended to make his associates nervous. Those associates in Central America were the most nervous of all.

"These Central American guys," I said, "which side were they on?"

Ryme shrugged. "Their own side." He straightened his shoulders, as though perhaps it had just occurred to him that he was not supposed to be like those other men.

"My last job," Ryme went on, "I met some people in a boat off the Louisiana coast. I went out with a guy I knew as Alfred Pitt. There were two men on the other boat. An American and a man named Ortiz. I was there to accept delivery of some cash. As it turned out, the two guys on the other boat, they were there to accept delivery of me."

Once the money was transferred, the shooting started. Ryme managed to jump clear with only a graze along his ribs. After swimming under the boat, he made his way back on board. When he jammed the throttles forward, Alfred Pitt was thrown against the gunwale. Ryme shot him twice and never looked back. Ortiz and the American fired after him, but the ocean is a big, dark place at night and he got away clean. On his way back in, Ryme used Pitt to feed the sharks. He kept the six million they'd picked up from Ortiz and the American.

I considered what Ryme had told me, tried to imagine the trail of phone calls and drops that led from the Gulf of Mexico to Montana.

"The other day," I said, "you wanted me to believe James Caldwell was nothing more than a head case."

"I'd think you'd know that by now, considering you're hip deep in corpses."

"But there's something you still don't want me to know. The American on the boat with Ortiz. You don't want me to know that was Caldwell."

Ryme licked his lips. "I don't suppose you'd believe I was about to tell you that."

"Sorry. I've bought all the Florida swampland I can afford. Anyway, it figures he has to have more in this than that line of Foreign Legion stuff you fed me the other day." I was curious about how far along I could pimp Ryme before telling him what I knew of his daughter's scheme to take him for a pile of money.

Ryme leaned his head back and scratched his throat below his neat beard. "Muscle. That's all Caldwell was. Same payroll as Ortiz. He was along on maybe half a dozen jobs I did. Always with the other side. I don't know where he stood in the chain of command, but I'm sure that at some point he made it clear to his superiors that he believed I couldn't be trusted."

"And how would he do that?"

"The Montoya incident, of course. That part was true. I cost him his future. Betrayed the unit for the sake of an outcast. For Caldwell and people like him—perhaps the people down south who hired him—that would make me an outcast, too. Especially once I began to talk about quitting."

"He's out of his mind," I said.

Ryme laughed. "You surely don't find that surprising."

When Ryme finally made his break, his daughter was in college. He used some of the six million to arrange for her future, then spent the next year bouncing around the country, stashing money in safe deposit boxes and watching his back to see if there was anybody on his trail. Once he was satisfied that his break was clean, he bought his place outside Rozette. After the incident in the Gulf, he never collected another retirement check from the Army. He abandoned his bank account and home. He quit filing income tax returns. He lived on a strictly local scale, paying the taxes on his home and licensing his truck. The modern federal bureaucracy is a computer wasteland, and Jacob Ryme set about the business of withering. Wither enough and you're automatically cut from the vine.

"Why not leave the country?" I asked.

"That was the alternative plan. If things here didn't work out. But leaving one's country requires dealing with a bureaucracy. That means either telling lies or paying bribes, both of which expose one to mistakes or betrayal. Then of course, an unattached man with money in a foreign country attracts attention. At home, an unattached man with money is simply retired.

"Anyway, getting lost is easier than people think. The most secure and effective lie is one that's never told. If you just refuse to participate—and expect nothing in return—then it's quite simple just to . . . fade . . . away." He made a flittering motion with his hand and looked out the window again.

"How were you found out?"

Ryme didn't answer for a while. Then he said, "Loneliness. I guess we both made the mistake of getting lonely. I went two years having no contact at all with Patricia. Then, a year ago last spring, she phoned. Said she wanted to see me. She was here for about a week that June. She came again last winter, and early this fall, she asked to come again. All three times, I knew better. I just couldn't say no."

"You think he followed her here?"

"How else?"

"What more do I need to know about Caldwell?" I asked. "I gather he was too young for Vietnam."

"Yes, yes. For God's sake, don't equate him with those men. Many of those men did terrible things in order to survive an outrage and then came home and put together normal lives. Now they get a lunatic rap, a very bad rap. Those men are heroes. Don't confuse them with men like Caldwell. War doesn't make men like Caldwell, men like that make war. It gives them someplace to go, something to do."

"Men like you," I said. I wasn't in the mood to let Ryme hide in a forest of ghosts.

"Men like me." You could have hung meat in the cold vault behind Ryme's eyes. "Young men die so that men like me can have the privilege of command. Our responsibility is to make sure that those deaths are necessary to the security of the homeland."

"You all fucked up."

Ryme waved it off. "A misinterpretation of history."

"And you satisfy that debt by ripping off six million dollars."

"Nice try, Banks." Then Ryme flashed a smile that made my hair stand on end. "But you'll have to try harder."

"What I intend to do, chum, is wrap up James Caldwell."

"And do you have a plan?"

"That's where you come in. I told you he's using me to get at you. Maybe you don't know it yet, but you're about to settle a tab."

"Really? And what is this *plan* going to accomplish? Do you plan to *arrest* him? Do you really think you can just go out and *arrest* a man like that, a man with those kind of connections? Jesus Christ, Banks, you'd have better luck cleaning an alligator's mouth with dental floss."

Ryme got up and looked down at the floor. Then he went in the bathroom and closed the door. I had Ryme for now, but what could I do with him? If all Caldwell wanted was Ryme dead, then why wasn't Ryme dead? Sure, I'd stashed him yesterday, but way back at the beginning, Caldwell surely could have murdered the father as easily as the daughter. It had to be the six million. There just wasn't any other hook. That meant that sooner or later, Caldwell would have to deal.

I heard the toilet flush. The plumbing sounded worse than the radiator. When Ryme came out of the bathroom, he was drying his face on a white towel with a green stripe down the center.

"When she was seventeen, Patricia went to the prom with a boy whose father was a master sergeant." He sat back down at the table and draped the towel over his shoulder. "I never really said anything. But I let her know I wasn't happy she was going out with a boy whose father was an enlisted man. Isn't that the stupidest thing you ever heard of?"

"Top ten, minimum."

"Your kids are young, you have all these ideas about what's right and wrong for them. What makes a good kid, bad kid. Aspirations. But hell, when you get right down to it, all you really want is that they should be able to take care of themselves. Be honest, not hurt people. Happy. What more should you want?"

"Alive."

Without saying anything, Ryme got up and went to the bed and dug through his black nylon jump bag. He took out a small cassette recorder, which he brought to the table and turned on.

Hello, it's me, Pat. I'm with a man. He says he won't hurt me, but you've got something he wants, some money and if you don't give it to him he's . . . he'll kill me he says. He says he'll contact you in a few days and to tell you not to try anything funny. He says for you to think a lot about something called The Blue Shark. *Please, Daddy, I think he—*

"How long have you had that?"

"It arrived in the mail a few days before you showed up. Local postmark."

"The Blue Shark's the boat you were on in the Gulf? When you turned the six million?"

"Yes."

"How long did you figure to hold this out? The tape?" I kept thinking about the tally of the dead, wondering how high the bodies would need to be stacked before Ryme's balance tipped.

"I held it until it was necessary for you to know. Now it's necessary."

"Did it occur to you that I might have done things differently if I'd heard this? That people might still be alive?"

"A miscalculation." He might have been describing a turn in the stock market. "I've made others, I'll make more. They're generally minimal. So this one wasn't."

I looked at him, reminding myself that he was my best chance to round up a killer. If Ryme's life were the only life at stake, I would have walked out of the room and let him fend for himself. I thought of Marian thrown wildly back into the room as the bullets slammed into her.

Ryme's voice slipped into the elaborately casual tone of an interrogator. "What would you have done differently?"

"I'd have left you at home, where Caldwell could take you on his own." What was the future in letting Ryme think a life like his meant more than spit to me?

He flashed a grim smile. "No. When you dug up Patricia's body, you loosed this thing in your town. You forced him from the shadows. Once you got involved, it stopped being a simple matter of him squeezing and me paying." Ryme laced his fingers behind his head and thought for a while. Then he said, "I can't get to the money right off, if that's what you're thinking."

That was exactly what I was thinking. If James Caldwell was willing to keep killing innocent people, I was more than willing to rip Ryme off for the money he'd clipped in the Gulf of Mexico.

You forced him from the shadows. Forced Caldwell, and who else? All along, I'd known Calvin Hoover was much more up to speed than your average federal bureaucrat. The only man who could have told Hoover that Patricia Ryme was dead was the only man who knew she was dead—James Caldwell. The man who killed her and planted her body like a message for Ryme in our park. I couldn't quite believe that any federal agency is jaded enough to set about murdering citizens to recover a cheesy six million dollars. Hell, by the time the feds got done with all the budgeting and overruns and the rest of the unpleasantness, they'd have more invested in the recovery than they recovered.

I asked Ryme if we were talking about finances or vengeance.

"Six million dollars," he said. "That's serious money to a barnyard army in Central America, Banks. More likely, though, the transaction, the arms sale, was completed without the money."

"So it's vengeance."

"Call it punishment. And silence."

"And the money? It's of no importance at all?"

Ryme shrugged. "Call that a finder's fee for Caldwell."

That made a kind of sense. With Ryme's booty on the table, Caldwell certainly wouldn't lack incentive. There was no start-up cost for either side, and if the job went critical, there was no traceable payroll. All Caldwell would need was someone to provide basic information.

I looked at Ryme. "Did anybody have your daughter under surveillance?"

"I assumed that they would. Why else would I stay away from her?"

"So why break the silence? Why did she come to see you that first time?"

Ryme massaged his temples. His eyes looked around for something to say. "I was her father," he said finally. "She got lonely for me."

"*She* got lonely for *you?*"

"Of course. But you're making it out worse than it was. I

missed her, sure, but it was Patricia who initiated the contact.
About eighteen months ago. First a letter, then a short visit.
Then more letters, phone calls. Visits."

"When did you last see her?"

"About two weeks ago," he said. "This visit was my idea. I
just got careless. I wanted her to stay, for at least another
month. All the rest, that night on the boat, the money, it all
seemed so long ago it couldn't matter anymore. Who would
care after all this time?" He was ignoring his own answer—
Caldwell would care.

"And that story you told me the other day about taking her
to the airport? Her return to Seattle?"

"Diversion. I didn't know how much I could trust you, so I
threw that out to fill up space. I had the tape by then. I didn't
know what else to do."

"Then why are you telling me this now?"

"Because it's all over, isn't it?"

I found myself thinking about Sky King Hudson, about the
wild edge in his voice—an animal voice—when he screamed,
Pig motherfucker, and the blood I didn't even feel splashed
down my throat. It was a voice that sounded, in its way, as
terrified and angry as I was, a voice I could understand. I
realized that it was never really Hudson that I'd hated, but the
fear he'd exposed in me. And then I'd made it worse by forcing
myself to be more or less satisfied to let it all go swirling
around the sink and down the drain we call justice. Even when
Hudson lay dead that night on the gurney, I could still feel the
dregs of a vague remorse. Hudson shouldn't have needed to
sell dope, I shouldn't have needed the thrill of trying to catch
him at it. Marian Tawney shouldn't have needed Hudson
enough to give me up that summer day, and to take him back
nearly two decades later. I imagined Patricia Ryme sitting up
late at night in a small apartment in Seattle, planning how she
could steal dirty money from her father to help the kind of
people he'd spent his life trying to exterminate, and wondering how far she could trust this other, newer man in her life,
a man who turned out to be even more murderous than her
father.

Remorse. I felt it settle over me like snow settling into the
thick, receptive needles of a cedar. Sex, money, and booze.
Find one of those and you've found your killer.

I smiled across the table at Jacob Ryme. "You're a lying asshole."

"What's that supposed to mean?" The words sounded distant and dark, as though spoken from the back of a cave.

"Simple," I said. "Means you're an asshole who isn't telling the truth. You can fix half that if you want to. You can tell the truth. You can tell me about how she was stealing from you." Once I had the words out, I felt as though Patricia Ryme had just died again, right there in that tacky room in a tacky hotel that should have become extinct back in the days when traveling salesmen began dealing in concepts rather than products.

As he turned back to the window, Jacob Ryme yawned, a tight clenched yawn that made his jaws quiver and made me scoot forward to the edge of my chair. "She's dead. What can it possibly matter now?"

"It matters," I said, "because Caldwell was helping her. It matters because one lie makes everything a lie. Mostly, I guess it matters because I don't like you and it does me good to hear you admit your own daughter was after you."

"The truth," Ryme said, nearly under his breath. "That's not the same as the facts, Banks. Truth is an interpretation of facts. Always an interpretation."

"She was after your money," I said. "Is that a fact?"

"Yes."

"How do you know?"

"I asked her. One day when I caught her returning some papers to my desk."

"What was she after?"

Ryme smiled. "Why should I care that much if you like me or not?"

I asked again what Patricia Ryme was after in his desk.

"Sorry."

What the cops do, they get a report of something that happened and they try to figure out who did it. They collect evidence. They dust for fingerprints and take photographs. They look for stolen property. They talk to witnesses and suspects. All this is a very past tense kind of work. Certain things happen and they can never be changed and when someone tries to change them, they only make the trail more bold. The cops wander around, in some kind of ordered fashion when we're lucky, and we try to document those things. The future exists only as one piece of documentation continues to lead to the next. If that process stops before we get an arrest, well, that's why God gave us file cabinets.

Like all police work, the Jacob Ryme job had its own interesting history. James Caldwell had found Ryme through his daughter. Maybe he had even manipulated her political sympathies from the very start, figuring to get the money for himself. But how had Caldwell found Patricia Ryme to begin with? That question brought me back to Calvin Hoover. And now, Hoover was here for damage control.

Less clear was the role of Roger Quill and the FBI. I had no reason to doubt that Quill was simply doing his job. Someone had come to him with information, and he'd gone cautiously about checking it out.

I looked at Jacob Ryme and tried to think of a plan, a plan not to fossilize the past, but to alter the future. Four people were dead. I couldn't afford to waste time letting the sediments in this case settle out at their own rate. My collection of trilobites was complete enough to last a lifetime.

Chapter 18

It was dark again, and again I was standing in the window of my apartment, looking down at the lights on the river. I might have been worried about James Caldwell seeing me there, except that I wanted him to know I was home. Only this time, I hoped he'd pick up a phone instead of a gun.

The weather had cleared and the temperature was falling, as though the valley had taken a deep breath of arctic air. I heard the rustle of a page, and turned to look at Jacob Ryme, who sat on my sofa. He was reading a dog-eared edition of Faulkner that he'd pulled from his bag.

"I'm from eastern Kentucky, you know," he said, lowering the book to his lap. "That's not Mississippi, but it's certainly southern enough that this feels very much at home."

We were waiting for the telephone. Waiting for James Caldwell.

"My father was an attorney. And an amateur historian of the Civil War." Ryme marked his place and set the book aside. "But then, many Southern men of his generation were students of that conflict."

Ryme was one of those people who seemed to think he could read Faulkner without getting dirt under his nails. "What did he learn?"

Ryme cleared his throat. "'Victory makes men voyeurs. In defeat, we are much more devout in our attention.'" That's what my father used to say."

"He sounds as crazy as you. I'll bet it was late at night and he was drunk when he thought up a thing like that."

Ryme wasn't about to let me get under his skin. He rearranged himself on the sofa and closed his eyes. "My father was also a Baptist."

"That supposed to mean he never sat up late and got drunk alone?"

"You have some knowledge of Baptists?"

"That's none of your business."

I had decided that as long as James Caldwell wanted something from Ryme, and wanted Ryme from me, we were both relatively safe. Those at risk were the people close to me. So it made sense to keep Ryme with me, and keep ourselves away from other people. At the same time, it was important for us to be accessible—both to Caldwell, and to the rest of the cops. That made my apartment the best place to hole up. The bullets in the ceiling said quite well that Caldwell knew the way to Banks's place.

"I was an only child." Ryme's eyes were still closed. "He took me on tours of all the old battlefields. Gettysburg. Antietam. Shiloh. I remember Shiloh best. The oak trees and the bronze statutes and plaques. Mostly I remember the absolute dignity and solitude of the hills, and the shafts of green light between the oaks, as if a great artist had created that single landscape just to give honorable men a worthy place to die."

"You're confusing honor with civil service gardeners," I said.

"Quite right. But I had an obsession with honor. I graduated from West Point in 1952. I was a student of honor even before that."

"What about your father?"

"He and my mother were killed in a car crash. That was in 1950. He was drunk—you were right. They were driving to New York to watch me play football."

"Did you go to Korea then?"

"No. I had to wait another fifteen years. Fifteen years of waiting for a chance."

"A chance for what?"

"Why, to prove what I knew about honor. What else?"

"And was it true? Did you have it all down straight?"

For once, Jacob Ryme didn't have a comeback.

After leaving the Congress, Ryme and I had gone by the station, where Blieker was organizing the evidence and paperwork from the Roebuck shooting. Frank Woodruff and Hanrahan were still at the Tawney house, along with Ardell Wings, our photographer and evidence technician. It was after-hours, so the place was quiet. I left Ryme alone in an interview room, and talked to Blieker in his office.

Blieker told me that Westhammer and Cassidy had taken Janice to a motel on the south side. He didn't tell me which motel, and for the time being I didn't want to know. I was studying the patch of carpet between my feet when I felt Blieker staring at me.

Blieker said, "My guess, he picked you up at the station last night, followed you there, then to your house, then back over to Marian's after his little confab with you."

It sounded so stupid and petty and obvious, hearing Blieker lay it out like that. Go ten years without seeing someone, then lead a killer to her doorstep. I wondered if he had watched us through a window. More than once, I had thought how glad I was I hadn't gone to Janice's instead, a thought that did not exactly boost my self-esteem. I felt like the carrier of a horrible disease.

"Suffer the little children," I said.

"What's that?" Blieker looked up from his papers and nudged his glasses up on his forehead.

"Suffer the little children. I read it under a bridge once. A long time ago."

"It's from the Bible," Blieker said. "It's got nice rhythm."

I told Blieker that when I talked to Marian Tawney last night, she tied the Hudson homicide into the rest of our nightmare. I also told him we needed to sit down and have a heart-to-heart with Mr. Calvin Hoover.

"Vic Fanning took on that job," Blieker said.

"Fanning's an idiot."

"Christ, I know that. But he knows when he's been trashed. If he didn't know it before, he did by the time Frank got done with him."

"And what does Hoover have to offer?"

"What he has is a disappearing act. He told Fanning earlier he was staying at the Riverside, but they never heard of him."

"I'm starting not to like this," I said.

Blieker nodded. "Roger Quill is making phone calls to Washington tonight. We've taken it upon ourselves to check Mr. Hoover's pedigree."

I told Blieker my plan to sit tight with Ryme at my apartment. He didn't like it, but he couldn't come up with anything better at the moment. As I was leaving to get Ryme, he called me back.

"Leo, these are intense people. *Devoted* people. Not shit-heads with big mouths who take off other shitheads with big mouths after the bars close." Blieker had that serious, rumpled look that always comes over him when he wants you to believe he's deeply concerned about your health and welfare. "Men like that are not to be toyed with. You hear what I'm saying?"

I heard.

"I know how you feel, Banks, but you can't risk being a cowboy on this thing. None of the rest of us can risk that, either."

I didn't plan to be a cowboy.

"If Caldwell contacts you, you get to us right away. We'll have something better by tomorrow. We just have to get through this one night."

I wanted to get through the night, too.

"You can't force Ryme to stay with you. But you can't allow him to run off on his own, either."

I knew that.

"And you can't trust him."

Now, in my apartment, I looked over at a man I didn't trust. He looked as though he were asleep, and then he opened his eyes and sat up.

"I met Patricia's mother when I was at Fort Bragg, just before my first tour in Southeast Asia. She'd just graduated from the University of North Carolina and had a job teaching school. She was a history teacher. Like me, she didn't have any family. She was ten years younger than me."

"How did she die?"

"She had a congenital heart condition, which we'd known about all along. It was a tremendous risk, just having Patricia but she insisted. She survived that, but it seemed to put her in a decline that she could never reverse."

He left her with a baby and a bad heart and he went to wa and then he came back. Twice more he did that and then it wa a new decade and his wife was dead, leaving him with a youn; daughter and no war to go off to.

"I wanted to be a complete father, a competent father," he said.

"Did you take her to battlefields?"

"Museums." Ryme's lips twitched behind his beard. "The refinements of battlefields."

I turned back to the window and tried to imagine some way that we could take Caldwell. I wanted him desperately, for Marian Tawney, and even for a poor dumb shit like Wattie Roebuck, for making me a moral accomplice in their deaths. But he had taken Ryme's daughter, the last of all his people. I could only imagine how badly Ryme must want him. I watched the figure of Jacob Ryme reflected in the dark window, waiting to see if would look at me. But he didn't. He didn't look up and for a long time he didn't speak.

Finally, I said, "Have you given any thought to a plan?"

"We can't devise tactics until we know how he wants to play it out. Once he calls, he won't give us any time, you can depend on that. Your people won't be able to help. We'll have to do it ourselves. The two of us. I am settled on the strategy, though. We have to kill him."

"Are you saying that because you believe it's true, or because you want it to be true? The part about killing him?"

"I didn't know there was a difference."

"Your father was a Baptist."

"That's right."

I left the window and sat in the battered reclining chair across the room from Ryme. The chair was broken, its back propped up by the wall, an artifact of several marriages. It's covered in heavy blue corduroy. A good chair for mulling over bad news.

"He'll probably call tonight," Ryme said. "He has to. The thing is, none of us can afford to let this business run on. Neither side can let the other have time to plan. That's still an advantage to him, because it's harder to plan a response when you don't know the nature of the initiative."

"So when he calls, we force him," I said. Ryme's logic was accurate and clear. Our only advantage lay in keeping Caldwell unsettled. He had to believe that his first chance was his only chance. "When he calls, we'll need some bait."

Ryme drummed his thighs softly with his hands as he

thought. "Tell him I'll bring him the keys to fourteen safe deposit boxes. Tell him I'll bring him a list of where the boxes are, and an example of all the signatures he'll need to get at them."

"And will you have those things?"

"He only needs to think I will."

"*Could* you have those things?"

Ryme didn't even bother to smile at that one.

"This is starting to feel," I said, "like I'm filling a role. Like I've sidestepped the normal course of things and taken on a part in something you're directing."

"I've done everything you've told me."

"I know that."

"I even shut myself up with Blondie and Dagwood last night."

"That's supposed to make you a hero?"

"You had to be there," Ryme said.

I had few doubts that Jacob Ryme was more than competent enough to handle this job on his own. He'd never struck me as a guy who did anything without a reason. And well thought-out reasons, at that. "Why trust something like this to a bunch of rube cops?"

"This guy murdered my daughter."

"Yes."

"He wants me dead, too. Wants me to suffer."

"That's right. And you still haven't answered my question."

"I never said that you were a bunch of rube cops."

Ryme fished in his pants pocket until he found a small knife. "I've known lots of cops." He shaved a small patch of hair from his left forearm, then used the knife to trim a cuticle. "The other day at my house, I liked the way you forced me into dealing with you."

"The pictures."

"That was part of it. I know you wouldn't have shown those pictures to just anybody. But you showed them to me, and it was the right move. That said you were reading me and doing a good job of it. Then, after we were done talking, you grabbed me. You didn't call somebody for instructions or help. You made your own plan and executed it."

"So you were just curious. Curious about me."

"Of course." Ryme examined the edge on his knife, then looked up at me and smiled. "You're a man who's had his throat cut. That makes you interesting. And the fact that you came back for more, that means maybe I can count on you when this thing turns to shit, which things like this always do." He snapped the knife closed. His voice had slipped into a gentle, east Kentucky drawl. "Besides, now he's gone and butchered that lady friend of yours, I know you won't quit on Mr. James Caldwell for anything."

I felt as though my wings had just been pinned to the back of a display case.

"You shouldn't think so hard about these things, Leo." Ryme settled back, extended his legs, and crossed his ankles. "Life, you know, sometimes it's kind of like a tracer round coming at you out of the deep woods. Deceptively slow and brilliant. You watch it chug along in this gentle, predictable arc, and you start to think how strange and wonderful it is and how you can always duck aside at the last minute if it gets too close." Ryme paused, as though he were recalling with pleasure the complete details of the incident upon which his homily rested. Then, he sounded as though he'd made up his mind about something. "You can't waste too much time contemplating it, Leo. Do that and sooner or later one of those rounds, it'll drill you. Right between the eyes."

"So what do you do? Keep your head down?"

"Kill the bastards."

Chapter 19

I had dropped off to sleep when the phone rang. I was dreaming about dinosaur digs along the Musselshell River and then I was wondering how there could be a phone buried among all those petrified bones and then I was awake. Jacob Ryme was already awake and looking at me, waiting for me to get up and answer. I lurched into the kitchen and snatched the receiver in mid-ring.

"You had me worried, Leo. I thought you'd lost interest."

"It's a safe bet I'm still interested." I nodded at Jacob Ryme, who was now standing. "What's on your mind?"

"You got Ryme there with you?"

"You want to talk to him?"

"No, Christ no. I'm happy talking to you, Leo."

"So talk."

"That's what I like, Leo, spirited give and take."

I listened for background noise, listened for some clue to where Caldwell might be. The only noise on the line was Caldwell. I looked at my watch. It was just after two-thirty.

"He tell you about the money?"

"He's told me."

"What else he tell you?"

"He told me you're an asshole. But I figured that on my own."

Caldwell laughed so hard I thought he might drop the phone.

"He told me to make you an offer. He said to tell you he ready to give you the keys to a bunch of safe deposit boxes around the country. He'll give you the keys, the location of all the boxes, and all the names and signatures you'll need to crack them."

For a moment, Caldwell didn't say anything. Ryme had moved past me into the kitchen and turned up the heat under a pot of coffee.

Finally, Caldwell made up his mind. "I'll get back—"

"No. We'll do it now," I said.

"I'll call you—"

"You're not listening, Caldwell. We'll do it now."

"If you think—"

"I don't think anything. *He* thinks. Ryme thinks. He says it's tonight, right now, or it's not at all."

"You think I'll stop just because—"

"I doubt it."

"So this is what Ryme thinks, huh?"

"What can I tell you, Caldwell? You got his attention."

"Yeah . . . yeah, I got his attention."

"Mine, too," I said.

Neither of us spoke for a moment, then Caldwell coughed slightly, as though he'd been trying to suppress a laugh. "You are a stupid shit, Leo," Caldwell said, finally.

I hoped that Caldwell was wrong. But I also hoped he kept on thinking that way. I said, "What's it going to be?"

"For starters," Caldwell said, "you better convince that sonofabitch there with you not to try to fuck me over this time. You better make him believe I can draw blood for a long time."

"He believes it, okay? He believes every fuckin' word you said. It's not the problem he doesn't believe it. What the problem is, he really doesn't give a shit."

"Hell, I know that." Caldwell laughed out loud this time. "He don't give a rat's ass about nothing. You think I don't know that? That's *your* department, Leo. You got to keep him in line."

"Caldwell, you murdered his daughter, for Christ's sake. She was all he had. It's not exactly like you put the guy in a generous frame of mind."

I waited for some response. When I didn't get one, I asked him if he was the one who tattooed the dragon on her hip.

"Think of me as an artist, Leo, a guy who likes to sign his work."

"What I can't figure is how come you did her so soon. How

come you didn't wait till after? You lazy, or what? You fuck up a little bit?"

"Hey, Leo, come on. I indulged myself, okay? So sue me."

"Right. Sure."

"Yeah. You tell Ryme this, tell him I believe in reincarnation. Tell him I wore his little girl out so I recycled her. Like it was a patriotic duty, you know?" He was laughing again. "You tell him that. Tell him right now, I want to hear you tell him."

I told Ryme. He didn't say anything and his expression didn't change. He took a sip of coffee.

"That's bullshit. You fucked up all right. You fucked up because you didn't figure she'd be found or identified before you made your move. You had her record that cassette and then you whacked her."

"Whacked her. I like that, Leo. You hear that on TV?"

"Sure, it was easier than peanut butter sandwiches and taking her to the toilet and worrying she was gonna get away. So you got a little lazy. I can understand that. It's just tough luck I went and told Ryme you'd already cashed her."

"If it's tough luck," Caldwell said, "it's all yours."

I'd been working on an explanation for Roger Quill and the FBI. I decided to try it out on Caldwell.

"You probably made up for it," I said, "calling the FBI like you did. That wasn't bad. You can't watch Ryme twenty-four hours a day, so you enlist the feds. You snitch him off to Quill and Quill helps keep him in one place.

"You liked that, did you?"

Caldwell knew Ryme would be sharp enough to realize that somebody—somebody besides Caldwell—was keeping tabs on him. It wouldn't tie him up completely, but perhaps it would impede him enough to give Caldwell an edge.

"As plans go," I said, "I've seen a few worse. I guess it was worth a try. But I wouldn't say it makes you the Einstein of crime."

"Have it any way you want," Caldwell said. "You just tell Ryme he deals on my terms or there'll be lots more bodies and you won't have any trouble finding them."

"I told you I tried that. He doesn't care. I guess he's as big a piece of shit as you."

"That's good," Caldwell said. "You hold that thought, Leo."

Caldwell was quiet for a few moments, and then he said, "Okay, here's what we'll do. We're going on a tour. In a minute here, I'm gonna tell you a phone booth and I'm gonna tell you to be there in a couple of minutes. Three minutes, say. Three minutes. You figure you can make that?"

"Depends on where it is."

"Oh, you can make it. Sure you can. You're a cop. You can drive fast and not get pinched, can't you? Cops are like that, aren't they, Leo?"

"Where do you want me to go?"

"*Us*. *Us* is the operative word here. You and your pal the colonel there. You stay together, and you use that raggedy-assed truck of yours, not the police car with the radio. By the time I call, you better be there. I call and the line's busy, I figure you're getting help. I figure that, and somebody else gets dead. Maybe that gal of yours out at the college."

Then he gave me directions to a pay phone downtown, an outside booth in the two hundred block of Hibbard, between McClean and Weaver. He told me to be there in three minutes for more delightful conversation, and then he hung up.

Ryme set his coffee cup down. "What's his move?"

"A tour." I got my gun from off the kitchen counter and slipped my arms through the shoulder holster. "He's going to lead us around town until he decides he can take us."

"Do you have to call somebody before we leave?"

I barely heard Ryme's question. *That gal of yours out at the college.* Caldwell might not be up to speed on the theory of relativity, but he wasn't bad with basic arithmetic.

"Shut up," I said, "and get your fucking coat."

Snow swirled on the pavement as we crossed the bridge. I turned up the heater, but the engine was still too cold to give up more than a cold blast. I hunched up my shoulders, trying to warm my ears inside the collar of my sheepskin coat. The streets were nearly deserted and I wasn't wasting seconds. By the time I pulled up at the booth on Hibbard, my toes were starting to get numb. Ryme waited in the truck, while I stood by the booth.

I should have called Blieker or Hanrahan or somebody. I knew that from the start. Alone, I was playing Caldwell's game as well as Ryme's, to say nothing of making Sam Blieker mad enough to kill me if nobody else got the job done. But hell, what could we do in three minutes? If things didn't work out, I'd be dead anyway, and Blieker would have to be content with abusing someone else. Think of death as the ultimate suspension, I told myself. Three days without pay, and then they bury you, cart you out to the boneyard at the head of a long column of red and blue lights.

I looked at my watch and tried to figure how long it had been since we left my place. The phone rang.

"Leo, old son. You made good time."

"What's next?"

"Easy, lad, easy. The colonel, he's there with you?"

"He's in the truck."

"That's good. Wait in the truck, boy. I like that."

"What's it gonna be, Jimmy? I'm freezin' my ass off out here."

"It's a cold country you got up here, Leo. Not like I'm used to. Ryme either, far as that goes. We're more your warm weather types."

"That's what I hear. Sun and fun in the Gulf."

"Yeah, there you go. He tell you about *The Blue Shark*?"

"Said you tried to kill him. You and a guy named Ortiz."

"Yeah, we sure enough did. Tried damned hard."

"Said he turned it into a six million dollar payday."

"Did he, now? That's good. Just dandy. You know the Safeway store way out on McClean? Out where it merges with Rankin?"

I knew it.

"Well, during the next three minutes while you're driving out there, why don't you ask the good colonel what happened to Ortiz's sister. Ask him what happened to my wife."

"He's running ahead of us," Ryme said. The truck was warm now. "He hasn't had time to line this out, get the phone numbers ahead of time, all that. The call to your house, tha had to come from that booth on Hibbard. The last call had to come from the Safeway where we're headed."

I felt reassured, knowing Ryme was smart enough to be an astronaut. My hair was wet from the snow. I felt drops of water slide down my scalp. The streets were getting slick. It was going to be tough, keeping time with Caldwell.

I hadn't asked Ryme about Ortiz's sister, and for the time being I didn't plan to. Right now, Caldwell was trying to drive a wedge between Ryme and me. I couldn't afford that. I couldn't be sure that Ryme was on our side, but I knew Caldwell was an enemy. I had the bodies to prove it.

The truck broke traction when I braked for the light at Flynn. I looked around for cops. I wasn't worried about getting pinched, but we couldn't afford the time it would take to explain—or the attention we would attract.

There weren't any cops around except me.

I took the light.

Ryme turned and looked behind us, then to his right. "Sooner or later he'll have to show himself. Wait for us at the next stop, double back, something. It won't be an ambush. He has to make sure I have the materials."

But was it really the money?

I said, "Any idea when?"

"No."

Caldwell was trying to tell me something, tell it to me in bits and pieces and let it work on me, let me get bogged down in doubt. Once Caldwell was done talking, that's when he'd go to work.

The phone at the Safeway store was just off the street at the edge of a large, bright parking lot. It was ringing when I slid to a stop.

"I was about to give up on you, Leo."

"Up yours."

"I'm glad the cold hasn't dampened your spirits. You ask him that like I told you?"

"Why should I? Because some half-assed jerk has a half-assed story? You got something to tell me, then get it told. Otherwise, type it up and mail to *Penthouse.*"

"Her name was Lucinda. I met her through her brother

Paulo. Paulo Ortiz. Cuban family. They were hooked up with some faction that doesn't even exist anymore. Anyway, Ortiz and I were doing business together, some trading. Ryme was our contact.

"Lucinda was twenty-three when we met. We got married in Honduras. The last time I saw her, her face was shot off.

"At the corner of Tenth and Pine, Leo. There's a phone in the kiosk at the bus stop."

And then he hung up.

The snow was steady now, falling in large white clusters that hung in the headlights until they exploded against the windshield. I felt my stomach tighten down, while at the same time the whole business began to take on a detached, improbable air. What could this frozen night possibly have to do with death in the tropics? With secret agents and clandestine money, the kind of deals those of us out here in the country only read about in the papers? Surely the dead girl in the park was just somebody's Halloween prank gone sour. Clever makeup. The best disguise at the party. How could she be the child of the man beside me in the truck? How could this man—himself a murderer?—have sat with her at the supper table and explained his trips to war in terms of the oaken silence at Shiloh? How could he have listened to her talk about her new life in Seattle, while he wondered to himself what she wanted from him and plotted getting away with giving her nothing. With her new politics, she must have grown into the kind of person he had come to hate most, a practitioner of noble sacrifice. How could he have known she would take his lectures on honor to heart, set out to cause him loss, and succeed only in being lost herself? How could he have raised such a fool?

No. It was impossible. Janice would agree. She would turn over and clip me with an elbow and I would wake up and tell her it was time for me to go home.

"He hates your guts," I said to Ryme.

"What's he been telling you?"

"Does it matter?"

"It must. Or you wouldn't have said that."

I was across the Defoe Street Bridge by now, and getting ready to turn off of Defoe onto Tenth, into a residential neighborhood. From there, it was five blocks to Pine. Darkness tightened around the truck when I left the corridor of light along Defoe. Suddenly, I was hot. I cracked the window and leaned into the cold draft and the snow nicking my face.

"He's a killer and he's got a big mouth," I said, partly to keep Ryme at a distance, and partly to remind myself that the man who lay ahead in the darkness deserved everything we hoped to do to him. I thought about the arrogant blond man I'd seen swagger past Angel's just last week, the languid pose there on the curb as Roger Quill drove by, the bait already in Quill's belly and the hook snared in his guts. I thought of Psyche pricking her finger on Cupid's deadly arrow.

"This is not a good place," Ryme said.

We were coming up on the kiosk. Light seeped out of it. Otherwise, the street was quiet as a mausoleum, the kiosk bright as an open crypt.

I pulled up short of the kiosk and parked in the shadows. I shut off the truck and rolled down the window. The phone was silent.

Without having to be told, Jacob Ryme got out and walked to a large tree about fifteen yards from the kiosk, where he stood motionless against the trunk. I got out, too, but stayed near the truck. I felt my gun bump against my ribs. It felt awkward and slow there, under my heavy coat, so I pulled it from the holster and held it in my right hand inside my coat pocket.

I imagined Caldwell's eyes watching me through a gun sight, as they must have watched Marian Tawney. Did she answer the door thinking it was me, her cosurvivor, back once more to make love that would stay made? Did he give her a chance to say she meant nothing to me? Or did she die without knowing why?

The phone rang once and I was on it.

"Feels like you're in a fishbowl, doesn't it, Banks?"

"How long are we going to fuck around with this?"

"That's kind of the way it felt when he lit up our boat with a spotlight. We'd already moved the money. Lucinda was down in the cockpit. When the light came on, she stuck her head up to see what was going on. Before I could get to her, he was shooting."

"That's a terrific story. I take it you're the only survivor." I looked to where Ryme was standing, but I couldn't make him out against the tree.

"Ortiz was dead. So was this guy who came out with Ryme. I never knew what his name was. It was his second, maybe third trip."

"You're telling me it was just money. That's what you're telling me?" I looked at my reflection in the scratched Plexiglas. The gray face that looked back was a stranger's.

"We'd made maybe a dozen deals like that. They were all the same, except that this time, he was supposed to take Lucinda, too, take her back to the States."

"To meet up with you?"

"That's right."

"So why did this one go wrong?" I was remembering what Ryme had told me, about the attempt on his own life.

"You're the cop, what do you think? He's a thief, man. Jesus Christ, what do you call it when a guy dumps a bunch of people and steals money?"

"I guess I'd call him the same as you'd call a guy who cultivates a young woman, then kills her once he's played her out."

"Women. Yeah. I was up to a house earlier tonight. Nice house up the end of some canyon on the south end of town. You know the house?"

Janice's house.

"There wasn't anybody home. What the hell. You can't hide her forever. I've waited years. What's a few days, you know, Leo?"

A few days was nothing. He was right, I couldn't hide her forever. I wondered if he was smiling. My teeth began to chatter. I wondered if Caldwell was calling from a warm place. I wondered if there were any warm places left.

Caldwell said, "I tried to get to her, but ended up going over the side. There was shooting for just a few seconds. He knew he didn't get me. He spent some time with the light, looking for me. But, you know, here I am.

"Anyway, after he gave up and I made it back onto the boat

she wasn't dead. She lived maybe another half hour. Breathing through a tear in her throat. A couple of times, she tried to talk, but her jaw was gone. Can't talk without a jaw, can you, Leo? Just her tongue, trying to talk and her breath making that sucking noise."

He stopped talking. I was out of snappy replies. Ryme still hadn't moved. We had talked about death so much, it seemed as though the whole world had plunged into silent, writhing sleep.

"Years, Leo. I still can't wash her blood off of me. I've done terrible things to get to this point. That's too long, too much to have him or you or anybody else calling the shots. I'll talk to you sometime."

Then he hung up. No instructions. No next stop on the line. Gently, I hung the receiver in its cradle.

Chapter 20

"He told me you're a killer."

Ryme sat in the truck dark and silent as a tumor. "Does that surprise you?"

"That he would say that, or that it's true?"

"Both."

I was far beyond surprise. The snow had stopped and the wind settled. We were almost back to my place. A sticky lifter under the hood beat out a faint, metallic pause. I parked and shut off the truck, silencing that pulse.

"I only deal with what I can prove," I said. "I can prove that James Caldwell committed murder in this town."

"That's an admirable statement." There was a lightness in his voice. Perhaps he was recalling his long lost days as a student of honor.

"It's a statement of fact. It would be wrong of you to take it as refuge."

"There is no refuge, Detective. There is only movement and countermovement."

We got out of the truck and walked through the thin carpet of new snow to the wooden stairway that led up the long side of the big old house where I lived. Halfway there, a saucer of light pinned us against the faded white clapboards.

I looked into the light and squinted, then looked away, forcing myself not to shield my eyes, to keep both my hands in my pockets. I wrapped my fingers around the rubber grips of the revolver and held on tight.

Ryme was just below me on the stairs. He started to back down, but Caldwell stopped him.

"Just stand still for a while," Caldwell said.

"I don't have the keys," Ryme said.

"I know that. I guess I never figured killing people would squeeze that money out of you. Not even killing your own daughter."

"From the first," Ryme said to him, "I wondered if it was you behind this. When Banks showed me that picture of the tattoo, I knew for sure."

Caldwell had spent months cultivating Patricia, once he found her in Seattle. Not that she took much cultivation.

"She was going to settle your sins," Caldwell said to Ryme. "Not the simple ones, like robbery and murder, which she didn't even know about. The more abstract kind, the ones behind the political clichés."

"She figured it out, didn't she?" I looked down at the light again. "All of it."

"I didn't want to do it that way," Caldwell said. "Didn't want to use her like that. I ain't like *him*."

"But she knew too much," I said.

"Seems like the whole goddamn *world* knows too much," Caldwell said. "You know the really funny part? That stroke about the kidnapping, the tape? That was all her idea. The only way she could figure to get anything out of this cheap sonofabitch."

I said, "She knew about *The Blue Shark*, too?"

Caldwell shook his head. "That was when she figured something was wrong, when I told her to put that in the tape. Then she knew I wasn't just some swingin' dick from Seattle. After that, I just went ahead with her own plan."

"Except the part about killing her," I said.

"An on-scene adjustment," Caldwell said. "Now do me a favor and take those hands out of your pockets, Leo."

"It's cold," I said. I shielded the hammer spur with my thumb, so it wouldn't snag.

"It's gonna get colder."

In one motion, I pulled the gun, fired a shot directly at the light, and tumbled over the railing. When I hit the ground, both feet went out from under me on the snow. I rolled twice to my left, toward the concealment of a large mock orange bush, straining to pick up Caldwell.

The light lay still on the ground, throwing a bright spike over the snow toward the street.

Caldwell fired toward Ryme, who was now at the foot of the stairs, digging in his coat pocket as he ran for the edge of the house. Three bullets smacked into the clapboards behind him, and a fourth showered splinters from the corner of the house as Ryme ducked out of sight.

I fired twice at the dark form silhouetted behind Caldwell's muzzle flashes.

Caldwell stood with his feet apart, slightly crouched, with the gun held in a two-handed grip before him. Classic combat style. Once Ryme was out of sight, he swung the gun toward me, keeping his feet in position and pivoting his hips. As he turned, I fired once more, then got my feet under me in the wet snow and sprinted toward the rear of a car that was parked behind my truck. I heard more shots from Caldwell, then lost my footing and took a dive headfirst toward the street. When I crashed into the cement curb, all the air went out of me.

By the time I managed to get to my knees and lay my gun over the trunk of the car, Caldwell had crouched lower and was backing swiftly toward my truck, all the while swinging the gun steadily from my direction toward Ryme's. His gun moved through the midpoint in its arc and I felt my hand squeeze into the trigger, when I saw flashes from the corner of the house and heard shots. The windshield of my truck exploded, and Caldwell dropped from view.

Slowly, I got to my feet and looked over the roof of the car. Caldwell was on his hands and knees near the front bumper of my truck. I could see that he was breathing heavily. There were dark stains on the snow under his chest and face. A strand of drool hung from his mouth. His gun lay on the ground about four feet from his right hand.

I stepped from behind the car and kept my gun level on Caldwell as I moved toward him. Just as he turned his head toward me and opened his mouth to say something, there was another shot from Ryme's direction. Caldwell pitched toward me and lay still on his back. I looked up and saw Jacob Ryme leaning against the side of the house.

I moved in closer to Caldwell and knelt beside his head.

"How come an arrow?" I said. It sounded crazy, but I really wanted to know. "How come you used that dumb gizmo and that stupid little arrow?"

Caldwell's bloody lips broke into a horrible grin.

"Fuck you," he said.

A thick, dark bubble flowered from Caldwell's nose, and then it broke. I felt under his jaw for a pulse. There wasn't one. I looked at Caldwell's gun, which I recognized as a Sig Sauer automatic. Even in the poor light, I could tell by the muzzle diameter and the size of the brass scattered on the snow that it was a 9mm.

When I stood up and looked for Jacob Ryme, I saw that he had moved away from the house and now stood near my truck. He held his gun, a small revolver, tight against his right thigh. When I met his eyes, he looked away.

I brought my own gun up and held it steady with both hands on the center of his chest.

"Tell me about Lucinda Ortiz."

He looked up and down the street, then back at me. "Leo, can't you just let this thing go?"

"Tell me!"

He shook his head.

"Put the gun down," I said. "Put the fucking gun down!"

He looked at the ground, and when he raised his face again, still silent, I knew it was true, what Caldwell had said. And I realized exactly how much I now knew about Jacob Ryme. In an instant, it was as though I heard all those dead whisper, *Yes*, and I saw myself at the head of a long line of red and blue lights.

"You've brought me a long way. Why me?"

"I've wondered about that. I think it's because you wanted to know. Not so you could decide what to do next, but because you wanted to know it all just for the sake of knowing."

"Now you've brought me too far for both of us." I nodded toward Caldwell's gun. "Hudson was killed with a .38."

Ryme seemed to settle into the notion that I would know it all. "He made himself a pain in the ass."

"And Marian Tawney? I don't know yet what kind of gun killed her, but I do know I didn't find any brass there. Not like it was an automatic. There may have been brass, but I sure as Christ didn't find any."

"She was a loose end," Ryme said. "Almost the last. There

was always the chance she'd go to the police. It was my mistake to wait too long."

"Put the gun down."

"You're a good policeman, Leo. That unsettled me for a long time. But it turns out it's okay that you're good, that you know and do exactly what's expected of you . . . when a threat exists, and when it ends."

Ryme started to laugh as he took a step backward. He was still laughing when I shot him. I shot him three times and kept pulling the trigger after the hammer started to click on empty chambers.

I was out of breath and I couldn't breathe. I looked at the house, and saw old Miss Hollingshead peering through the curtains of her bedroom window. Then, as though falling through cold water, I sat back on the ground and took the deepest breath imaginable.

"Real patriotic."

I swallowed my heart and looked up to see Calvin Hoover standing behind my truck. He was wearing a dark parka and watch cap. He didn't have a gun that I could see.

I got up and went to Ryme. His eyes were open. It had started to snow again. The snow stuck to his hair and beard, but melted when it struck the bare skin around his eyes. Soon, the snow would fill his eyes. I kicked his gun away.

To Hoover, I said, "You're lucky I'm out of bullets." Then I looked down at Caldwell's automatic, and at Jacob Ryme's revolver, which both lay nearby in the snow, and which both probably still held live rounds.

Hoover wasn't shaking in his boots. "I followed you on that little tour around town."

"Secret agents," I said. "Bullshit."

"I couldn't believe it," Hoover said. "When he called the FBI, I mean. It was bad enough when he called and said he'd done that. And then he turned around and killed that goddamned girl. He was out of his mind. Out of control."

"And you were the stopper."

Hoover laughed. I'd never heard him laugh before. It was colder than the snow, emptier than the street. "Never trust a job to a man with a grudge. That's what I said all along."

"How did he get a line on Ryme's daughter?"

Hoover's failure to answer was itself an answer.

I told Hoover what I'd learned about the life and times of Jacob Ryme, the Army career, the death of his wife, his flight to Montana. About the soldier, Hector Montoya, whom Caldwell had cut free to fall to his death.

"He told you all that?"

"Yes."

"That's not bad. It's as good as anything."

"What's that supposed to mean?"

"It means I can't tell you."

"Can't or won't?"

"I thought they were the same subject."

"Can you tell me this, was she really his daughter?"

"Yes."

"Can you tell me about Lucinda Ortiz?"

"Cuban. Pretty, I gather. Caldwell had some sort of attachment to her. Dead. Anything else?"

"Was all this really necessary?"

"Yes. I can also tell you he was a good soldier one time. Ryme. I wish I could tell you he was a good man. Once, the two were the same. I don't know if the definition has changed, or my perception. Both, I suspect."

I pulled the coat tighter around my shoulders. My ankles were starting to ache from the fall. I heard sirens in the distance. I started around the truck for Hoover. After two steps, I was limping.

"Where does it go from here?"

"Why, nowhere. I go home, you write your report."

"Where's home?"

Hoover smiled and dipped his head toward the east. "That way."

"And that's it?"

"What else is there? You have your local homicides. You have the men who did those homicides. Conveniently dead. You've got two good shootings and no trials. There may be external *motives* that people will wonder about, but those motives don't alter the fact that you have done what the people who hired you expect you to do. Your loose ends are my solution."

"You're a witness. *My* witness."

"And you're an honorable man. People will believe you. That's very important." He sounded amused.

I said, "And what about you? What are you?"

Hoover shrugged and pulled his watch cap closer around his ears. "Just another of your banal bureaucrats."

"What if this hadn't worked?" I said. "What if it was one of these guys, instead of me, who was standing here?"

"Then we'd have to think up another story," Hoover said.

The sirens were louder now, and Hoover seemed to gather himself up, as if he'd just heard them. Without another word, he turned and walked off down Eau Claire Street.

Chapter 21

An honorable man. For weeks, when I went to bed and closed my eyes, I would see Hoover's back as he faded into the snow that night. Lying there in the dark, I would watch his upright, clipped gait and hear the sirens bearing down on us and then I would look down at the two dead men and I would think: *An honorable man*.

Well, hell.

After the cops got there, I turned the whole mess over to Herm Fenstermacher, who smoked half a pack of cigarettes while he called for lots and lots of supervisors. Then I went to the station, where I spent two hours explaining things to Sam Blieker, Frank Woodruff, and Vic Fanning, who had left Red Hanrahan in charge of picking up the bodies. I told them the whole story, exactly as I knew it.

When I was done, Blieker stubbed out his last Camel and shook his head. "It's too outrageous not to be true." That seemed to be the prevailing mood there in Fanning's office.

Finally, Blieker sent me off to Janice Bowie's house in the canyon, where Linda Westhammer and Thomas Cassidy had taken her after the shooting. *Chez Banks* remained in the middle of a crime scene, so I spent the rest of the night at Janice's.

"I didn't like it," she said after we were settled in. "It was like being a prisoner." The pale light of an early winter dawn filtered through the blinds, casting gray bands across the bed. I was cold, and tried to get closer to her.

"He would have killed you." As I told her that, just hours after the shooting, it already sounded absurd.

Janice wanted to know when I had stopped believing that Caldwell killed Marian Tawney. I couldn't answer that exactly.

I'd been troubled about the setup all along, but I hadn't been smart. Seeing all that 9mm brass around Caldwell's body was, I guess, what tipped the scales. As it turned out, all Caldwell had done to Marian Tawney, it seemed, was find her body. Patricia Ryme must have trusted him more than she'd trusted Marian, since Caldwell would have had no reason to go to her house, unless he'd known she was a player.

And why hadn't Jacob Ryme shot me, too? That was what I kept wondering, lying there in the dark.

Sometimes, people force a deadly confrontation with the police because they want to end it all and don't have the stomach to perform the act themselves. But that wasn't Ryme, not for a minute. I like to think he had some reluctance to kill me in particular, but given the kind of life he had led, the dreadful things I knew he had done, I didn't relish being the sort of man who might have made Jacob Ryme pause to consider compassion. I do know, too, that every man can reach the point where he wants nothing more than for another human being to know his story. Maybe that's where Ryme was, and the time it took for me to learn was simply all the time he had left. I'm glad he never knew what shooting Hudson had done for me. Jacob Ryme would have enjoyed a thing like that.

We never found the money. Red Hanrahan and I tossed Ryme's house three times, but we never found the fourteen safe deposit keys or any records. Who knows, perhaps he kept them buried in the woods, the way a bear will hide its kill. Anyway, I figure the money is still out there, like little green cancers, in fourteen banks across America. The keys remain Ryme's secret as much as his reason for allowing me the chance to live.

There was no Calvin Hoover, of course. Quill made official inquiries, and called in favors, too. But the man we knew as Calvin Hoover had vanished that morning in the snow.

It's easy to live in our town, here in the pretty mountains on the fringe of America, and imagine that the rest of the world is no more than a headline, a glib phrase spoken on TV by some guy who makes too much money and always talks in complete sentences. Sex, money, and booze, self-solving mysteries. That's what we're used to. That's the sort of crime we like, in our smug, terrible way.

One night near Valentine's Day, I was listening to this suit of clothes with a two-hundred-dollar haircut enunciate the network news from New York City. I wasn't paying much attention, until the screen was filled with Calvin Hoover's face. Only this guy with the blow-dried hair wasn't calling him Calvin Hoover, he was calling him Martin Summers, saying he was a deputy something-or-other in a federal office that sounded too innocuous to be without weight. Martin Summers had been found dead that morning at his home in Arlington, Virginia. A single gunshot wound in the head. The only thing that made his death news was that, tomorrow, Summers was supposed to testify before a bunch of senators on the latest round of shady business among what we in America innocently refer to as our intelligence community. Probably the stress of becoming the next day's sound bite just got to Martin Summers. That's what the Arlington cops apparently thought; they weren't having any trouble at all calling it suicide. What the hell, it was their town, they could call it anything they liked. Maybe some cop in Arlington had a few friends he was happier having alive.

To torture him, I might have asked Roger Quill to poke around about the death of Martin Summers, but soon after Christmas, Quill had been transferred to Puerto Rico, which is the closest thing the Bureau can do, short of setting an agent on fire, to sending him to hell.

I, apparently, was not important enough to dispose of. Or maybe it was as Calvin Hoover had said, I had done a public service. Maybe a handful of men talked about me as they milled around on the links of a private club and worried about slices and hooks, sat in their quiet electric carts and called me a patriot along the seventh fairway, a hero while teeing off on the back nine, and by the eighteenth green decided to let me live for my trouble. More likely, they would look at one another over sour mash in the clubhouse and agree that I just was not worth killing, that being a two-bit cop in a two-bit town was disposal enough.

So, they left me to wonder about it all, especially about Patricia Ryme and her two lives, the one I had invented for her and the one she had lived for herself, both of them teetering like the arm of a scales on the tip of James Caldwell's unexplained arrow. Sometimes, I would remember her voice from the tape her father had played that day, and I could hear her asking Caldwell what he planned to do with that ridiculous gizmo and its toy arrow. And I could hear him answer her, answer me, answer all of us: "Fuck you."

Janice and I spent the winter more or less together. Sometimes, I caught myself longing for those innocent days when all I had to do was drink beer and hate a piece of shit named Sky King, who cut my throat one time, the days before I became an honorable man. Red Hanrahan and I went fishing in the spring, and in June, after she was out of classes, Janice and I took off for a week and went exploring over around Missoula.

One day, we were driving the frontage road along I-90 between Missoula and a place called Bearmouth. The road follows the Clark Fork River. Near mid-afternoon, we stopped because I wanted to climb up through the rocks above the river and look for fossils. It was a hot, still summer afternoon when I set off with a rock hammer and canvas satchel. Janice stayed behind to explore along the river.

I had climbed for maybe half an hour when I came upon a narrow cave. I sat on the lip of the cave, breathing hard, and watched Janice standing below in the shallows of the green river. I thought about it for a long time, and then I dug out my glasses and put them on, so I could see more clearly the texture of the rock. I tried to imagine how it must have been centuries ago, carrying a charred stick and pigments up here, then crawling to the back of the cave to make your mark for all time, while outside the country shimmered away in every direction through the stone-brown air and no stranger was on his way from far off, coming closer with every heartbeat to tell you none of this was true.

ABOUT THE AUTHOR

Originally from Winchester, Illinois, Robert Sims Reid now lives in Missoula, Montana, where for the last ten years he has worked on the Missoula City Police Department. He has published two previous novels, MAX HOLLY and BIG SKY BLUES. Bantam will publish his second Leo Banks novel, BENEDICTION, in Fall 1991.

Praise for Joseph Wambaugh

"Joseph Wambaugh's characters have altered America's view of police." —*Time*

"Wambaugh is a master artist of the street scene."
—*Publishers Weekly*

"Wambaugh is a writer of genuine power."
—*New York Times Book Review*

"Perhaps better than any other contemporary writer, Wambaugh is able to convey just what it is that makes cops different from the rest of us and, more important, why."
—*Library Journal*

Nobody Writes About Cops Better Than Wambaugh
Don't Miss Any Of These Bantam Bestsellers

☐	27386	DELTA STAR	$4.95
☐	27259	GLITTER DOME	$4.95
☐	27148	LINES AND SHADOWS	$5.95
☐	27430	SECRETS OF HARRY BRIGHT	$5.95
☐	26932	ECHOES IN THE DARKNESS	$5.95
☐	28281	THE BLOODING	$5.95

Look for the above books at your local bookstore or use this page to order.

Bantam Books, Dept. JW3, 414 East Golf Road, Des Plaines, IL 60016

Please send me the items I have checked above. I am enclosing $_____ (please add $2.00 to cover postage and handling). Send check or money order, no cash or C.O.D.s please.

Mr/Ms _____

Address _____

City/State _____ Zip _____

JW3-11/90

Please allow four to six weeks for delivery.
Prices and availability subject to change without notice.

Now there are two great ways to catch up with your favorite thrillers

Audio:

☐ 45116 **Final Flight** *by Stephen Coonts*
    Performance by George Kennedy
    180 mins. Double Cassette $14.95

☐ 45170 **The Negotiator** *by Frederick Forsyth*
    Performance by Anthony Zerbe
    180 mins. Double Cassette $14.95

☐ 45207 **Black Sand** *by William J. Caunitz*
    Performance by Tony Roberts
    180 mins. Double Cassette $14.95

☐ 45156 **The Butcher's Theater** *by Jonathan Kellerman*
    Performance by Ben Kingsley
    180 mins. Double Cassette $14.95

☐ 45211 **The Day Before Midnight** *by Stephen Hunter*
    Performance by Philip Bosco
    180 mins. Double Cassette $14.95

☐ 45202 **The Minotaur** *by Stephen Coonts*
    Performance by Joseph Campanella
    180 mins. Double Cassette $14.95

Paperbacks:

☐ 26705 **Suspects** *by William J. Caunitz* $4.95
☐ 27430 **Secrets of Harry Bright** *by Joseph Wambaugh* $4.95
☐ 27510 **Butcher's Theater** *by Jonathan Kellerman* $4.95
☐ 28063 **The Rhineman Exchange** *by Robert Ludlum* $5.95
☐ 26757 **The Little Drummer Girl** *by John le Carre* $5.95
☐ 28359 **Black Sand** *by William J. Caunitz* $5.95
☐ 27523 **One Police Plaza** *by William J. Caunitz* $4.95

Buy them at your local bookstore or use this page to order:

Bantam Books, Dept. FBB, 414 East Golf Road, Des Plaines, IL 60016

Please send me the items I have checked above. I am enclosing $_____
(please add $2.00 to cover postage and handling). Send check or money
order, no cash or C.O.D.s please. (Tape offer good in USA only.)

Mr/Ms _____

Address _____

City/State _____ Zip_____

                                                    FBB—8/90
Please allow four to six weeks for delivery.
Prices and availability subject to change without notice.

BANTAM AUDIO PUBLISHING

FICTION'S HOTTEST DETECTIVES TACKLE THE TOUGHEST CASES OF THEIR CAREERS IN 180-MINUTE ABRIDGEMENTS READ BY TODAY'S FINEST ACTORS:

Nero Wolf, the orchid-growing, gourmandizing sleuth, who solves his cases from the snug comfort of an armchair in his New York townhouse is back in:

By Robert Goldsborough:

		ISBN#	PRICE
☐	**THE BLOODIED IVY**	45141-3	$14.95
☐	**THE LAST COINCIDENCE**	45182-0	$14.95
	Read by Michael Murphy		

Alex Delaware, the psychologist-detective, who handles cases in the eccentric, electric environs of California in:

By Jonathan Kellerman

		ISBN#	PRICE
☐	**BLOOD TEST**	45175-8	$14.95
☐	**SILENT PARTNER**	45191-X	$14.95
☐	**OVER THE EDGE**	45122-7	$14.95
☐	**WHEN THE BOUGH BREAKS**	45138-3	$14.95
	Read by John Rubinstein		
☐	**THE BUTCHER'S THEATER**	45156-1	$14.95
	Read by Ben Kingsley		

V.I. Warshawski, a tough female private eye who wears stiletto heels and carries a revolver faces down some desperate characters in gritty, corrupt Chicago:

By Sara Paretsky

		ISBN#	PRICE
☐	**BURN MARKS**	45208-8	$14.95
☐	**BLOOD SHOT**	45215-0	$14.95
	Read by Kathy Bates		

Buy them at your local bookstore or use this handy page for ordering:

Bantam Books, Dept. BAP11, 414 East Golf Road, Des Plaines, IL 60016

Please send me the items I have checked above. I am enclosing $_____ (please add $2.00 to cover postage and handling). Send check or money order, no cash or C.O.D.s please. (Tape offer good in USA only.)

Mr/Ms _____

Address _____

City/State _____ Zip _____

BAP11–11/90

Please allow four to six weeks for delivery.
Prices and availability subject to change without notice.